THE
ADVANTAGED

MARK ALLAN GUNNELLS

If I had to guess, I'd say this confession is probably a first in one of these admission essays. At the very least, at this point I'd guess I have your full attention.

I don't think of myself as a bad person, not even now, but I am a liar. It started out feeling small and inconsequential, but the speed at which it escalated into a full-blown disaster has left me breathless. And the inevitable collapse of the lie, leaving my life in a bit of a ruin, has taught me something about honesty. A very valuable lesson.

And what I've learned is that honesty is the most important thing, and it's an all-or-nothing proposition. There is no such thing as a little white lie or a harmless lie. All lies hurt. Half-truths and lies of omission are not any better or less damaging. Small lies lead inexorably to bigger lies and those to even bigger lies, the way that streams lead to rivers and rivers to oceans. I've used the phrase, "it snowballed out of control," and yet what that ignores is that if you never make the snowball and start it rolling in the first place, it has no chance to grow.

So am I saying that you should tell your wife those pants make her look fat or your grandmother that her cookies taste like ass? Well, there are better and more tactful ways to get those points across, but essentially yes, the goal should always be honesty. Because once you start down the road of dishonesty, however slight it seems at the time, you quickly learn there are few off-ramps from that road. And it's a road that leads nowhere good.

So you ask how important the concept of honesty is to me. Extremely important, in a way it can only be to someone who has been a horrible liar in the past and seen the devastating consequences.

And that's the truth.

This book is dedicated to the 2018 Furman TEDx crew who were so awesome and taught me that the future of the world is in good hands with young people so passionate and intelligent.

FALL 2018

CHAPTER ONE

Silas noticed the group of students as they settled onto the grass near the bell tower, only a few feet from where he sat on a bench by the lake, but he didn't pay them much attention. Furman University sprawled over seven hundred and fifty acres and had almost three thousand students enrolled, so the campus was usually crowded any time of day. Add in all the non-students who loved to come here to walk and bike and picnic because of the school's picturesque beauty, and one would find it difficult to locate an isolated spot. Especially on a lovely late September day like this, when the weather wasn't too hot or too cold. Just right, as that breaking-and-entering felon Goldilocks might say.

The group consisted of six students, four young men and two young women. The tall guy with the athletic build and mega-watt smile seemed to be the epicenter, the planet around which the other five orbited like moons. He had that leadership air about him, an easy confidence that didn't come off as arrogance but more like he simply knew what he had to say was worth listening to.

Okay, so maybe Silas was paying a little bit of attention to the group.

He couldn't stay focused on the math book open on his lap, having worked on the problems for so long that the numbers all started to jumble together until they looked like alien hieroglyphics, so his mind hungered for a distraction. Besides, he heard the tall one mention *Fahrenheit 451*, a book by one of Silas's favorite authors. He continued to stare at the math text while surreptitiously tuning in on the group's conversation.

"I'm not saying I didn't like the novel," said a chunky guy

with a cap of curly black hair. "I simply pointed out I'm more a fan of his works like *Something Wicked This Way Comes* and *Dandelion Wine*. Pieces like that have more emotional resonance for me."

"Those are definitely more personal books," the tall one conceded. "About growing up and growing older, but for me the scope is much more limited."

A willowy girl in a flowing peach dress, hair done in pigtails, laughed. "The human experience is limited in scope?"

"What I'm saying is that with *Fahrenheit* Bradbury was making a commentary on society as a whole, exploring Big Ideas, and extrapolating where he thought we were heading culturally. With amazing prescience, I might add."

"That's true," said a short guy wearing a T-shirt which sported a picture of the President of the United States rendered in a cartoonish caricature, under which were written the words *Make America MAD Again*. "It's crazy how much stuff Bradbury predicted in that novel. Bluetooth technology, wall-mounted flat screen television, ATMs, CCTV cameras, not to mention people being glued to their devices and the fact that this all started not because people were forced to stop reading but because they merely *chose* to stop."

A slight young man with glasses and Chipmunk cheeks looked around the group as if seeking permission to speak before saying, "I don't know, I have to agree with Kris."

"Big surprise," said the young lady with the black jeans and rider boots. "Although I'll admit, the science feels really wonky to me, not remotely plausible. It's distracting and makes it hard for me to suspend my disbelief. I had a similar reaction to *The Martian Chronicles*."

The tall one's voice was full of passion as he gestured with a paperback copy of *Fahrenheit 451*. "Bradbury wasn't a writer of hard science fiction. That was never his interest. He used science fiction tropes, in this case the dystopian society, to get at deeper, emotional truths. And Franco is right, he had an almost spooky eye for the future. That made him a bit of an outcast in his own time. Look at his views on racism. In a pre-Civil Rights world, he already recognized the ridiculousness of judging people based on skin color. What's the name of that story in *The Illustrated Man*? You know, the one where white people have sent all the black people to live in exile on Mars then have to go asking for asylum after they finally make Earth uninhabitable. Damn it, I can't think of what it's called. Anybody?"

The other five offered only blank stares and shrugs.

"'The Other Foot,'" Silas said without thinking, only realizing he had spoken once the words were out of his mouth.

He looked up to find the six staring at him, and heat suffused his face. He didn't like scrutiny and had spent his high school years trying to will himself into invisibility to escape any undue attention. It was out of character for him to speak up, especially when he wasn't being spoken to, but the one topic that could usually get him involved was books.

Silas considered muttering an apology and scurrying away but then the tall one stood up and said loudly, "Finally, someone who actually knows his Bradbury. What is your name, young man?"

"Um, Silas. Silas Granger."

The tall one strode toward the bench and held out his free hand. "Name's August Monroe, but my friends call me Gus. Come join our little confab."

Silas reached out and shook, his own hand limp inside Gus's firm grip. A familiar suspicion rose up inside him. In high school, an extension of kindness toward him usually turned out to be nothing more than a ploy to humiliate him even further.

You're not in high school anymore. You're on a University campus filled with students from all over the country. All over the world. You're in the presence of a group discussing Ray Bradbury; in high school, you'd have been hard pressed to find anyone who'd even heard of the author. Be brave for once. Put yourself out there. Take a risk.

"I would, but I have an assignment due tomorrow," Silas said, not able to overcome his misgivings.

Gus reached down and closed Silas's math book. "Obviously your mind isn't on the assignment, or you wouldn't have been eavesdropping on us."

"Oh no, I mean, I wasn't—"

"Don't sweat it, my friend. We're a very interesting crowd.

The assignment can wait. For now, scintillating conversation is in the cards for you."

The guy with the curly hair rolled his eyes and said, "Gus can come on a little strong, but he's basically harmless. The rest of us skew closer to the side of normal."

"Speak for yourself," said the girl in the rider boots.

They all continued to stare at him, and Silas imagined his face must be the glowing red of a stoplight. Counterintuitive as it seemed on the surface, he felt the easiest way to get their attention diverted away from him was to join them. Perhaps then they'd return to their discussion, their usual group dynamics would kick in, and they'd almost forget he was there.

Clutching the math text to his chest like a shield, he stood and walked with Gus to the loose circle the group had made on the grass. Gus made introductions. The guy with the curly hair was Kris Wellford, the guy with the chipmunk cheeks next to him Philip Greene. The girl in the peach dress was Paige Sinclair, the girl in the riding boots Sheila Lee. The guy with the *M.A.M.A.* T-shirt introduced himself as Franco Johnson.

"If you've ever been to the improv show at Coffee Underground on Friday nights, you've probably seen me," Franco said.

Silas shook his head. "Sorry, I don't go to Coffee Underground much."

"Of course not," said Sheila. "All the *cool* people go to the Village Grind."

"Very funny, Sheila, but I'm the comedian of the group."

Paige leaned over and placed a hand on Franco's shoulder. "It's very brave of you to think so."

Silas found himself smiling at the group's easy banter. He'd seen these kinds of friendships before, but always from a distance. Never from the inside.

Kris scooted over, creating a gap between himself and Philip. "Have a seat, Silas."

Silas settled onto the ground, noting the fleeting look of disappointment and hurt that tightened Philip's features. The group continued to gaze at him, but only with open inquisitiveness. Nothing malicious that Silas could detect.

"So," Gus said, taking his position between Paige and Franco again, "I can only assume since you know 'The Other Foot,' not one of his most recognizable works, that you are a Bradbury enthusiast."

"Yeah."

Gus waited a moment then made a "go on" gesture with the hand holding the copy of *Fahrenheit 451*. "Give me more. When did you first start reading him?"

"Oh, last year, but I've read a ton since then."

"That's when I first discovered him as well. I was in a Lit class with Paige and Sheila where we were assigned *Dandelion Wine*, and we just fell in love with the magic of the man's prose. We formed a sort of unofficial book club where we periodically pick one of the man's books to read and discuss. What was your first Bradbury?"

"*The October Country*."

"Was it assigned for a class?" Franco asked.

"No. Um, honestly, I had never heard of Bradbury until I found this weird YouTube video."

"'Fuck Me Ray Bradbury'?" Sheila asked with smile.

"Yeah."

"That's some funny shit."

"Sophomoric," Gus said, "but vaguely humorous for those with an unrefined palate, I suppose."

Kris nudged Silas with an elbow and gave him a knowing wink, as if they were two old friends sharing a private joke instead of strangers who had met literally only seconds before. "This coming from a guy who thinks that *Schitt's Creek* show is hilarious."

"Hey!" Gus said. "That show actually has a lot of intelligent commentary on class systems and the haves versus the have-nots. It's quite sophisticated, masquerading as silly antics in order to slip by people who work at fast-food establishments and go to community college."

The heat, which had started to leave Silas's face, suddenly roared back like a fire reigniting from a few errant embers. He held the math book even tighter against his chest.

"You're such an elitist snob," Paige said, tugging on her

pigtails. "Here you are talking about class systems, and then making cracks about community college."

Gus laughed and held up his hands as if in surrender. "Okay, a charge that is perhaps not totally without merit, I will concede that. Truly though, you guys should watch the show. You're missing out."

"I watch it," Silas said in a quiet voice, staring down at a single ant making a lonely trek through the blades of grass which must seem like a jungle to it, perhaps seeking a group to which it could belong. "I think Catherine O'Hara is a riot."

Gus slapped his hands on his thighs. "Yes, I knew we were kindred spirits. An appreciation for good literature *and* good television, it's like we were separated at birth."

Silas sputtered a laugh and loosened his hold on the math book, letting it settle across his knees.

"I don't know that I've seen you around before," Franco said. "You a freshman?"

After hesitating a moment, Silas tripped over his words. "I, um, well, yeah, I am."

"Nothing to be ashamed of," Gus assured. "We all started out that way. In fact, little Philip here is a member of your newbie tribe."

Philip glanced at Silas, seeming a bit more guarded than the rest. Perhaps because he, too, was relatively new to the group and still unsure of his place. Silas offered a sympathetic smile, and Philip's lips twitched up like a tic.

"Which dorm are you in?" Kris asked.

"Oh, I don't live on campus."

"A local?" Paige said as if spotting a rare and endangered species. "I thought you guys were a myth. Sometimes it seems all I meet on this campus are people who've come from other states."

"I live in Greer with my dad," Silas said. "So none of you guys are from the area?"

As with the introductions, Gus took the initiative to go around the circle and announce everyone's state of origin. Gus himself was from Pennsylvania, Franco from Florida, Philip from Wisconsin, Kris from Texas, Paige from West Virginia, and

Sheila won the distance award being from Washington State.

"Wow," Silas said. "And I've barely been out of South Carolina."

Kris bumped him lightly with his shoulder. "You're not missing much. Everywhere looks pretty much the same. Besides, Greenville is a great place. Close enough to the mountains for some good hiking, a thriving theater scene, a lot of great restaurants and clubs."

"There's more culture here than I would have guessed before coming to Furman," Gus said.

Franco made an *ehhhh* sound and held up a hand, tilting it from side to side. "The stand-up scene here isn't the greatest. There's that Comedy Zone place downtown, but it's pretty lame. Never get any decent acts. Once in a while, a big name will come to the Peace Center or the Bon Secours Arena, but there aren't a lot of places for up-and-comers like me to really hone our craft. I like doing the open mic nights and being involved with the improv group at Coffee Underground, not to mention the Furman group Improvable Cause, but I wish I had more opportunities."

"You ever do your act here?" Silas asked.

Franco frowned. "Here? You mean, on campus?"

"Sure. They do plays and recitals in the auditorium, right? Why not a stand-up act?"

"You know, that's not a bad idea," Paige said, pulling a Ziploc baggie of carrot sticks from her backpack and beginning to nibble. "Who's your theater advisor, Dr. Wells? You should talk to her and see if you can set something up."

Franco's frown inverted itself. "I think I will. Makes sense, stand-up is pretty big on college campuses."

"Or used to be before the PC Police started finding everything offensive," Shelia said.

Franco reached across the circle and shook Silas's hand. "Thanks for the suggestion, Si. You're my new best friend."

Silas felt the blush returning to his cheeks and he realized he was pulling at the grass, plucking out blades and tossing them aside. He forced himself to stop and fold his hands over the book on his lap.

Philip leaned forward so he could look around Silas and said, "Hey Kris, you still going to help me study for my World History quiz tonight?"

"Sure thing, buddy. What are friends for?"

Silas noted that Philip winced, almost as if expecting a physical blow, at both the words "buddy" and "friends." A realization struck Silas like the proverbial ton of bricks.

Philip has a crush on Kris, and a pretty big one from the looks of it. I wonder if Kris knows.

Silas had learned that what seemed obvious to him wasn't always obvious to those around him. The one perk of being socially awkward was that it provided ample opportunity to fade into the shadows and merely observe other people. Over time, you could hone some pretty impressive skills analyzing human behavior.

"I'm hungry," Sheila announced, and when Paige offered her a carrot stick, she made a face like she'd been offered a live worm. "I need real food. I skipped lunch. What do you say we head over to the DH and continue our *Fahrenheit* dissection there?"

"Works for me," Gus said, hopping to his feet. "I could go for some grub."

The rest of the gang also stood, dusting themselves off, leaving only Silas sitting on the ground. Kris looked down at him and lifted his chin slightly. "Feel free to join us."

"Absolutely," Gus said. "The food here on campus isn't exactly four-star cuisine, but it's not half bad either."

"Oh, I'd love to, but I can't," Silas said, scrambling to his feet, dropping the math book then snatching it up again. "I really do need to finish this assignment. I've been putting it off all week, and now it's do-or-die time. Besides, I promised my dad I'd be home for dinner. He's making my favorite. Spaghetti, lots of oregano."

Silas realized he was babbling but was powerless to stop himself. This served as a good reminder as to why he didn't talk much, because he hadn't really mastered the art of conversation.

"You know where we'll be if you change your mind," Gus said, walking away backwards. "And I'm sure we'll see you around."

"We hang out down by the amphitheater a lot," Kris said. "In case you're interested in joining our little unofficial book club, our next read is going to be *Death is a Lonely Business*."

They all said goodbye, even Philip, and started down the walkway that led away from the bell tower. Silas offered a weak wave and watched them go, feeling dazed and...well, an emotion he couldn't immediately put a name to. It was warm and kind of fizzy like the carbonation in a soda.

When he finally recognized this alien feeling, he laughed out loud. Happy, he was feeling happy. It wasn't that he'd never felt happy before, but what usually made him happy was a good book, or constructing a perfect paragraph himself, not the camaraderie of a group of people his own age. That was, in fact, quite foreign to him.

He started making his way around the lake toward the parking lot. The sun dipped low in the sky, getting ready to make its nightly departure, sending a glaze of auburn light shimmering across the water, making it appear as if the ducks and swans swam through fiery lava. A cool breeze wafted his face, cooling the sweat that had formed there. It felt like one of those perfect, golden moments, and he tried to hold onto that feeling so that he could describe it later in one of his stories. Such moments were rare and needed to be cherished.

The only thing that tainted his mood was the nagging guilt at all the lies he'd told the group of students who had been so welcoming to him.

CHAPTER TWO

You didn't actually tell them any lies, Silas told himself as he finished up his math assignment at the little wooden desk in his bedroom. *They merely made certain assumptions that you didn't correct.*

He recognized that as a technicality, a semantic justification that in no way absolved him of his culpability. He'd had ample opportunity to set the record straight, and he'd made the conscious choice to allow Gus and his friends to continue thinking that Silas was a Furman student.

After he completed the final equation, not at all certain the answer he'd come up with was correct and not really caring, he closed the text and placed it in his backpack. Next to the desk was a three-shelf bookcase, and he scanned the titles until he found his copy of *Death is a Lonely Business* and slid it out. Silas of course had no intention of joining Gus's book club, but he'd been meaning to read Bradbury's mysteries anyway.

He kicked off his shoes and reclined on his bed, propped against the headboard, and tried to lose himself in the book. In this past, this had proven an effective escape from his problems, but this time it didn't seem to be working. He couldn't stay focused on the words, and his mind kept worrying over the events on the Furman campus like a splinter in his brain.

The first people his age who had shown him true kindness in quite a while and he had completely lied to them. If only Gus hadn't made that crack about community college, maybe Silas would have felt comfortable telling them that he wasn't a Furman student, but actually enrolled at Greenville Technical College.

You already lied to them; don't start lying to yourself as well.

Okay, good advice. The truth was that he liked that they thought he attended Furman. It gave him a thrill because ever since his father had started taking him to the campus to walk the trail around the lake when he was twelve years old, Silas had dreamed of attending the university. The campus was beautiful, and there always seemed to be so many interesting things going on there. Sometimes he liked to go through the buildings and look at the flyers posted on the bulletin boards. Plays, discussion panels, concerts, guest speakers, classes on diverse and fascinating subjects. The atmosphere at Furman buzzed with excitement and intellectual stimulation. He dreamed of matriculating with the lucky souls who crisscrossed the grounds on a daily basis.

However, as his senior year of high school had drawn to a close, reality had set in. And the reality was that Silas's father made little money at the hardware store and Silas's grades were mediocre at best. A school like Furman was simply unattainable. And so, he had ended up at Greenville Tech.

For which he was grateful. GTC offered a solid two-year degree track that would give him a firm foundation, and it was definitely more education than anyone else in his family had ever received. It would be self-indulgent and churlish to wish for anything more.

And yet, most days after he finished his last class, he drove over to Furman and spent time on the campus. Studying, doing assignments, sometimes just wandering around the lake. The dream continued, unrealistic as it might be, so when Gus's group had come along and assumed he was one of them, it fed into that not-so-latent desire, and he'd found himself unable to correct them. Their assumption didn't make the dream any more true, but it felt more solid when other people believed in it as well.

Silas was distracted from his distraction by the feel of his cell buzzing in his pocket. He fished it out and frowned at the little head-and-shoulders notification in the upper left corner of the screen, indicating he had a new Friend request on Facebook. He didn't use his Facebook much anymore, in fact couldn't remember exactly the last time he'd been on the site. Even longer since he'd received any new Friend requests.

He swiped down and saw this message: "Kristopher J. Wellford sent you a friend request."

Silas bolted to a sitting position on the bed, hand clutching the phone as if his flesh had become welded to it. Kristopher J. Wellford. Kris. The chunky guy with the curly hair. He'd somehow tracked Silas down.

Tracked me down? Don't be so melodramatic. It's the social media age. That's what people do when they meet anyone new, look that person up on social media.

Silas supposed he simply wasn't used to being looked up on social media. Most people that met him found him weird and awkward, not someone about which they wanted to get to know more. He knew he was being too hard on himself, but self-deprecation was easier to take than deprecation from others.

He opened his Facebook app and went to the notifications page, ignoring the request and navigating instead straight to Kris's page. The young man's profile picture was a close-up candid shot of him in mid-laughter, face practically glowing with mirth. The cover photo behind it showed Kris dressed in a tux with Paige on one arm and Shelia on the other. Both young women wore dresses, Paige's pink and Sheila's a cobalt blue. Nothing else was visible on the page, Kris's account apparently being locked so that only Friends could view what he posted.

Should he accept the request? His finger hovered over the "Confirm" button. Most people his age probably didn't think twice about these things, and yet Silas debated the pros and cons as if he were making a decision that could impact the trajectory of the rest of his life.

While he hemmed and hawed, he received another notification, this one the little word bubble icon that indicated a private message. Also, from Kris. Because they were not yet Friends, Silas couldn't actually view even a preview of the message without first accepting it, which meant Kris would be able to see on his end that Silas had opened the message. Which would pretty much obligate him to accept the Friend request.

Ah, the complications of online interaction. Jesus, stop being such a baby and just accept the Friend request already.

Silas pressed his thumb against the "Confirm" button, imagining he felt a tiny static shock as he did so, then opened the message Kris had sent.

Hey Silas, my man. Not sure if you remember me, we met out by the bell tower at school earlier. You're a hard man to track down. First I tried Instagram and then Snapchat and couldn't find a profile for you on either. So I dusted off my Facebook and here you are. I swear you update your Facebook even more infrequently than I do. It still has you as being in high school. :p

Track down. Kris used the words himself. He hadn't merely sent a casual Friend request; he'd put in some effort, going to the trouble of searching for Silas along several social media platforms before finally *tracking him down.* Why bother for someone he'd met for only ten minutes?

Silas pushed past his innate paranoia and suspicion and focused on the latter part of Kris's message. The young man was right, Silas rarely updated his Facebook, and his profile did indeed state that he still attended Riverside High. He hadn't bothered to change that status after he graduated and started Greenville Tech. A quick scan of his page, mostly links to YouTube videos by the Vlogbrothers, confirmed that he'd never posted anything about Greenville Tech. Not when he got accepted, not when he started, nothing. Which meant the lie was still safe, if he wanted to preserve it. Of course, now was the perfect time to come clean and fess up. His thumbs beat against the screen as he composed his reply.

Of course I remember you. And yeah I don't have much of an online presence. Have to keep it low pro when you're in the CIA. lol Nah seriously though I'm not big into social media really. Facebook is pretty much it and as you noticed I don't exactly keep up with that either. I enjoyed meeting you and your friends, you're a cool bunch.

Silas hesitated only a fraction of a second before sending the message, cursing his cowardice for not telling the truth but also not quite ready to give up the fantasy of being a Furman student interesting enough that other people sought him out to keep the conversation going. Besides, to continue the semantic acrobatics, he still hadn't told any outright lies.

Underneath his last message, the three dots appeared

indicating that Kris was composing a follow up response. While Silas waited, he went back to Kris's profile to snoop around.

Studies Psychology at Furman University
Went to Llano High School
Lives in Greenville, South Carolina
From Llano, Texas

His profile and cover photos had been updated in the last hour, but before that his last post was from August 3rd. A photo of Kris in a T shirt, cargo shorts, and hiking books, standing by a lake with the sun setting behind him. The caption read, "It sure is ENCHANTING here." The most recent post before that was from April 27th, a meme of Samuel L. Jackson in a suit pointing a gun, which read, "Say Hillary's Emails one more time, motherfucker!"

Silas found himself chuckling when Kris's next message popped up.

Right back atcha. I have to tell you Franco is so excited about your idea of him doing a standup show on campus that he's about to burst. He says he's going to talk to Dr. Wells first thing in the morning. Haven't seen him this jazzed about anything since Kinky Boots came to the Peace Center. I should warn you though if Dr. Wells shoots him down on this, he'll probably be in an incredibly grouchy mood for the next month.

Yikes! I hope he gets the thumbs up then. I'd hate to be the cause of grouchiness.

So Silas, at the risk of asking a totally clichéd question...what's your major?

Haven't really settled on one yet. Just taking my general ed course right now.

I hear ya. I'm doing a BS in Psychology. Thinking of becoming a counselor.

That's awesome. What year are you?

Sophomore. Before Phil came along I was the baby of our little clique.

Oh everybody else seniors?

Gus Paige and Sheila are. Franco's a junior. That makes you and

Phil the only two freshmen in our group.

Silas couldn't help but notice that Kris had casually included him in "our group." This for some reason caused a fluttering in his stomach, not quite a cramp or queasiness but something akin to that feeling right as the rollercoaster nears the apex of the first big hill, the nervous anticipation of the plunge.

A knock at his bedroom door startled Silas, and he quickly tucked his phone under his pillow as if he'd been watching porn or something. "Come in, Dad."

His father pushed open the door and stuck his head inside. "Hey fella, you finished with your homework?"

"Yeah. Can't guarantee I got any of the answers right, but it's done."

"I'd offer to look it over, but I'm no good with numbers. You should see me trying to make change down at the store."

Silas smiled. "So what's up?"

"Nothing much. Just figured, my shift doesn't start until eleven tomorrow, and I think you're first class is at ten, right?"

"Right."

"Then what do you say I make us a big bag of popcorn and we stay up late binge-watching *Supernatural* on Netflix?"

"Sounds good, Dad. I'll be out in a minute."

"Great. I'll get the corn a'popping."

His father shut the door, and Silas reached beneath the pillow to retrieve his phone. Kris had sent him another message.

I have to admit that I feel like some of Fahrenheit is going right over my head. Maybe we can discuss it sometime and you can tell me what I'm missing.

Sure thing. I gotta go for now.

Okay have a good night. I'm sure I'll see you around campus.

Yeah, we're bound to run into each other.

Silas tossed the phone onto the foot of the bed, the fluttering in his stomach becoming more a churning. This feeling he had no trouble identifying. Guilt, plain and simple. He didn't like to think of himself as a dishonest person, so why hadn't he simply told Kris he wasn't a Furman student?

Because he didn't ask. All he asked about was your major, and you gave him an honest answer.

True, but Silas realized it would be better if he avoided any more chats with Kris and didn't seek out the group when on the Furman campus. In fact, maybe he should not spend time at the school for a while to ensure he didn't run into them.

Silas got up, leaving his phone on the bed, and padded across the room in his bare feet. When he opened the door to the hall, he could already smell the popcorn and hear the muffled explosions as the kernels bloomed to life in the bag. Lingering in the air was the aroma of the spaghetti his father had made for supper.

As much as Silas had once dreamed of attending Furman University, he didn't belong there. This was where he belonged, and it wasn't a bad place to be.

He headed down the hall to help his father in the kitchen.

CHAPTER THREE

He stayed away from Furman for over a week. Kris sent him a few more Facebook messages, but Silas did not even open them. He'd received Facebook Friend requests from Franco and Sheila but had ignored them. Clean break, he figured that would be the best way not to dig himself any deeper and get himself into trouble.

But after only nine days, he began to actually miss the campus, found his mind wandering in the middle of his classes to those green quads, the elaborate fountains, the stately buildings. All while experiencing something like hunger pains, only higher up in his chest. He thought he was actually feeling homesick for Furman, which was of course ridiculous. Being ridiculous, however, did not make it any less true.

After his last class of the day, he'd had every intention of driving straight home to Greer but instead had found himself steering the twenty-year-old Nissan Altima toward Furman. Maybe it would be okay if he spent a little time on the grounds, just to get a fix.

He laughed at his own geekiness. Only a true nerd would consider college his drug of choice. And only a nerd with mental issues would consider as his drug of choice a college that wasn't even the one he went to.

Instead of parking down by the lake, this time he found a spot in the lot by McAlister Auditorium. He wanted to avoid the bell tower and the amphitheater. He told himself that on a campus Furman's size, chances were slim he'd run into the group again. Still, he didn't want to risk it.

He took his History book and left the car, wandering around the back of McAlister and the Daniel Music Building.

He considered setting up shop in the rose garden or even the Asian garden, but both those locations were located right off the lake. In the end, he settled on the Place of Peace, a small Japanese temple that had actually been originally built in Japan then later disassembled and donated to Furman, reconstructed at the top of a hill in a copse of trees. Seemed a good place to study and hide out all at the same time.

He approached the building from the back, planning to take a seat on the steps and learn as much as he could about the Revolutionary War. Only when he came around the side of the temple, he discovered that someone else had already taken up residence on the steps. Someone he knew.

He froze for a moment, wondering if he could turn and scurry away without being noticed, but then the young woman on the steps looked up from the notebook in which she was scribbling and spotted him. Her lips curled in a gentle smile of recognition. "Hey, stranger. Long time no see."

Silas tried to smile back, but it felt more like a grimace. "Hi, Paige. How are you?"

She sighed and closed her notebook. "Fine, albeit creatively frustrated. I'm working on a new poem, and it isn't coming together."

"Oh, are you a writer, too?" Silas asked, taking a step forward, momentarily forgetting his commitment to avoid the group to which Paige belonged.

"Trying to be. Do you dabble in poetry?"

"I'm more a short fiction kind of guy."

"Are you on the Writing track? Kris said that you hadn't declared a major."

This gave Silas pause, the idea that people talked about him when he wasn't around. Hell, that people *thought* about him when he wasn't around. "Um, he's right. Writing is a passion of mine, but the reality is that it isn't likely to pay the bills. I'm still trying to figure out what I want to do to actually, you know, make a living."

Paige laughed and rose from the steps, moving with an easy grace. "You sound like my parents. They're always talking to me about making 'practical choices.'"

"My dad is pretty cool about my writing. Encourages me and stuff."

"Maybe you can put him in touch with my folks." Paige pulled her phone from her purse and checked the time. "I'm about to head down to the amphitheater to meet the rest of the gang. You should come with."

"Oh, um, I was just going to—"

"Don't try the 'I have to study' line again," she said, coming over and taking his arm. "Everyone would love to see you again. Especially Kris, he's been worried about you."

Silas allowed himself to be maneuvered onto the path that led down toward the lake, almost as if he had no will of his own. "Worried about me? Why?"

Paige cut a glance at him, and one corner of her lips pulled up in a half-smile. "Guys are so adorable when they are oblivious."

Silas frowned, not at all sure what she meant, which to her probably made him even more adorable. They walked by the Asian Garden in the direction of the bell tower, passing four little cabins on their right.

"I live in the one on the end," Paige said, pointing to the last cabin in the row which was also the biggest.

"These are eco-friendly, right? Solar-powered and all that?"

"Yeah, it's all about teaching sustainability. Low-flow shower heads, composting. It's pretty cool, actually."

They turned right past the cabins. As they approached the amphitheater, dread settled over Silas like a fine coating of ash. He should make his excuses and slip away while he still could, but he didn't want to be rude. He didn't want to reject an extension of kindness toward him.

"Who do you have for History?" Paige asked, nodding toward the text he carried. "I hope it's not Dr. Carver. I never had him personally, but I've heard he's a real hard-ass."

"Oh, I haven't heard that," Silas said, not really answering the question at all.

At the amphitheater, several students gathered in clusters on the tiers that made up the "seats," but Paige led him over to the stage itself. Forming a loose square in the center were Gus, Franco, Kris, and Sheila. The whole gang, minus Philip.

"Hey guys," Paige called out as she started up the steps. "Look who I ran into."

The four looked up. "Silas, where the hell ya been?" Gus shouted, causing several out on the grounds to glance toward the stage. Sheila tossed Silas a half wave/half salute, while Kris merely smiled at him. Franco, however, had the most extreme reaction to seeing him.

Franco leapt to his feet and charged forward. Silas took a step backward and braced himself, convinced that for some reason he was about to be tackled. Instead, Franco engulfed him in a bear hug and actually lifted him off his feet for a moment.

"Silas, you beautiful bastard! I was beginning to think you were my guardian angel or fairy godfather or something. Came down, did your deed, then disappeared."

When Franco finally released him, Silas laughed and shook his head. "What are you talking about?"

"Dr. Wells loved the idea of me putting together a stand-up act. She's helping me jump through all the necessary hoops with the administration, but we're tentatively scheduling it for early January just after the holiday break. I'm talking to some of the guys from Coffee Underground and Improvable Cause about doing a set as well. When it happens, you have to be in the front row, man. My guest of honor."

Silas didn't think he'd ever seen anyone brimming with quite so much joy and excitement in his life. Franco bounced up and down, as if his good mood wouldn't quite allow him to be completely stationary. It delighted Silas to know that he'd had even a small hand in making someone else that happy.

"I'm sure you'll do great," Silas said.

"Of course. Come sit with us for a bit."

Paige had already taken her place between Gus and Sheila. Kris patted the cement next to him and Silas had a seat.

"You been okay?" Kris asked.

"Yeah. Busy with school work and stuff, but otherwise can't complain."

"So then…we're cool?"

"Why wouldn't we be?"

"Kris here thought he'd run you off from our little group," Gus said.

Silas cocked his head toward Kris. "What?"

Kris shot a glance at Gus that seemed to be the literal exemplification of the phrase *if looks could kill.* "No, it's just that…I mean, after we chatted that first night, I didn't hear from you again and you never even opened any of my other messages. I thought maybe I'd said something that offended you or, you know, you found me so boring you didn't want to talk to me anymore."

"He even had some of us send you Friend requests on Facebook like it was the Dark Ages of the Internet or something," Shelia added. "When they went unaccepted, he figured you thought we were all a bunch of dorks and were avoiding us like the proverbial plague."

Silas studied Kris for a moment, bemused by the young man's obvious discomfort as he rocked from side to side on his sit bones like he'd settled on a tack. The idea that Kris would worry that Silas considered *them* too dorky to hang out with was confounding.

"Sorry, it wasn't anything like that," he assured the group. "I don't check my Facebook very often, that's all."

"I don't even have a Facebook," Gus said. "It's for old people."

Paige laughed. "It really is. My grandmother has a Facebook now."

"When grandparents embrace something," Franco said, "you know it's a dead platform."

Paige nodded. "I know, but she's so proud of it, I don't have the heart to tell her. I think she thinks she's hip or something."

Kris nudged Silas with an elbow. "What's been keeping you so busy that you dropped off the face of the planet?"

"I had a paper to write for Psychology, and I have a big test next week in History that I'm grossly unprepared for."

"Silas has Dr. Carver for History this semester," Paige said.

Collectively, the group groaned.

"I feel your pain, man," Franco said, leaning back and propping up on his elbows. "I had him my freshman year and barely made it out alive. Ended up with a C minus but was grateful for it."

"Phil has him this semester," Kris said. "You two in the same class?"

"No, I'm pretty sure we're not."

"Well, maybe you can be study-buddies. I'm trying to help him out, but honestly I think I'm doing more damage than good."

"Where is Philip?" Silas asked, desperate to change the subject.

"He's got a late Bio lab on Fridays," Gus said with a smirk and a shake of his head. "Typical rookie mistake. Your science class might be at ten a.m., but you have to pay attention to when the labs meet. Nothing worse than having a late class on a Friday."

"What about cholera?" Sheila asked. "Isn't that worse?"

"Eaten alive by ants?" Kris suggested.

"Dropped in a vat of sulfuric acid," was Paige's contribution.

Franco gave it some thought before saying, "Finding out your new girlfriend is actually your long-lost sister who used to be your long-lost brother before the sex change."

Silas laughed along with the rest until he realized they were all now looking at him, as if it were his turn. He blurted out the first thing that came to mind. "Being the center of attention for all the wrong reasons, like having a wet spot on the front of your pants or spinach in your teeth."

Not the best retort, but everyone laughed politely and for a golden moment Silas felt that he fit in here, that he was one of them, a feeling he'd never experienced before. The sensation was warm and comfortable, like a fur-lined coat. Only this coat wasn't really his to wear but knowing that didn't make him any more willing to take it off quite yet.

"As soon as Philip is out of the purgatory of lab, we're all headed downtown," Gus said. "You should tag along, Si."

"Oh, well—"

"Don't even think about blowing us off," Kris said. "If you've got homework, so do the rest of us. That's what Sunday night is for. Friday night is for hanging out and having some fun."

Silas turned to him with a defiant lift of his chin. "If you'd let me finish, I was going to say, 'Oh, well, I'd love to.'"

"Awesome," Franco said. "Some people I know that are involved with the Warehouse Theater are putting on an impromptu production of *Waiting for Godot* in Falls Park. We're going to check that out then split a pizza at Mellow Mushroom."

Silas pulled out his cell. "Sounds like a plan. I just need to call my dad and let him know I won't be home for dinner."

"Hope he's not making your favorite again," Kris said with a wink. "You know, spaghetti. Lots of oregano."

Silas's thumb paused over his father's number in the contact list. How weird that Kris would remember such a random fact from something Silas had said a week and a half ago.

The phone rang three times before his father answered. "Son of mine, you on your way home? I just got in myself. Don't feel like cooking. What if we order out?"

"Actually, I was calling to say I'm going out tonight with some friends from school, so I won't be home 'til later."

A brief silence on the other end then, "That's great. I hope you have a good time."

"Thanks. We're going to see a play and then grab a bite. I'm not sure what time I'll be in."

"No worries. If I'm already asleep, you can tell me all about your evening tomorrow morning over breakfast. Pancakes and eggs?"

"It's a date. Have a good night, dad."

"You too, buddy."

After Silas disconnected the call, Shelia said, "That was so sweet. You have to love a man that's close with his father like that."

Something about her tone made Silas instinctively duck his head down and tense his shoulders.

"Oh no, that wasn't a crack," Shelia said, leaning forward. "I was being sincere, though I realize it's hard to tell. You know how some people are said to have resting bitch face? I have resting bitch voice; everything I say comes out sounding sarcastic and snarky. It's a curse."

Silas allowed himself to relax and smiled. "It's okay. Everything I say comes out sounding like I'm a total spaz. We all have our curses."

"Let's get over to Plyer," Gus said, rising to his feet. "Philip should be getting out of lab shortly and we can head straight out."

The group left the amphitheater and meandered back toward the main part of campus. Silas lagged toward the back, and Kris slowed his pace so that they walked side by side. "I'm really glad you're coming with us," Kris said. "And I'm glad you're not mad at me. I really thought I might have inadvertently insulted you or something. You're not the only one with the spaz curse."

Silas gave the young man another bemused smile. "I can't believe you thought I was mad at you. That's silly."

"Well, silly is another of my curses. I don't have it as bad as our pal Franco, but I definitely have it."

They shared an easy laugh then picked up their pace to catch up with the rest of the gang.

What are you doing, Silas? This is the exact opposite of avoiding them and is only digging you deeper into an already deep hole. If you're not careful, you'll find it impossible to climb back out. You're being stupid.

Silas recognized the truth in this, but he also was not yet ready to give up this feeling of acceptance and belonging. When he'd heard himself say "friends from school" earlier, he'd been as stunned by the words as his father. It wasn't a phrase he'd ever used before. Just as hanging out in downtown Greenville on a Friday night was something he'd never done before. Shouldn't he get to experience it at least once in his life, even if under somewhat false pretenses? Sure, it was wrong, but it wasn't like *murder wrong.*

Right?

What's worse than having a late class on Friday? How about lying to good people and trying to convince yourself that it doesn't make you a bad person?

CHAPTER FOUR

Gus, Franco, Paige, and Sheila went together in Gus's Lincoln SUV, while Philip rode with Kris in Kris's Honda Fit. Kris offered to let Silas ride with them, but it made little sense for them to bring Silas back to campus after their night out. More practical for Silas to take his own Nissan and go straight home from downtown.

The group caravanned from campus to the West End of downtown Greenville, Gus's shiny SUV in the lead with Silas's heap bringing up the rear. He felt more than a bit self-conscious following their nice new cars in his jalopy, but when the others had driven around to meet him at the parking lot by the auditorium, no one had given him any grief about it.

They parked in the free lot at County Square, next to the Governor's School. After everyone had climbed out, Gus said, "We're a little early for the show, so let's walk down to O-CHA and get some bubble teas."

Silas had no clue what a bubble tea was, but he simply nodded along with everyone else. They left the parking lot and headed past the Governor's School, taking the paved path that led down to Fall's Park. The day was slightly overcast and chilly but still pleasant enough on a Friday evening for the place to be nearly packed. Families splashed down by the Reedy River, couples reclined on the grass, some guys tossed a Frisbee back and forth. Laughter and the white-noise chatter of crowds buzzed like static. To their left, Silas saw that the theater troupe already hard at work setting up the little round stage for the production. Franco called to a few of them and exchanged waves.

After taking the steps up toward Main Street, the group

turned at the Passerell French Bistro and onto the suspension bridge that curved over the river, offering a nice view of the waterfall for which the park got its name. Halfway across, Silas slowed then stopped, transfixed by the water rushing over the rocks down below. He didn't get downtown much, and he still found it a marvel that there was a waterfall right by Main Street.

"Pretty, isn't it?" Kris said, leaning on the rail next to him.

The rest of the gang had stopped a few feet further down the bridge, taking selfies with the waterfall in the background. Everyone except Philip, who stood off to the side, cutting occasional glances back toward Silas and Kris.

"You know," Silas said, "my dad told me that when he was young, this area of Greenville was a real cesspool."

Kris frowned. "Really? I've never heard that."

"Yeah, he says that back then you only went downtown if you were looking for trouble, and this park in particular was where you went to score drugs or have sex in the bushes."

"Interesting. You'd never guess that now."

"No. Apparently the city invested a ton of money into revitalizing the downtown area. Then the theaters and art galleries and fine-dining restaurants moved in, and the rest, as they say, is history."

Kris stared silently down at the water for a moment before saying, "Gives me a whole new appreciation for the place. Thanks for that."

"I guess my dad is really the one owed the thanks."

"Well, when I meet him, remind me to thank him."

Silas laughed. "Yeah, I'll be sure to do that."

"You guys coming or what?" Philip yelled their way. The rest of the group had continued on to the end of the bridge and were waiting for them.

Kris leaned over and nudged Silas with his elbow. "Come on, little bee, let's rejoin the hive."

The O-CHA tea bar was a five-minute walk, a space so tiny that once the six of them were inside, they jostled each other for room at the counter. Silas kept to the back and stared up at the menu mounted on the wall, lips curled in a slight frown.

Kris bent his head close to Silas's ear and said, "Never had bubble tea before?"

Silas shook his head.

"I recommend you get the milk-based. It's kind of like a smoothie."

"I appreciate the help," Silas said gratefully. "Embarrassing to be the only one not in the know."

"Don't worry about it. Last year we went to this place called Hibachi Café, and Gus ordered us all an appetizer of edamame. I'd never even heard of it before, and I popped a whole pod in my mouth. Realized right quick that you weren't supposed to eat it that way."

When Silas's turn to order came, he asked for a milk-based strawberry flavored bubble tea. The cashier, a rather androgynous teenaged boy with a veil of dyed-black hair falling over one eye like a pirate's patch, asked, "Jellies and pearls?"

Silas gawked at him for a moment, brain working overtime to make sense of the word salad he'd been presented. "I'm sorry, what?"

"Jellies and pearls," the cashier repeated, looking at Silas as if he were the one talking crazy.

Kris came to the rescue again. "Jellies are gummies they put in the tea, and pearls are little tapioca balls."

Little tapioca balls. There's a phrase I never thought I'd hear.

Swallowing a chuckle, Silas started to tell the cashier no thanks but then thought better of it. If he was going to try something entirely new to him, why not go all out and get the full experience? Jellies and pearls, it was.

They took their drinks and meandered back down to the river, stopping at the base of the waterfall and setting up shop on the grass. Silas sipped at his drink, which was indeed quite tasty, though the jellies and pearls seemed unnecessary add-ons that only served to clog his straw.

"So," Sheila said to Paige, "how was the Muse today? Did you create something profound and beautiful?"

"No. I haven't written a poem I really like in weeks. It's like I'm creatively constipated or something."

"Simple solution for that," Franco said. "Just need to find an enema for the brain."

Paige made a gagging sound then laughed. "Nice imagery. Thanks for that."

"I do what I can."

"You know, Silas here is a writer as well."

All eyes turned toward Silas, and he coughed on a pearl that nearly got lodged in his throat. "I dabble, that's all."

"I can respect a dabbler," Gus said. "What kind of stuff do you write?"

Silas thought about it for a moment then shrugged. "I don't know exactly how you'd categorize it. Slice-of-life vignettes, maybe. I don't do anything terribly plot-heavy, mostly character studies and pieces that focus on emotion rather than action."

"Sounds really interesting," Kris said. "I'd love to read some of it."

"Oh, um, I don't know," Silas stammered. He'd never let anyone read any of his stuff before, not even his father, and he'd never even worked up the nerve to submit anything to his high school literary journal. His work was deeply personal. Maybe it was no good or maybe it was brilliant; as long as he never showed it to anyone else, it could be either. A Schrodinger's cat situation. If it turned out the cat was dead, part of him would rather not know.

"Don't be afraid to share your talent," Gus said. "Life's too short for false modesty and shit like that."

"Hub City Books in Spartanburg does an open mic night once a month," Paige said. "I've read my poems there from time to time. Sometimes the crowd can be a little light, but you usually get good feedback."

The very idea sent a shiver of panic through Silas. Hard enough to imagine giving his work to someone else to read and judge; impossible to imagine standing up in front of a group of people and opening himself up in that way.

Paige, perhaps sensing his discomfort, waved off the suggestion and said, "Just something to think about. No pressure."

"So when are you leaving us, Gus?" Sheila asked, and Silas

almost shuddered from relief at the subject change.

Gus slurped up the last of his drink before answering. "Second week of January."

"Where are you going?" Silas asked.

Franco snorted. "You mean there's someone on campus Gus hasn't told? He's headed up to Executive City to rub elbows with all the corrupt politicians."

"I'm going to Washington D.C. to intern at the House of Representatives for spring semester," Gus said. "I'm majoring in Politics and International Affairs."

"Cool. I know Kris is doing Psych and Paige is a future poet laureate. What about the rest of you?"

"I'm majoring in Theater Arts, of course," Franco said. "Sheila here has majored in just about everything. Isn't that right?"

Sheila gave Franco some major side-eye and a dainty bird. "I simply have many different interests, and it's hard for me to settle on just one."

"How many majors have you been through?" Franco asked.

Sheila tilted her head back as she thought. "Let's see. I started in English Lit then switched to History. Very briefly I tried Sociology before going back to English Lit. Oh, wait, sophomore year there was the temporary insanity that was Economics."

Franco laughed. "See, she's had more majors than women on soap operas have husbands."

"Well, I finally settled on Communications."

"The major for the person who doesn't know what they want to do," Gus said. "One step up from Undeclared."

The dainty bird flew Gus's way. "Need I remind you, the Communications department sponsors your little debate team. And just so happens that a Communications degree is going to come in very handy. The world is already largely digitized. Look at the Green brothers, they've built a multi-million-dollar media empire almost exclusively from making digital content for the masses."

"So you're going to be a YouTuber for a living?" Silas asked.

"Please, in five years YouTube will have gone the way of

Myspace, but I'll be ready to take full advantage of whatever the next big thing is to come along."

Silas turned to Philip. "What about you?"

"Sustainability Sciences."

"What's that?"

"It's an environmental major. Sort of looks at the interconnectivity of the environment, society, and economics."

Silas took a moment to try to mentally digest this information. "Wow, sounds...intimidating. You should be living in echo-lodges like Paige."

"Oh, I'll get to live in one of those cabins eventually, at least for one semester. For now, I'm stuck in SoHo."

"SoHo?"

"You know, South Housing, the freshman dorms. I'm in McGlothlin."

"Oh yeah," Silas said. "South Housing, of course. Sorry, I guess I still don't know all the campus lingo."

"So," Franco said, turning toward Gus, "when you're up in the Capital, think you'll get to meet our turd of a fake president?"

Gus shook his head. "Look, I don't like the guy any more than you do, but enough with the 'fake' bit. He won the election fair and square."

Franco's mouth dropped open like that of a broken nutcracker. "Are you serious? Even if you ignore the outside interference from foreign enemies, he still lost the election by millions of votes."

"Do I really need to school you on the importance of the electoral college again? Without it, there are a lot of states that wouldn't get fair representation in the governmental process. That might seem unimportant to you, but..."

Kris leaned toward Silas again and whispered, "This could go on for a while. Among all his other accomplishments, Gus is captain of the debate team. Once you get him wound up, it's hard to stop him again."

Silas listened but couldn't say he entirely followed all the political discourse. A lot of it went over his head. He liked to think of himself as civic-minded, and he definitely planned to vote in the next election now that he was able, but he didn't follow politics much. For all the doomsayers out there prophesizing the end of civilization if one side or the other got into power, none of it seemed to affect Silas's day-to-day life in any kind of meaningful way.

Gus was mid-sentence when Sheila stood up and announced, "We should head on over if we want to get good seats."

Everyone else stood but Gus, who sat for a moment longer before getting to his feet. "Fine, but we're merely shelving this topic for later discussion."

"Great," Paige deadpanned. "Something to look forward to."

A crowd had already started to flank the round stage, some sitting on blankets while others had brought canvas chairs. Near the front, a tall, lanky man with greying hair waved at the group. He sat next to a lovely woman with flawless skin and two young kids, a boy and a girl.

"Hey, it's Dr. Flem," Gus said and started over.

"Phlegm," Silas said to Kris as they followed. "His name is Phlegm, as in mucus?"

Kris laughed. "F-l-e-m. Actually, his name is Flemming, but everyone calls him Dr. Flem. He's head of the Philosophy department and the academic advisor for the debate team."

"Dr. Flem, Mrs. Flem, Little Flems," Gus said, shaking the professor's hand. "Here to see the show?"

"We love live theater," Dr. Flem said. "And *Waiting for Godot* is a great exercise in existentialism."

"Think we're ready for the meet with William and Mary next week, coach?"

"Definitely. The new freshmen we've got on the team are looking solid." Dr. Flem turned toward the rest of the group. "How are the rest of the rabble?"

They all mumbled their hellos.

Dr. Flem focused his attention on Silas. "I do believe there's an extra member in the band. Who do we have here?"

"This is our new friend, Silas," Kris said, throwing his arm around Silas's shoulders. "We met him last week, but we think we're going to keep him."

"Nice to meet you, Silas."

"You too, Dr. Flem…ming," he said, not able to bring himself to use the shortened sobriquet.

"Wanna join us?" Mrs. Flemming asked, the two toddlers crawling on her like a jungle gym. "It'll be a tight squeeze, but we can make room."

"Nah, you have your family time," Gus said. "See you on campus next week, Dr. Flem."

The group located a spot not too far back and slightly to the left of the stage. Silas noticed there wasn't much of a set, just a few raised wooden platforms painted to resemble rocks and right in the center of the stage a thin, crooked tree that looked to be made of papier-mâché.

Kris looked at him and smiled, wide and bright. "Glad you joined us?"

Silas found himself returning that smile. "I am. I'm having a great time."

"Good to hear. Before you leave, I'd love to exchange numbers. You know, to keep in touch. Easier than Facebook. Besides, the six of us get into some pretty interesting group texts sometimes. Would be nice to have a lucky seventh involved."

Feeling uncharacteristically bold, Silas took out his phone and handed it to Kris. "Just enter your number in my contacts."

Kris took Silas's phone then held out his own. "You do the same."

After the numbers exchange, Silas leaned back, staring up at the sky. It wasn't yet twilight, but already a crescent moon hung like a sliver of clipped fingernail, and only a few scattered clouds remained to dot the sky, a Morse code message from God. The breeze was cool but not downright cold, and the air smelled of a variety of foods, the intermingled scents wafting down from all the nearby restaurants.

This is one of those golden moments again. Usually, a person only recognizes them in retrospect, after they've passed, but I'm fully cognizant of being smack dab in the middle of one.

Buoyed by a wave of unaccountable optimism, Silas closed his eyes and waited for *Waiting for Godot*.

CHAPTER FIVE

"How was your evening?" his father asked as Silas walked into the living room.

Silas lingered by the door, jangling his keys like a baby's rattle. "Good. I enjoyed myself."

His father reclined on the sofa, feet propped on the round glass-topped coffee table. He had a Budweiser in one hand, the remote in the other. On the television across the room, just beside the front door, an episode of *Modern Family* played at low volume. "That's great. What play did you see?"

"*Waiting for Godot.*"

"Hmm, not familiar with that. What's it about?"

"Nothing, really."

His father laughed. "A play about nothing. Was Kramer in it?"

Silas wasn't sure what his father meant, but he often made references that were lost on his son. Silas figured he was referencing some old movie or song or something and let it go. "It was about two guys waiting for a third guy that never actually shows up. A lot of talking, philosophical musing, that sort of thing."

"Oh, so not a musical then?"

"No, dad. Not a musical."

"You know, for our first date I took your mother to see *Company* at the Gaffney Little Theater. She got such a kick out of that song, 'Not Getting Married Today.'"

Silas opened his mouth to say, "You've told me that story a million times, dad," but then kept silent. His father loved to tell the story, it made him happy, so why should Silas try to take that away from him? So little seemed to make his father truly happy these days.

"I'd never been to a play before, not in my whole life," his father said, his gaze directed at the television but unfocused, clearly looking beyond the sitcom flickering on the screen and into the past. "But your mother seemed so classy, I wanted her to think I was classy, too. I mean, I know it wasn't like I was taking her to Broadway or nothing, just a rinky-dink theater in a Podunk town like Gaffney, but it was something artsy and sophisticated, you know?"

Silas took off his jacket and sat on the love seat placed cattycorner to the sofa. "Yeah, dad, I know."

"I actually bought a jacket from the Salvation Army Thrift Store. A ridiculous pale green thing that came with a bowtie, but I felt fancy. Your mother was dressed in this gorgeous strapless number. Now when we got there, we were definitely the only people in the theater dressed that way. I saw more than a few pairs of overalls out there in the audience. We didn't care, though. It was almost like we were in our own little bubble and only saw each other. To this day, I couldn't tell you exactly what the play was about because I spent most of the play watching your mother watch the play."

His father's gaze dropped down to his beer, which he swished around in the can before taking a swig. Silas could see the familiar melancholy seeping in, the way it inevitably did when his father talked about his mother. She had died when Silas was only four, he honestly had very little memory of her, but he could tell his father still felt her absence every day, like that one missing piece of the puzzle that will leave it eternally incomplete.

"I'm glad you had a good time," his father said after a moment. "I'd like to meet these new friends of yours sometime."

Not likely, Silas thought but said, "Sure, dad."

The two exchanged a brief hug then Silas went down the short hallway to the right of the door, his bedroom at the end of the hall. He found it somewhat sweet that his father had waited up for him, and there was no doubt this was what his father had done. It wasn't so much the fact that his father was still up at nearly midnight that gave it away, his father had notoriously bad insomnia, but he typically watched television in his own bedroom at the opposite end of the trailer. The only reason he would have set up shop in the living room was so he could talk to Silas when he got home.

Once in his room with the door closed, Silas threw his keys on the desk and draped his jacket over the chair, then kicked his shoes off and collapsed onto the bed. Head propped on the pillow, he took out his phone and scrolled through his memories of the night. He'd taken several photos of the play itself (which he would have probably found very boring if the actors hadn't made the choice to do all their lines in really bad, stereotypically New York accents, adding in more profanity than one would find in a Tarantino film), shots of the crowd, of the gang. His favorite photo was one Dr. Flemming took of the entire group, all seven of them, Silas sandwiched between Kris and Paige. He thought that to any outside observer who happened to glimpse the photo, Silas wouldn't stand out. In fact, he would blend in, just another college kid among college kids. Nothing to indicate his traumatic high school years, his sometimes-crippling social anxiety, his struggles with feelings of inferiority, his fears that he would never achieve the dreams he harbored like wanted fugitives. No, in the photo he looked like a guy simply having a good time with his friends. Happy, comfortable, *normal*.

The phone vibrated with another text. True to his word, Kris had included Silas in on the gang's group texts. Gus had posed the question, *"If time travl were possible who wuld you go back n time to kill in order to make th world a beter place?"* The answers ranged from the predictable (Hitler, Lee Harvey Oswald, the 9/11 hijackers) to the more humorous (Miley Cyrus, Paris Hilton, the television executives who canceled *Firefly*). Silas hadn't responded yet, but after giving it some thought, he typed out a reply.

Thing about altering the past is that you never know what effect it will have. May seem like you're doing a good thing but could have unforeseen consequences that make the future even worse. So I'd go back and kill whoever invented time travel thus saving us from any potentially devastating timeline deviations.

Gus's response was quick and, as Silas was learning, characteristically full of typos.

Ding ding din! Thats th rite answer Si wins the prze give that guy a cupie doll!

Silas smiled then pulled up the other message. Apart from the group text, Kris had also sent him a personal, private text. It had come in only five minutes after Silas had pulled out of the County Square lot to head back home. Silas had not yet responded, but he'd read the message several times already.

Silas, I just wanted to thank you for joining us tonight. You're an interesting guy and I look forward to getting to know you better. Hope I didn't offend you with the "I think we'll keep" him joke to Dr. Flem. I routinely make a fine meal of my foot if you know what I mean. Too bad you can't join us for the movie tomorrow but I understand how it is when you let your schoolwork pile up. I'm sure we'll run into each other on campus. Anyway drive safe and have a great weekend. Talk to you soon.

Silas felt dazed and slightly euphoric. He wondered if this was what it felt like to be drunk. The group was so dynamic and funny and passionate, and yet Kris found *him* interesting, worried about offending *him*. It was almost as if Silas had stepped into *The Twilight Zone* or something, the world turned topsy-turvy, up becoming down.

An insidious line of guilt began to thread its way through his contentment, but he quickly snipped that string. Sure, this situation he'd created for himself was ultimately unsustainable and would have to come to an inevitable end at some point. Probably sooner rather than later. Already he found himself thinking of an end game. He could completely ghost the group, simply disappearing, deactivating his Facebook and changing his cell number. That seemed cruel, however. He could simply send a group text saying that his father got transferred to another state and Silas had to withdrawal from Furman and move suddenly. Of course, what kind of transfer happened so suddenly that there was no time to say goodbye to friends? Obviously, this would take more planning, but Silas wasn't in the mood to think about it now.

He typed out a quick *Thank you* to Kris then put his phone aside. He climbed off the bed and went to his desk, opening the laptop and pulling up the Word doc for his latest story-in-progress. A simple tale from the point of view of an old woman looking at a snapshot of herself as a child, musing about all the choices that had brought her from then to now, the moments that had seemed inconsequential at the time, but which had proved to be quite consequential in the long run.

As Silas's fingers tap-danced over the keys, sometimes in a fast staccato and sometimes with longer pauses between, he mused on how his fiction had once seemed like a wonderful escape from his real life, but now his real life had become a fiction, a yarn he spun for an audience of six.

Perhaps there was some kind of irony there.

CHAPTER SIX

Wednesday morning, just as Silas pulled into the parking lot at Greenville Tech, he received a text from Kris.

Hey man why don't you meet us at the DH for lunch at 1230?

Silas sat in the car, staring down at the phone. Since Friday, he'd participated in more group texts and exchanged a few messages with Kris, but he hadn't seen any of them. In fact, he'd made a point of staying away from Furman since then, and he'd found excuses to decline all their subsequent invites to get together. He figured it would be easier to live out this fantasy if he didn't have to do it in person. Besides, Friday night had been so perfect, he thought it could only go downhill from there.

A part of him wanted to get together again, to re-experience that feeling of fitting in, but he recognized the more he did, the greater the chances he would wreck things and it would be revealed that he didn't fit in at all.

Wish I could but I won't be on campus for lunch. Have some stuff to take care of down on S Pleasantburg. Sorry.

Silas's thumb hovered over the screen before hitting Send. He still avoided telling any outright lies in some futile attempt to assuage his guilt, as if this somehow mitigated all the lies of omission, the failures to correct misconceptions. Like if the gang found out he wasn't a Furman student, he could just say, "Well, I never said I was," and all would be forgiven.

Talk about living in a fantasy world.

Kris's response came a moment later.

Then tonight Village Grind @ 6. Won't take no for an answer this time. I really want to see you again.

The next message came only seconds later, before Silas even had time to begin typing a response.

We all want to see you again.

Silas knew he would be late for class if he didn't go in soon, but nonetheless he contemplated a moment before composing a response text. It would only get increasingly harder to put off their offers to hang out without raising their suspicions, so the time had probably come for him to put an end to this charade. And yet if that were the case, then might he not allow himself one more evening of fun and friendship before putting this dream to bed and returning to his normal humdrum life? After all, he'd allowed the fraud to persist this long, what could one more night hurt?

Decision made, he quickly typed out a message before he could change his mind.

I can make that work but won't be able to stay long. Gotta run for now. See you tonight.

With that, Silas turned off his phone and stowed it away in his backpack.

Silas found it hard to concentrate on Dr. Gordon's History lecture. Although to be fair, he always found it hard to concentrate when Dr. Gordon was talking. The man spoke in a flat monotone devoid of inflection or emotion. Like a robot, only even a robot had more modulation in the voice. Typically Silas ended up scribbling out story ideas or entire pieces of flash fiction in the back of his notebook.

Today, however, his mind kept turning to his impulsive and reckless decision to go to the Village Grind tonight to hang with the gang. Second thoughts were creeping in. Second, third, and fourth thoughts, actually. Of course, he could still back out. Send Kris a text and say something came up, or simply not show.

You can't do that. It would be terribly rude.

Of course, that led to the question would it be more rude to not show up or to continue lying to people he'd begun to tentatively think of as friends?

Silas was jerked out of his reverie when he realized Dr. Gordon had said his name.

"I'm sorry, sir. What was that?"

Dr. Gordon's face tended to remain as affectless as his

voice, so it was impossible to tell from his expression if he was annoyed by Silas's inattention or not. "I asked if you could name anyone other than Paul Revere who made those desperate horseback rides to warn the colonists that the British forces were advancing?"

"Oh, um, let's see, William Dawes, Samuel Prescott, there was a woman. Sybil something."

"Ludington. Very good, Mr. Granger. Yes, because of the famous Longfellow poem, Revere is the name everyone knows and associates with 'The British are Coming,' and yet he was not the only one. Sybil Ludington, in fact, rode over twice the distance as Revere and was only sixteen at the time. You see…"

Silas tuned out again. He actually found the subject matter rather interesting, but Dr. Gordon's delivery made even the most fascinating stories dull and plodding. Besides, Silas's moral dilemma took up too much space in his brain to allow room for anything else.

His fingers itched to sneak his cell from his backpack and shoot a quick text to Kris, saying that he'd started throwing up or his car had broken down or his grandmother was in the hospital with a broken hip. Of course, neither of Silas's grandmothers were living, but Kris had no way of knowing that, and what was one more lie on top of all the others?

And yet another part of him wanted nothing more than to be there at the coffee shop with the gang tonight, laughing and talking and having a good time. It felt almost as if he were two different people.

You are. You're Silas Granger, Greenville Tech student, and you're also Silas Granger, Furman student. Of course, one of those people is real and the other is fictitious. You should be careful that you don't get in so deep that you forget which is which.

Silas stood in front of the mirror affixed to his closet door, scrutinizing his reflection. This was the fourth outfit he'd tried on, and he felt ridiculous. He'd never been one to give much thought to clothes. He typically opened the closet every morning, reached in and blindly picked the first shirt and pair of pants his fingers touched. Now he found himself wondering things like, "Are these pants flattering?" and "Does this shirt make it seem I'm trying too hard to be cool?"

Then again, the writer side of him understood why he was putting so much more effort into dressing himself tonight. He was basically building a character, and every detail counted.

"Screw it," he muttered to himself, deciding that the Iron Man T-shirt and the faded jeans he currently wore would have to do.

He grabbed his jacket and left his room, heading down the hallway into the living room. His father stood in the kitchen, separated from the living room only by a short bar that jutted out like a peninsula, staring into the fridge.

"Sure I can't make you something to eat before you head out?" he asked. "A quick sandwich or something?"

"That's okay, Dad. I'll grab something at the coffee shop."

His father closed the fridge door and pulled his wallet from his back pocket. "Need some extra cash?"

"No, I'm fine."

Undeterred, his father came into the living room and held out a twenty. "Just take it. You can never have too much cash."

Silas hesitated for a second longer, but he knew his father would persist and ultimately it would hurt his father's feelings if Silas refused the money. "Thanks, Dad," he said, taking the bill and stuffing it into a pocket.

Taking money from his father always made Silas feel a bit weird. They weren't exactly destitute and starving, but Silas knew that finances were an issue. He'd talked about getting a part-time job, but his father insisted that while he was in school, focusing on his studies should be his job. Financial aid covered tuition and even books, but Silas relied on his father to pay for his cell phone, car insurance every month as well as gas money, and an additional fifty-dollar-a-week allowance had to cover everything else. Silas already felt like enough of a mooch without taking any additional money.

And yet he knew that it made his father feel good to give it.

"So," his father said, adjusting the collar on Silas's jacket, "tell me about these new friends of yours."

"I already told you about them."

"No, you told me their names. I want to know about *them*."

Silas shrugged. "I don't know what to tell you. They're cool, smart. Like to read, discuss politics."

"Are they a biker gang?" his father asked. "I bet they're a biker gang."

Silas sputtered a laugh. "Yeah, Dad. They all ride Harleys and are covered in tattoos and piercings. They're going to initiate me into the gang tonight, so you might not recognize me under all the ink and studs when I get home."

"You'll have to get a new name. Silas is good but not for a biker. Maybe Pisser or Crusher, something like that."

"I'll keep that in mind."

His father gave him a brief hug then said, "Have a good time. It is a school night, so back by ten, okay?"

"Promise."

Outside, Silas cranked his car but didn't pull out right away. Looking back at the trailer, he could see his father by the kitchen window, probably preparing his own sandwich by the sink. An almost overwhelming sense of love crashed over Silas, followed by a bitter wind of sadness.

Until this moment, he hadn't considered how his pretense of being a Furman student was actually a betrayal of his father. A man who worked so hard to provide for Silas, to make his life full and happy despite meager means. A man who despite his own hardships and pain always managed to make Silas laugh. By pretending to be someone else, was Silas actually denigrating the life his father worked so hard to give him?

More kindling for the guilt bonfire. At this rate, Silas would soon burn to ash.

CHAPTER SEVEN

Not only had Silas never been to the Village Grind, he'd never been to this part of Greenville before. He relied on Google Maps to lead the way. He passed through a pretty sketchy neighborhood before entering another area that had obviously been revitalized and beautified. He found himself wondering about the people who lived in the sketchy neighborhood he'd just come through. Did they appreciate the revitalization, or did they feel they were being pushed out the way wild animals did as their natural habitats were destroyed to put up housing developments and parking lots?

The Village Grind came up on his right, but he didn't see any available parking. He continued on, found a place to turn around, then made another pass. He did this a couple of times before branching off to the side streets and finally locating a spot a few blocks away. It was a tight squeeze, but after starting to back in, stopping to reposition himself, then repeating the process, he finally managed a halfway decent parallel parking job.

By this point, it was already five after six, so he expected to be the last one there, but when he entered the coffee shop, he looked around and spotted Kris sitting alone on a tall stool by a bar that ran along one of the windows. Kris smiled, waved, then hopped off the stool, walking over with an oversized coffee cup in his hands.

"Hey, man. I was worried you weren't going to make it."

"Sorry about that. I had a little trouble finding a place to park."

"Oh yeah, should have warned you about that."

Silas glanced at Kris's coffee cup, half empty. "How long you been here?"

"A while. I'm obsessive-compulsively early for everything."

"Not a bad trait to have."

"You'd think, but it extends even to stuff I don't want to be early for. Dentist appointments, visits with Grandma, *class*."

Silas laughed. "Well, you could always drive around the block a few times to put off the inevitable."

"Good idea. Come on, let's get you a drink."

Behind the counter was a chalk board with the menu scrawled across it. Kris ordered another coffee, and Silas settled on a chai latte. They didn't serve sandwiches or anything like that, but they had a selection of pastries. Silas went for a lemon poppy seed muffin and a donut. Kris offered to pay, but Silas wouldn't allow it. He had left the house feeling like a mooch already; he didn't want to compound the problem.

The barista, a young woman with vibrant violet hair, handed over the pastries on a plate and said she'd bring their drinks out to them.

A trio that had set up shop in a corner with a leather couch and two plastic chairs with a wood plank table between them vacated at that moment, so Silas and Kris headed there, Silas taking the couch and Kris sitting in the chair directly across from him.

Silas took a moment to really look around the coffee shop. It was small but cozy, exposed brick walls and rough wood rafters overhead. Overpriced artwork from local artists were on prominent display, and the large windows lent the place an open atmosphere that actually made it feel larger than it was. The air smelled strongly of coffee, a scent that Silas had always liked, despite the fact that he didn't actually like the drink itself.

"Your first time here?" Kris asked.

"Yeah. Actually, I'd never even heard of this place before Sheila mentioned it."

"It's just far enough outside the hub of downtown that it isn't totally crowded all the time."

"So where are the rest of the guys?" Silas asked. "Are they as habitually late as you are early?"

Kris took a sip of his coffee, added more Splenda, stirred it in, blew on the surface though at this point it couldn't still be hot, and took another sip before answering. "It's only me tonight."

"Oh. I'm sorry, I guess I misunderstood. I thought the whole gang was getting together."

"Yeah, I suppose my text may have made it sound like everyone would be here, though technically I never said that."

Silas paused with a hunk of donut halfway to his mouth. Kris's comment sounded so much like one of Silas's own justifications that for a moment he wondered if Kris knew the truth and was messing with him.

"I wasn't trying to lie to you," Kris said. "I guess part of me worried you wouldn't want to come if you knew I'd be the only one here. Hope you're not terribly disappointed."

"Why would I be disappointed?"

"I don't know. I mean, I'm not the most dynamic member of the group."

"What are you talking about? You're great, probably the easiest one to talk to."

Kris smiled then held his coffee cup up, as if trying to hide behind its bulky shape. "Thanks. I know what you mean. They're my friends and I love them, but some of them can be a bit much to take."

Silas nodded then leaned forward, lowering his voice. "I have to admit, I don't always understand everything Gus is saying."

Kris had just taken another sip, and his surprised laugh sent a sprinkling of coffee onto his lap. He apologized and used a napkin to clean himself up. "Yeah, Gus is a really great guy, but he can lay the whole intellectual act on pretty thick sometimes. He always feels he has to prove he's the smartest person in the room. Then again, that might be a good trait in a future politician."

"Don't get me wrong," Silas said, "I like him a lot. It's just that I find him a bit...intimidating."

"He can get a little grandstandy in the group, but if you ever get to talk to him one-on-one, he's much more down to earth. A surprisingly good listener."

A few moments passed in an awkward silence. Silas had

only started to feel comfortable with the group dynamic. Anything more intimate still had him feeling out of his depth.

"So," Kris said, "how are you doing in Dr. Carver's class?"

Silas took a bite of his muffin and chewed longer than necessary as he ran the name through his memory banks. Dr. Carver, Dr. Carver...ah yes, the history professor from hell.

"Um, History isn't my best subject, but I'm managing. Think I might get out of there with a B."

"Philip is really struggling."

"You still tutoring him?" Silas asked.

"If you can call it that."

"Well, I'm sure he appreciates the attention."

Kris stared at him, one side of his mouth raised slightly. "Yeah, I know he does. I guess I need to do something about that."

"What do you mean?"

"I think you know what I mean. I'm not blind to the fact that Philip has feelings for me, and I like him. I just don't *like* him. I'm not sure how to address it. I certainly don't want to hurt his feelings or make him feel bad. Got any suggestions?"

Silas found it almost laughable that he would be solicited for suggestions relating to interpersonal relationships, but before he could formulate any response, Violet Hair came over with their drinks. Kris traded his now-drained coffee cup for one brimming with the aromatic brew.

"Any idea when Katie will be working again?" he asked as the barista turned to go.

"Not off the top of my head," the girl said, "but I can check the schedule in the back."

"Nah, it's not that important. Just curious."

After Violet Hair had returned to her place behind the counter, Silas said, "Who's Katie?"

"Another barista that works here. We're sort of friendly, and sometimes she gives me free drinks. She hopes to transfer to Furman in the fall."

"Oh, where does she go to school now?"

"Greenville Tech."

A chunk of muffin lodged in Silas's throat, and he coughed

and sputtered. Kris actually half-stood and patted him on the back. Silas waved him back to his seat and took a large gulp of his chai latte, the drink burning away the blockage.

"Sorry, swallowed it down the wrong pipe. You were, um, saying that your friend Katie goes to Greenville Tech but wants to transfer to Furman?"

"Oh yeah. She says a lot of people do that. Furman, as you know, can be pretty pricey, so it's cheaper for some to get a lot of the basic education courses at Tech. Plus, a chance to boost your GPA and increase your likelihood of being accepted. Katie's a smart cookie, I doubt she'll have any trouble getting in."

Silas found himself looking around the coffee shop, as if afraid that despite Violet Hair's assertion, Katie really was here and would recognize Silas as a fellow Tech student and rat him out.

"Does the rest of the gang know her?" Silas asked, trying to sound nonchalant but failing.

"Sure. She writes poetry, too, so she's gone with Paige to that open mic night at Hub City. And though Gus hasn't copped to it yet, I think he has a thing for her."

Silas sipped at his drink, thoughts ricocheting inside his skull. He'd been so afraid to tell them that he wasn't a Furman student but instead went to Greenville Tech, fearing they would see him as an outsider and not someone they would want to hang out with, and yet according to Kris they had no issue with Katie, the barista Tech student who went to poetry readings with Paige and was the object of Gus's untold affections.

Since first encountering the group that day by the bell tower, Silas had reimagined that meeting. A reimagining where he immediately corrected their assumption that he attended Furman and they turned cold, talking to him only in clipped monosyllables, making excuses to leave and not offering to have him join them. No follow-up Friend request and message from Kris, no night out in downtown Greenville, no entertaining group texts. He found this alternate timeline oddly comforting because it somehow made him feel better about the deception.

Only now he was forced to reimagine that meeting a different way. He immediately comes clean about his status as a Tech student, and nothing changes. The group is still warm and welcoming. They still treat him as an equal; they still treat him as a friend.

Could it be that the deception was unnecessary, born only from his own insecurity and apprehension? It took the pressure off himself to think that they had unwittingly walled him into this corner, but perhaps he'd been the one laying the bricks one by one, building the wall to his prison all by himself.

Which led to the question…was it too late to get himself out? Had he reached the point of no return, or could the friendships he had only started to build still be salvaged once the wall was knocked down?

"You okay?" Kris asked, sitting down his coffee cup. "You look upset."

Silas still had half a muffin left, but his appetite had fled. He pushed aside the plate and his drink, steeling himself. His heart trip-hammered in his chest, loud in his own ears like the pounding of drums at a rock concert, and he felt sweat beading on his forehead. Twin lumps formed in his gut and his throat, blockages that seemed designed to keep the truth from escaping. He fought past them, took a deep breath, and said, "Kris, I have to be honest with you about something."

Kris took a deep breath of his own and nodded. "Okay. You can tell me anything."

"Well, you see, I don't know exactly where to start. The thing is—"

Silas leaned forward and put both hands on the plank table between them. Kris immediately responded by leaning forward and taking his hands. The move was so unexpected that Silas quickly pulled back, jerking his hands away as if he'd just come into contact with something gross, like a pile of vomit.

From the crestfallen expression on Kris's face, he obviously read the reaction the same and saw himself as that something gross, as that pile of vomit. "Oh shit, man. I'm so sorry. I thought you wanted me to. I guess I totally misread the situation."

Silas stared down at his own hands as if they were suddenly alien to him, as if Kris's touch had transformed them into something other than extensions of his own body. "I don't understand. Did you invite me here on a...*date?*"

Kris fidgeted in his seat, stuttering and stammering and gesturing so emphatically when he spoke that he nearly knocked over his coffee cup. "No, not exactly. I mean, I guess the truth is that I was hoping that if we spent some time alone, just the two of us, that I would work up the courage to ask you out on a date. I should have gotten the picture when you wouldn't let me pay for your stuff."

Silas's mind fought to play catchup. Clearly, he was the one who had misread the situation, and now he looked back over everything since he'd arrived at the coffee shop—actually everything from the moment he'd received that Facebook message from Kris—and discovered new meaning in it. He hadn't let Kris pay so he wouldn't feel like a freeloader, but Kris had read into that a statement of a lack of interest.

"That wasn't it," Silas said. "I had no idea that you were interested in me in that way. No idea at all."

"Really? That's surprising, because according to Paige it's quite obvious."

"So the whole gang knows?"

"I think so. Paige and Franco for sure, and Philip definitely knows."

Pieces continued to fall into place. Now he understood why Philip was more standoffish toward him than the rest. He saw Silas as a threat, an invader trying to stake claim to a territory in which Philip himself wanted to plant his flag.

"You really had no idea?" Kris asked shyly.

Silas shook his head. "It never even crossed my mind."

"Well, it was stupid of me to think that you'd be interested in someone like me anyway."

This statement shocked Silas anew. "What do you mean, *someone like you?*"

Kris began to fidget again, his gaze darting everywhere but at Silas. He looked like a man who wanted to be anywhere but here, even if that meant dissolving and melting into the floor. Silas knew that feeling, he experienced it a lot.

"You know," Kris said, "I'm just some chubby guy with sloppy hair. No one special."

Silas was stunned into silence by this. The idea that Kris thought he wasn't special, that he wasn't good-looking enough, that he harbored his own insecurities...it baffled Silas completely. To him, the group had taken on mythic proportions; it had never occurred to him that they could be so *human*. Of course, he now recognized the notion as absurd.

"You're crazy," Silas said then realized how that sounded. "I mean, crazy to think you're not special. You're great, truly."

Kris finally allowed his gaze to settle on Silas. "So does that mean you might be interested in going out on a date with me?"

Now it was Silas's turn to fidget and not make eye contact.

"Guess I'm a real glutton for punishment, huh?" Kris said with a strained laugh. "Can we just pretend I never asked?"

"It's not that, I—" Silas started but paused as he tried to figure out exactly what he did think, exactly what he did feel. "I'm still trying to wrap my head around this. I meant it when I said it never crossed my mind. I never would have dreamed *you* would be interested in *me*. And honestly, this is uncharted territory for me."

"You've never been asked out on a date before?"

Silas shook his head, staring down into his cup like a two-bit psychic trying to read tea leaves. "Never been on a date, never kissed anyone, never even held hands before."

"That's nothing to be ashamed of. I mean, I'm not exactly what you would call experienced in that arena myself. Last year I dated a guy from the theater department for a couple of months, but that ended in disaster."

Eager to get the spotlight off himself, Silas said, "What happened?"

Kris didn't answer right away, his silence stretching out until it seemed he wasn't going to reply. Then he finished his coffee, took a deep breath, and plunged on. "Brandon said from the get-go that he didn't want anything serious. 'Keep it casual,' is what he said. Nothing exclusive. After a couple of months, I told him that I wasn't built for 'casual,' and I wanted more of a commitment."

"I'm guessing that didn't go over well with him?"

"He actually laughed at me then told me that while I was

fun to be around, I wasn't 'boyfriend' material. He said maybe if I lost some weight and got a better haircut."

"Jesus," Silas said. "This Brandon guy sounds like a real asshole."

Kris smiled. "That seems to be the general consensus. In fact, everyone else picked up on that long before I did. I've sort of shied away from dating since then."

"Then why ask me out?"

"Usual reasons," Kris said. "I like you. You're funny and you're sweet. You actually listen when I talk. You seem like someone who wouldn't lie to me or purposefully try to make me feel bad. Plus, icing on the cake, you're cute as hell."

This bombardment of compliments caught Silas off guard, and he wasn't sure how to react. And a bombardment is exactly how it felt, as if each one was a pebble pelting his body. Ridiculous, but the experience was so new to him that it felt utterly foreign. Most confusing of all, Kris seemed to genuinely mean everything he said.

Then there was that one statement that rang in Silas's mind like an accusation: *You seem like someone who wouldn't lie to me...*

"I don't think I can go out with you," Silas said. "At least, not right now. Like I said, this is uncharted territory. It's not that I don't like you, and it certainly isn't because I don't find you attractive. This really is about me, about not being sure I'm ready. I've got my own stuff I need to work on. I'd like it if we could still be friends and just see how things go from there."

"Absolutely!" Kris said with a touch too much enthusiasm to be completely convincing. "Friends is good for me. I worried that if you weren't interested, you wouldn't want anything to do with me anymore."

"That's silly. Friends it is."

Silas wondered why that felt like such a lie.

They sat in silence for a few moments, invisible walls suddenly constructed around them, putting them each in a separate sound-proofed booth. Silas wondered what excuse he could give for having to leave without coming off like a total douche. Kris beat him to it.

"I should get back to campus," he said. "I have some

studying to do for an Abnormal Psych test tomorrow."

"Yeah, I promised my dad I'd be home early."

Outside on the sidewalk, Kris asked, "Where did you park?"

Silas pointed toward one of the side streets. "A few blocks down that way."

"I'll walk you to your car."

"You don't have to do that."

"I know I don't have to, but I want to."

Silas didn't protest. The walk started off silent, but he had a question nagging him that he felt he had to ask. "Could you tell I was gay right away?"

Kris glanced over at him. "You're not super obvious or anything, but yeah, I sort of got that vibe. Can't you just sort of tell about people?"

"I guess so. I've never really had the opportunity to confirm whether or not my gaydar is functioning properly before."

Kris laughed and nudged him with his elbow. Something Silas now realized he'd never seen the young man do to anyone else. It was Kris's nonverbal way of expressing affection. So much more suddenly made sense.

"We're all going to the Acoustic Café down on Augusta Saturday night," Kris said. "You should join us."

Silas glanced at him and tilted his head. "Like legit you're all going or..."

"No, for real the rest of the gang will be there this time. We know some guys who are in a band that will be performing. The Redneck Raiders. Stupid name, I know, but they're actually pretty good. We'll have dinner there. They serve these fantastic teriyaki steak bites."

"Sounds fun. I'll think about it."

"Seriously, don't let my extreme oafishness put you off from spending time with the rest of the gang."

They had reached Silas's Nissan and stopped, Silas leaning against the passenger's door. "It's not that."

"Then what? You always seem so hesitant to hang out with us."

"It's just that...well, I don't exactly feel I fit in with you guys."

Kris stood on the sidewalk, keeping a respectful distance

between them, hands stuffed in his pockets. "Don't fit in? That's crazy talk. Everyone thinks you're awesome."

"Even Philip?"

"There may be a little jealousy there, but yes, even Philip likes you."

Silas dropped his eyes to the cracked pavement. "Can I tell you something personal?"

"Of course."

"I've already confessed I've never been on a date before, but truth is I've never really had friends before. I mean, *never*. From pretty much the first day of kindergarten, I didn't seem to fit in with the other kids, and they sensed it like a scent on the wind. I was quiet and bookish, awkward in social situations, and because my father didn't make much money, my clothes were usually thrift store specials. I was the perfect target for my peers, and the older I got, the worse their torment became. Ridicule and rejection I know how to handle from, you know, the years of experience. Acceptance and kindness...that's a new one for me and I'm a little less sure how to act."

Kris didn't say anything right away, though Silas could sense him stepping closer, then he reached out and put a hand on Silas's shoulder. "Hey, we've all been there, man."

Silas looked up quickly. "What do you mean?"

"What do you think drew the six of us together? We were all outcasts before coming to Furman. You're not the only one with scars that need healing."

Just when Silas began to think everything made sense, he got thrown for another loop. "I never would have guessed that. You guys all seem so confident."

"Well, college is a time of rebranding, redefining yourself. Becoming the person you've always wanted to be instead of the person you've been told you are."

Silas laughed softly to himself. "I can certainly relate to that."

"And you don't have to worry about being rejected," Kris said, hand still resting on Silas's shoulder. "You have friends now. You're totally one of us."

Tears prickled at the corners of Silas's eyes, for a myriad of complicated reasons. He pushed them down and muttered a distorted thank you.

Kris removed his hand, and the absence of the weight on Silas's shoulder seemed profound with metaphorical meaning. "You're a cool guy, Silas. After all, you managed not to make me feel like the biggest fool in the world after my botched attempt at asking you out. That's quite a feat in and of itself."

What happened next was an act not of thought but of pure gut instinct. Silas didn't even know he was going to do it until a second before he started to move. He pressed forward, put his hands on the sides of Kris's face, and planted a tentative but definite kiss on the other man's lips.

The kiss lasted only three seconds, and Kris seemed too stunned to react, but it was the first time Silas's lips had ever touched another man's, and the thrill that followed was all-consuming and dizzying. He actually stumbled back a step and swayed slightly, as if having trouble keeping his feet.

Kris remained frozen for a moment, his expression a monument to both surprise and delight. "I, um, I thought you only wanted to do the friend thing."

"I'm sorry, I went with an impulse."

"You don't have to apologize. It was a good impulse, a very good impulse. You should definitely follow that impulse."

Silas couldn't say who initiated the second kiss, but this one was reciprocal and lasted longer. Kris's arms enfolded him and pulled him in tight, an embrace that was warm and secure and comforting. When the kiss broke, Silas felt breathless and flushed, and he couldn't stop smiling.

"Have lunch with me tomorrow," Kris asked, his voice soft and shy and somewhat fragile. "Please."

Silas thought quickly, formulating a story in record time. "Sure, but not in the dining hall. It's so crowded and noisy. I actually will be coming to campus late tomorrow, so how about I pick us up something and we can meet in the Rose Garden? We'll have sort of a picnic in the gazebo."

"Sounds romantic," Kris said. He too seemed to suffer from the rictus that twisted his lips into a permanent smile.

"12:30?" Silas asked.

"Awesome. So it's a...date?"

"Yes, it is. I'll be there. Any preferences on the food?"

"Doesn't matter to me. As long as you're there."

Silas nodded. They were no longer embracing, but they lightly held hands. "This probably means Philip is going to hate me now for sure."

"Possibly, at least for a little while, but he'll get used to it. You could even win extra points if you help him get through Dr. Carver's class."

Acting on instinct instead of thought again, Silas crossed the line he'd been toeing and said, "Yeah, that Dr. Carver is tough. Sometimes I wish I hadn't ended up in his class."

CHAPTER EIGHT

His father wasn't waiting for him in the living room when he got home this time, though Silas could hear the television playing in his father's bedroom. Silas went into the kitchen to grab a soda out of the fridge when the television muted.

"Back already?"

Silas walked past the cramped laundry area and into his father's bedroom to find his father sitting up on the bed, on top of the covers, back against the headboard. "Home earlier than I expected," he said.

"Yeah, it was just coffee."

"Get anything to eat?"

"Some pastry."

"I can make you a sandwich if you're still hungry."

"Don't bother. I can do it."

"Was a good time had by all?" his father asked.

"It was only two of us tonight. Me and Kris."

"I see. Sounds...cozy."

Silas laughed at his father's struggle. He could tell the man didn't want to pry into his son's private life, but as it was the first time in eighteen years that Silas actually had a private life, the curiosity must be overwhelming.

"I had a nice time," Silas said. "In fact, I kissed him."

His father immediately turned off the television and scooted over on the bed. Silas kicked off his shoes and stretched out next to him. Silas felt transported back to his childhood when he used to routinely crawl into his father's bed. Not because of bad dreams or fears of monsters in the closet. Merely because he enjoyed his father's presence. Back then, it had made him feel safe, like nothing could hurt him. It still felt that way, if he were being honest.

"So," his father said, "big-time grown-up stuff, huh?"

"It was just a kiss, Dad. Let's not make too big a deal out of it."

"If it didn't feel like a big deal when you kissed him, then I think you might not have been doing it right."

Heat flushed Silas's cheeks, and he glanced at the black television screen, offering a distorted reflection of the two of them. He and his father had always had a very open relationship where they could talk about anything, but this was the first time they'd ever had anything of a truly intimate nature to discuss.

"Okay," Silas said. "Maybe it was a little bit of a big deal. At least a medium-sized deal."

His father nodded and folded his hands over his gut, what he liked to call his potbelly. "You know, you've mentioned this guy's name in passing before, but never anything that suggested to me that he was something special to you, that you had feelings for him. What changed?"

"I don't know. I guess I didn't realize I had feelings for him, or maybe didn't want to admit to myself I did because I thought they wouldn't be reciprocated."

"I understand. It was that way with your mother and I at first."

Silas glanced over at his father, head tilted slightly. "Really? You never told me that?"

"Well, you know we met at the old Bloom grocery store where we both worked. She was a cashier, I worked in the deli."

"Yeah, I know. It took you six months to work up the nerve to ask her out."

"That's both true and not exactly true at the same time."

This grabbed Silas's attention. He would have thought he'd heard all the stories about his parents, from their courtship to their wedding when his mother was already four months pregnant with Silas, to their all-too-brief marriage to the aftermath of the accident that made his father into a single dad. The idea that there might be a story he hadn't yet heard intrigued him greatly. To him, his mother was little more than a character in stories his father told, so he welcomed any opportunity to flesh that character out a little more.

"It did take me six months after meeting her to ask her out," his father said, "but I wasn't spending that time trying to work up my nerve. Truth is, it didn't occur to me to ask her out. I mean, she was undeniably attractive, and whenever we would chat on breaks and such, she seemed smart and funny. Yet the idea of asking her out wasn't even on my radar. Looking back, I think I saw her as so far out of my league that to even consider that she'd go out with me was insane. So for all those months, she was just this nice girl I worked with, not someone I actively had a crush on or anything."

"So what happened?" Silas asked. "When did you know you liked her?"

"We both got off at the same time one night and were just shooting the breeze in the parking lot. Something we'd done plenty of times before, but this time there was something different. I don't know if I can explain what. She looked so adorable, with her hair in braided pigtails and she was wearing this sparkly lipstick she liked to wear, but then she was always adorable. It was fall, and the day was chilly, and she started to shiver, and I gave her my jacket. She smelled so good, like vanilla. She was talking about this musical in Gaffney she wanted to see but she hated going to these things by herself. She always swore after that she wasn't hinting, but almost before I knew I was going to, I asked if I could take her out to dinner and the play. Just like that, as if in an instant she went from just someone I knew to someone I wanted to know so much more."

Silas smiled and squeezed his father's knee. "Then you ran out to the Salvation Army for the jacket and tie."

"That's right. And the rest, as they say, is history. After that, you couldn't pry your mother and me apart. It was hard to imagine that I had spent half a year around this wonderful creature and somehow not realized she was the most special person on the planet."

A familiar ache started in Silas's chest. "I wish you'd gotten more time with her."

His father blinked rapidly a few times, as if trying to clear dust from his eyes. "And I wish you'd had a chance to know her. She'd be every bit as proud of you as I am."

Silas began to shift uncomfortably on the bed. Not because he was embarrassed by the sentiment, but because he didn't particularly feel like someone to be proud of at the moment.

"So," his father said, slapping his thigh, "I'm going to have to meet this Kris fella, of course."

With a groan and an eye-roll, Silas climbed off the bed. "Come on, Dad, it was one kiss. It's not like we're engaged or anything."

"It's my boy's first romance. I need to scope the guy out, make sure he meets with my approval."

"Again, *one kiss*. I don't know that we can classify that as a romance."

"When are you seeing him again?"

"We're having lunch tomorrow."

"The whole group, or just the two of you?"

"The two of us."

His father nodded decisively. "It's a romance, at least the beginning of one. And the beginning is often the most exciting part."

Silas found himself remembering the almost electrical tingling that had left his lips buzzing after kissing Kris, the sudden but undeniable impulse that had led him to uncharacteristic boldness to initiate the kiss in the first place. Silas's only experience with romance came from books and movies, but yes, he had to admit this felt like one. And it was exciting.

And frightening.

"I'm going to grab a bite and get some homework done," Silas said.

"Okay, I'll let you off the hook for the time being, but we'll talk more about this. Consider that not just a promise, but a threat."

Silas laughed, grabbed his shoes, and headed back to the kitchen. With a fried bologna sandwich and a soda, he closed himself up in his bedroom. At his desk, he ate quietly while staring out the window. The neighbors in the trailer next door, a young couple with two small kids, were sitting on their back deck, their voices quiet murmurs in the night. A rare and welcome change. They often engaged in loud, vicious arguments right outside for the entire trailer park to hear. Usually about money, occasionally about infidelity, but always full of cursing and name-calling. Not exactly the model for a healthy relationship.

Look who's talking! Starting off your very first relationship with deception.

Silas hated that voice in his head, particularly because it so often spoke the truth.

The truth...a concept from which he was growing more and more distant.

And yet, he tried to convince himself, it wasn't as if everything he'd shared with Kris and the rest of the group were lies. Most of what he'd shared had been the truth, only with that one little fib underlying it all. One little fib that could destroy everything for him, not least of which was what had only started to develop between him and Kris.

"How did I get myself into this?" he asked himself, looking down at his half-eaten sandwich and finding it too repulsive to finish. Although he knew what really repulsed him was himself. He had always thought of himself as a decent person, and at his core he still believed that to be true, otherwise this wouldn't be eating him up the way it was.

So how could he get himself out of this situation with the least amount of collateral damage?

Katie.

At first, Silas wasn't sure why the barista he'd never met sprang to mind, but then it came clear like the proverbial lightning bolt or cartoon lightbulb flickering on over his head.

Was there possibly a way to take a lie and retroactively make it true?

He recognized the fallacy of his thinking but chose to ignore it for the moment, and instead opened his laptop and pulled up the Furman website. From the tabs along the top of the screen, he clicked on the one labeled, "ADMISSIONS & AID."

CHAPTER NINE

As Silas walked beneath the overhanging Magnolia branches and into the rose garden, he found the gazebo already occupied by a group of three young women, talking and giggling. He glanced around, grasping the bags of food in his fists, and spotted Kris at the far end of the garden, sitting on the rim of the fountain nestled in the alcove between the two sets of brick steps that led up to the backside of the library.

The Lib. Don't forget, Furman students call it the Lib.

Kris, who sat hunched over a book, suddenly looked up as if he could sense Silas's presence, smiled and waved. Silas tried to wave back, but his hands were burdened by the food, and he hurried quickly through the center of the garden, past the trio in the gazebo, and to the fountain with the baffling statuary of a cherubic angel clutching a fish almost as large as it was, water shooting out of the fish's mouth.

"Hey there," Silas said, taking a seat next to Kris. "Studying?"

Kris shook his head and held up the book, a tattered paperback of *The Halloween Tree*. "Just getting started on the next Bradbury."

Last night, Gus had sent out a text to the group telling them that he had started the novel, but Silas hadn't paid much attention or responded. One, he'd already read *The Halloween Tree*. Two, he'd been otherwise occupied. Not only looking into the proper process to become a transfer student to Furman and apply for financial aid, but also just researching the school itself. Professors, class schedules, accessing photos of buildings he'd never been in before. He threw himself into it the way he did his fiction, weaving a story he hoped would be plausible and convincing.

"Our romantic picnic spot was commandeered by the Giggle Brigade," Kris said, lifting his chin toward the three girls in the gazebo.

"That's okay. This spot is even better. More private."

Kris wagged his eyebrows and said, "So we could make out if we wanted to and no one would know but the fish angel."

Silas gave a nervous laugh and squirmed around on the cement fountain rim, though it wasn't particularly uncomfortable.

Kris grimaced. "Sorry. Whenever I try to flirt, I turn into Super Spaz."

Silas still had trouble accepting the fact that anyone wanted to flirt with him, and he certainly didn't know how to flirt back. If Kris was Super Spaz then Silas would surely be the Spaz King of the Universe. Instead, he merely held up the bags and said, "Hungry?"

"Yes. What do we have?"

Silas didn't want to admit the inordinate amount of time he'd spent deciding what to bring for lunch. The decision had taken on momentous importance. This was, after all, his first real date, something he would likely remember for the rest of his life, a story he could potentially tell over and over the way his father told the story of his first date with his mother. The right food choice seemed pivotal.

He'd immediately dismissed any fast-food options because that didn't strike the correct tone, seemed too transitory and easy, like he didn't consider the date significant enough to put any thought into. He'd briefly considered splurging on meals from one of the nicer, more expensive restaurants in town like Larkin's but then dismissed that as too presumptuous, like he'd assigned too much significance to the date. He had to strike the right balance. Had he succeeded? He wasn't sure.

"Thai," he said, holding up the bags. "From a little place in Greer."

"Awesome, I love Thai."

With an inner sigh of relief, Silas handed him one of the bags. Not knowing how daring Kris's pallet may be, he'd taken the safe route and gotten them both Pad See-U. A simple dish consisting of noodles, broccoli, carrots, egg, and chicken, drenched in soy sauce. He'd gotten bottled waters for them to drink.

Both of them balanced their takeout containers on their laps, opening the lids to release puffs of steam. Silas took the plastic fork and began to twirl the noodles around; Kris stabbed into a carrot slice then merely stared at it for a moment.

"Okay, there's something we need to get out of the way before we eat," Kris said, closing the container and placing it next to him.

Silas followed suit. "What's that?"

The kiss that followed was soft and tender and every bit as electrifying. Silas could still hear the soft chatter of the girls in the gazebo, but he didn't care if they were looking. Everything melted away until all he was aware of was the press of Kris's lips, the faint peach scent he assumed came from Kris's shampoo, the weight of Kris's hand resting on his knee.

When the kiss broke, they were both smiling.

"There," Kris said, retrieving his food. "I figured that would get us past the first date jitters so we could relax."

"Good call."

At first, a bit of residual awkwardness lingered despite the kiss, and they ate in silence. The trio left the gazebo, but the two young men remained by the fountain. Silas couldn't speak for Kris, but he enjoyed the secluded feeling of the alcove, as if they were in their own little private grotto together.

Clearing his throat, Kris broke the silence. "So, did you not have any classes this morning?"

"I had a few things to take care of, so I skipped out on my morning classes," Silas said, which was at least half true. He had gone to his eight o'clock but blew off his ten so he could go back home, shower again, change, pick up the food and get to Furman.

"I haven't been able to stop thinking about last night," Kris said then popped a broccoli stalk in his mouth.

Silas took a bite, chewed methodically, and swallowed before answering. "Me either."

"And I want you to know, we'll take things as slow as you

want. I don't ever want to make you feel like I'm pressuring you or rushing you."

"I appreciate that," Silas said with a smile. "Means a lot, really."

"But I also want you to know that I like you a lot. I don't say that to scare you off by coming on too strong, but I need to be upfront and honest."

Silas stared glumly down at his cooling food. "Upfront and honest. Yeah, those are good traits to have."

"Christ, I am coming on too strong, aren't I?"

"No, you're not," Silas sand, reaching out and taking Kris's hand. "You're very sweet. This will take some getting used to for me, that's all. I don't have a great deal of experience with sweet."

"Well, get ready because I'm going to smother you in sweet. Okay, that sounds creepy, but you know what I mean."

"I do, and I look forward to suffocating on kindness."

They laughed then returned to eating. After a couple of moments, Silas asked, "Did you tell any of the others about us?"

"Yeah. They wanted to know why I wasn't having lunch with them, so I told them. I hope that's okay. Did you want to keep it a secret?"

"No, that's fine. In fact, I told my dad last night."

Kris paused with a forkful of noodles halfway to his mouth, one noodle hanging down like an unfurled streamer. "Seriously? You told your dad?"

"Yeah. Do your parents not know that you're gay?"

"They know, and for the most part they're pretty cool about it. At least, in the sense that they aren't trying to ship me off to conversion therapy or anything, but honestly, it isn't something we really discuss much. I told them, they said okay, but I don't share anything about my social life with them and they don't ask."

"My dad and I are the opposite. We're pretty open about everything. Probably because for most of my life, it has been just the two of us."

"Wow," Kris said. "My family isn't close like that. I mean, we all get along and everything, but we're more like friendly acquaintances than anything else. Honestly, the friends I've made here at school feel more like actual family to me."

"Created families are often the most close-knit," Silas said, though his only experience with that came from television shows and movies. He'd never before had the opportunity to create a family from friends. In fact, corny as it sounded, his father was for all intents and purposes his best friend.

Kris took a swig of water. "You know, I'd like to meet your father sometime."

"Funny, he said the same thing about you."

"Really?" Kris said with a beaming smile.

Silas realized he was wading into dangerous territory and had to quickly retreat before he sank into the bog. "Yeah, but I told him it was way too early for the whole meeting-the-fam thing."

"Oh, you're right. That makes sense. As I said, I'm not rushing you."

Silas appreciated Kris's words, and he could tell they were sincere, but he also sensed that Kris's feelings had been bruised. Just as he'd sensed his father's feelings had been bruised last night. And honestly, he had no issue with the two of them meeting, in fact thought they'd get along well, but he couldn't risk it. His father was sure to ask Kris something about Greenville Tech, Kris was sure to mention life at Furman. Silas's real life and his imaginary life would not withstand being together in the same room; keeping them separate was imperative.

"When's your next class?" Kris asked.

Silas had prepared for questions like this, had the answer ready to go, but still he hesitated. Lying did not come naturally to him.

Which is a good thing. You'll really have to start worrying when it does.

"Two o'clock. I have English Comp with Dr. Riddle in Furman Hall."

Kris laughed. "Okay, that's specific."

Inwardly, Silas chastised himself for the excessive detail but forced a laugh as well. "Sorry, you make me a little nervous."

"In a good way, I hope."

"Definitely a good way."

"Glad to hear I'm not the only nervous one. So, how about after lunch I walk you to class like a true gentleman? I'll even carry your books."

"Thanks, but I actually have to go by the library before class."

Silas started to launch into his planned spiel about the research paper he was doing but stopped himself in the nick of time. He made a mental note that too much detail didn't bolster a lie but actually exposed its fragile framework.

"Way to step on my attempt at gallantry."

"Sorry, but if we see any puddles, I'll let you throw your coat on top of it so I can cross."

"Very kind of you, but how about we settle for me taking you to dinner tonight? You wouldn't let me treat at the Grind, you bought lunch, so I insist that you let me buy you dinner."

Silas smiled around a mouthful of noodles and nodded. Once he swallowed, he said, "Okay, you have a deal. Want to meet me by the bookstore around 5:30?"

"Or you could come by dorm. I'm in Judson."

"Oh, um, I don't know…"

"It's okay," Kris said, reaching out and taking his hand. "My roommate Pete will be there."

"Of course, I didn't think… Anyway, sure, I'll come by."

"Great, just text me when you get there, and I'll come let you in."

"Yeah, great."

Silas resumed eating, not sure if he was grateful Kris's roommate would be there or disappointed.

CHAPTER TEN

Smiley's Acoustic Café was a small place with exposed brick walls (exposed brick seemed to be very popular among Greenville's more trendy places, Silas thought), tables cramped together, a bar off to the right, and near the front a small stage above which hung a banner of photos. Silas recognized a few faces like Johnny Cash and Tina Turner so assumed the rest were singers as well. The stage was empty, and only a few patrons filled the space. A group of four sat at a table near the stage, and Gus occupied a stool at the end of the bar. He looked up from his drink, spotted Silas, and waved him over.

"Hey," Silas said, taking the stool next to Gus. A female bartender with a ponytail came over and Silas asked for a Coke. After she gave it to him and went down to the far end of the bar to clean glasses, Silas glanced at the beer in Gus's hand. "I didn't realize you were twenty-one already."

Gus made a "keep it down" gesture with his free hand and spoke in a soft voice. "In January, but I have an ID in my wallet that says I turned twenty-one in April. Which is technically true."

"How do you figure that?"

"I would have already been conceived in April, which means I technically existed."

Silas laughed. "So life begins at conception, huh?"

"I'm not trying to tell women what to do with their bodies, just want to enjoy a little drink to unwind."

"No judgements from me."

"Glad to hear it." Gus took a sip then began peeling the label off the bottle. "So, you probably want to know why I asked you to meet me here early."

"Did cross my mind."

In fact, it had done more than cross Silas's mind. It had obsessed him since he'd received the text from Gus asking if they could meet at the café shortly after it opened to have a private conversation before the rest of the group arrived. Silas had convinced himself that somehow Gus had found out the truth and this was to be the confrontation. Silas took a deep breath and braced himself.

"I like you," Gus said. "Not the way Kris likes you, of course, but you seem like a good guy."

Silas's blinked and frowned. This wasn't at all what he'd been expecting. "Um, okay. I...I like you, too."

After another sip of beer, Gus said, "I'm making a mess of this, I know, but what I'm getting at is that while I like you, and I hope we become good friends, I love Kris. He's family, and family look out for one another."

The frown began to relax as Silas found his moorings in the conversation. "I understand. Basically, you want to know what my intentions are."

"Something like that. Kris is a sensitive guy, and he's been through a lot. It's left him with some self-esteem issues that he's working through. The last guy he dated was a real asshat that screwed him over and only made matters worse."

"Yeah, Brandon. From what I've heard about him, I agree with the asshat assessment."

Gus nodded, staring down at the shredded bits of the beer label. "I don't know how much Kris told you about that whole debacle, but it left him crushed for several months. We could barely get him out of his dorm room, he was skipping classes, and his grades began to slip. All of us rallied to try to bring him out of the depression before he ended up flunking out of school. He managed to pass all his classes at the end of spring semester but just barely. To be honest, he's only started to really recover from all that. A little more withdrawn and reserved than he was before, though he's been more like his old self ever since..."

"Ever since what?" Silas asked when the silence stretched out.

Gus met his gaze. "Ever since he met you."

"Oh."

Gus finished off his beer and sat the bottle on the bar with a decisive *clunk*. "All I'm asking is that you be gentle with him. His wounds are still fresh. He doesn't need to be hurt again."

"I don't want to hurt him," Silas said quietly, swirling the melting ice cubes around in his soda. "And I don't want to be hurt, either."

Gus reached over and gripped his shoulder. "I know, man, and I don't mean to come off all protective big brother. Honestly, I think you're good for Kris. It's about time one of us had a successful relationship. Sometimes I think the whole group of us is cursed, though maybe my luck will turn around tonight."

"What do you mean?"

"Well, there's a certain barista I've been crushing on for a while. I finally worked up the nerve and asked her to join us tonight."

Silas had just taken a sip of his soda and began to cough and sputter. "You mean Katie?"

"Yeah, I went to...hey, wait, how do you know about Katie?"

"Kris mentioned her when we were at the Village Grind earlier in the week."

"Kris sometimes has a big mouth," Gus said, but with an affectionate smile. "Anyway, it's not an official date or anything. I just stopped in for a coffee when I happened to know she'd be on the schedule and casually mentioned we were coming to hear the band, said she could tag along if she wanted. So just a group outing, you know. She said yes, and maybe I imagined it, but I think she winked at me. Or maybe she had something in her eye. Either way, she's supposed to be here."

Silas heard Gus's words, but they didn't truly register. All he could think was that Katie was going to be here, and that could prove disastrous. He'd never even met the barista, but she attended Greenville Tech. She and Silas walked the same campus every day, possibly passed one another regularly, it wasn't even out of the realm of possibility that they could share a class or two. What if she recognized him? What if she blew his whole cover? What if—

The thought spiral disintegrated when Gus snapped his

fingers in front of Silas's face and said, "Earth to Silas, where'd you go?"

"Oh, sorry. What were you saying?"

Gus laughed. "Don't worry about it. I don't blame you for drifting. I have a tendency to babble when I'm nervous, and I'm incredibly nervous right now."

As mired as Silas was into his own worries, his natural sense of empathy kicked in as he recognized that he wasn't the only one at the bar with worries. Gus had taken the torn strips of label and was ripping them into even smaller, confetti-sized bits.

"You're nervous about meeting Katie tonight?" Silas asked.

Gus shrugged then nodded then laughed. "To be honest with you, I'm not exactly a Casanova when it comes to women. Not ones I'm interested in, at least. I lose all my smooth and become a blathering idiot."

"You managed to ask her out for tonight. That's something."

Gus winced and slapped a hand over his eyes. "It was all kinds of pathetic. I intended to ask her out on an actual date, I really did, but at the last minute I chickened out. When I told her about the outing tonight, I said we didn't have enough estrogen in the group, and she could help even things out. That's exactly what I said to her. 'We don't have enough estrogen in the group.' Real sweet-talker I am."

"She said yes, though. And there was that wink."

"That *possible* wink."

"Possible is better than impossible, right?"

Gus looked at him for a moment then unleashed that smile. Silas couldn't figure how anyone with a smile like that could lack confidence in matters of the heart. "You're a pretty good pep-talker. If the writing thing doesn't work out, maybe you could do that professionally. Just convince poor saps that they aren't quite so poor-sappy."

"I'll keep that in mind for a potential career choice."

"I'm going to get another beer. Want me to get you one?"

Silas pretended to think it over for a moment then shook his head. "No thanks. I'm a lightweight and the night's early."

"I hear that. Besides, I wouldn't want to contribute to the

delinquency of a minor. I mean, unless your mother had an unusually long gestation, I don't think my whole conception justification will work for you."

With a laugh, Silas took another sip of his diluted soda. He didn't want to admit that he'd never had a beer before, or any type of alcoholic beverage for that matter. The strongest drink he'd ever had was NyQuil.

"So," Gus said after receiving his second beer from the bartender, "what classes are you taking this semester?"

Silas took a deep breath and began flipping through the mental files he'd memorized of courses and professors. He'd spent time scouring the Furman website, creating a fictional schedule for himself, writing it down and studying it until he had it committed to memory.

Feeling like a total shit but repeating to himself, *It's only a lie until you make it true*, Silas opened his mouth and began to spin his fiction.

Kris arrived a half an hour later, the rest of the group following shortly behind. Paige and Sheila greeted Silas with hugs, but the biggest hug came from Franco. Silas thought it was like getting a Heimlich from the front. Philip remained reserved, only more so than usual. Silas had expected that and decided to give him space to adjust to the idea of Silas and Kris as a...

As a what? A couple? It seemed too early for that designation. Dating? Yes, they were dating, and the mere thought was enough to send a shiver through Silas. Yet he could easily imagine what it felt like for Philip to see the man he had feelings for with someone else. Silas could imagine it because he'd lived it. He'd been the Philip in so many situations before that he found it hard to believe he was the envied instead of the envier. Like being through the Looking Glass, or in the Twilight Zone, or the Upside Down. More pleasant than any of those fictions suggested, but no less surreal.

Gus was even more animated than usual, hyper and agitated, repeating himself a lot and constantly in movement as if being still for more than five seconds may result in his death. Silas wasn't the only one who noticed.

"What the hell is wrong with you?" Sheila asked as they settled at a table.

"Nothing," Gus said, but his nervous laugh and the way he constantly turned to watch the door belied that statement.

Paige poked him in the side to get his attention. "Who are you looking for?"

When Gus didn't answer right away, Silas decided to put him out of his misery. "He asked Katie from the Village Grind to join us."

This revelation elicited a few approving nods and whistles.

"About time," Sheila said. "The unrequited mooning had started to get old."

Franco slapped Gus on the back. "Good for you, man. Fortune favors the brave, as my granddad likes to say. Hell, even if she doesn't show up—" He cut off abruptly when he saw the venomous stare Gus shot him then continued with a lame attempt at recovery. "I mean, she'll show up, I'm sure. You know chicks, always late. Probably can't get her hair or her lipstick right."

Paige and Sheila exchanged a pointed glance, and Sheila spoke for both of them. "You know, Franco, gender stereotypes only make you look ignorant. I had no idea you were such a Neanderthal."

Leaning across the table, Franco said, "Hey, I'm just trying to make Gus here feel better."

"You're all making me feel like a million bucks!" Gus said loudly, causing some of the patrons at nearby tables to glance his way. "So how about we all start talking about something else. *Anything else!* Wouldn't that be a fun game?"

Silas felt his emotions splitting in opposing directions again, as if he were two different people. The kind, empathetic Silas hoped that Katie would show up because he wanted to see the way Gus's face was sure to light up when she did. The selfish, deceptive Silas hoped Katie would blow Gus off, because there was still that risk she would recognize Silas and wreck his charade. The warring impulses, the contradicting voices in his head, left him feeling a bit schizophrenic. It was difficult to maintain a double life, especially when Silas was unaccustomed to having even one.

Gus sank down in his seat and muttered something into his beer, so softly that only Silas sitting right next to him could hear. "There's nothing worse than being stood up."

This pierced Silas's heart and the selfish side of him took a backseat. Leaning over, and speaking in a hushed voice meant only for Gus, he said, "What about uncontrollable flatulence in church? Would that be worse?"

Gus glanced at him, gave a half-hearted smile, and said, "Thanks, Si, but not now."

Silas straightened up, fidgeted with his glass of melting ice cubes, then started slightly when Kris planted a kiss on his cheek. "What was that for?"

Kris reached up and gave a playful tug on Silas's earlobe. "For being the sweetest guy ever."

In his periphery, Silas caught the glare coming from Philip but chose to ignore it. Instead, he took Kris's hand and squeezed it.

"So you don't want to talk about Katie at all?" Franco asked, propping his elbows on the table.

Gus groaned and extended his middle finger toward Franco.

A strange, enigmatic smile lifted one side of Sheila's mouth. "So there is absolutely no circumstance under which you would want us to bring up Katie's name?"

Gus slapped an open palm onto the table. "What is wrong with you guys? I said I wanted to change the subject, so let's change the damn subject. I don't want to hear another word about Katie."

"Not even if she just walked in?" Franco asked.

Gus froze with his beer halfway to his lips. "You better not be messing with me, man."

"See for yourself," Sheila said, pointing back toward the entrance.

He hesitated for a moment, but then Gus turned in his seat. Katie spotted him, smiled, and waved. Gus's entire demeanor changed in an instant, his glum moodiness dissipating and leaving behind his usual manic energy. He stood abruptly, nearly sending his chair toppling over, waving back at Katie and motioning her to the table.

"Katie, hey, didn't know if you were going to make it or not," he said, taking one of her hands in both of his and shaking vigorously.

"Doesn't exactly have game, does he?" Kris whispered.

"It's always a bitch finding parking downtown," Katie said. "I parked down at County Square and hoofed it over. My dogs are barking, so how about someone offer me a seat?"

Gus quickly scooted out of the way and let her take his. He grabbed a chair from a nearby empty table and squeezed in between Katie and Philip.

"I think you know everybody," Gus said, "except for our friend Silas. He's a new addition to our little confab."

Katie turned to the right and fixed Silas with an appraising look. "So they've sucked another one in, huh?"

Silas laughed and said, "Nice to meet you."

Katie didn't respond, just continue to stare at him in mute contemplation. The seconds stretched out to an uncomfortable degree. He'd often scoffed at writers who used the phrase, "I felt like a specimen under a microscope," but he now realized how true that cliché could be.

After nearly a full minute, Katie said, "You look awfully familiar. Have we met?"

Silas froze and sweat instantly popped up on his forehead. He tried to breathe normally, move normally, but everything he did felt jerky and spastic, as if he were a marionette being worked by someone with cerebral palsy. Katie didn't look familiar to him; he couldn't remember ever having run into her on the Tech campus, but that didn't mean they hadn't crossed paths. He tended to drift along with his head down, not making eye contact with most people.

"Um, I don't think so."

"Hmm, I can't put my finger on it, but your face really rings a bell."

"Guess I just have one of those generic faces."

"Do you go to the Village Grind much?"

Silas shook his head. "I only went there for the first time earlier this week. You weren't working."

She continued to stare at him for a moment more. "Damn,

this is going to bother me until I figure it out. Oh well, I'm sure it'll come to me eventually."

She turned back to Gus, and they started chatting, and next to him Kris said something, but Silas didn't register the words. Dread enclosed him on all sides, squeezing him tighter and tighter, and his mind could only focus on one thought that repeated on an endless loop: *she recognizes me, she recognizes me, she recognizes me...*

"...then I rubbed macaroni salad all over myself and sacrificed a squirrel to Cthulhu."

These words penetrated Silas's self-absorbed reverie and he frowned at Kris. "What did you say?"

Kris laughed. "Sorry, just trying to get your attention."

Silas released his own shaky laugh. "Forgive me. My mind has a tendency to wander."

"Maybe this will help keep it more grounded," Kris said then kissed Silas.

And the kiss did help ground Silas's thoughts...but not completely. Katie continued to sit right next to him, the proverbial other shoe balanced precariously on the edge simply waiting for the slightest vibration to drop.

CHAPTER ELEVEN

The Redneck Raiders sucked.

At least, Silas thought so. Most of the crowd in the café seemed to enjoy their loud, aggressive music, all snarling guitar riffs and unintelligible lyrics screeched into microphones whining with feedback. Not exactly Silas's taste.

Not that he exactly had a taste in music. He liked a few Adele songs, and sometimes he enjoyed listening to some of his father's old albums from bands like The Beatles, The Rolling Stones, and The Who. Silas wasn't sure if he actually enjoyed the music itself or just the nostalgia. Those albums seemed to always be playing in the background when he was growing up, making up the soundtrack of his childhood.

Silas certainly didn't like music this frenetic and angry and relentless. However, he had enough couth to keep that opinion to himself. To each his own, as the saying went, and Silas had always thought that would make a good motto. If he was the kind of person who felt the need to have a motto.

After a few songs, the band took a break, and Silas breathed an inward sigh of relief. He glanced over and caught Katie giving him that scrutinizing look again, as if he were a puzzle to be solved. This made Silas uncomfortable, and he took Kris's hand and said, "Want to go get some drinks?"

"Sure."

Silas wasn't really thirsty, he simply wanted to get away from Katie. The less he was in her line of sight, the less chance she'd recognize him and blow his cover.

"Like the band?" Kris asked after they'd gotten their sodas.

He hesitated for a moment, took a sip, then said, "Interesting, but not really up my alley."

Kris smiled and kissed him. "I love that you won't just come right out and lie."

If you only knew, man. If you only knew.

"What would you think if we cut out early?" Silas asked. "Maybe found something else to do? Something a little quieter, more private?"

Now it was Kris who hesitated and took a stalling sip of soda. "Well, Pete went home for the weekend. We could go back to my room. We'd have the place to ourselves."

A tingling sensation spread over Silas's skin. The thought of being alone with Kris in his dorm room was simultaneously exciting and frightening. Of course, there may have been nothing provocative in Kris's suggestion.

But if Silas was honest with himself, he wanted to think there was.

"Yeah," he said after a moment. "Sounds like a plan."

They walked back to the table, where Gus and Sheila were in the midst of a heated debate on the nature of sense of humor, pondering the question if anything was ever objectively funny or was it all a matter of subjective perception? Katie sat next to Gus, watching over the whole affair with a look of wry amusement. Gus seemed to have gotten over his initial bout of nerves and insecurity, settling back into his old bombastic self. Silas and Kris waited next to the table for a break in the discussion.

"You going to hover all night?" Paige asked them. "Or are you going to sit back down?"

Suddenly the examination of humor ceased, and all eyes turned to the couple. Silas hung back, as if trying to hide behind Kris. For someone who had spent the bulk of his high school years trying to be invisible, since meeting this group Silas had found himself the center of attention far too often.

"Well," Kris started, seeming as nervous as Silas felt, "I don't think we're going to stick around for the Raider's second set. Tell Kevin and Lenny that they were great as usual."

Silas thought he detected a knowing smirk from Gus and Sheila, and he quickly stared down at his shoes.

Jeez, stop acting like you two are going off to commit espionage and high treason. You've been with him in his dorm room before.

Yes, but never alone. His roommate was there last time, a chaperon to ensure nothing happened.

And if something does happen…so what? You're both adults.

"I'm not feeling too well," Philip said, breaking up Silas's inner debate. "Kris, do you think you could give me a ride back to the dorms?"

Kris hesitated, glancing over at Silas. "Um, well, I…"

"I'll take you, Phil," Paige said, coming to the rescue. "I'm a little beat myself."

Philip shot her a look of pure poison that dissipated almost instantly into disappointment. "Sure," he muttered. "Thanks."

Paige pushed back from the table. "I just need to hit the restroom then we'll head back to campus. Kris, Silas, you guys have a nice evening."

Arms folded tersely across his chest, Philip sank down in his chair, lips pulled down in a rather childish pout. Again, Silas had the out-of-body-experience where he couldn't help but put himself in Philip's shoes, having been there so many times himself.

Kris apparently also felt that sympathy, saying, "Hey Phil, want to work in a study session for history sometime tomorrow afternoon?"

At first it seemed that Philip wasn't going to reply, but then he lifted one shoulder in a half-hearted shrug. "I don't know," he muttered. "We'll see."

"Ha!" Katie suddenly cried out, pointing a finger toward Silas. "I finally figured out why you look so familiar to me."

A dread heavy as chainmail settled over Silas, suffocating him to the point that he had trouble drawing air into his lungs. He imagined he could hear the creaking and cracking as his world prepared to crash down all around him.

"You look like one of Frankie's sons on that *Grace & Frankie* show. You guys know the one I'm talking about? The one with the funny name?"

The group focused all their attention on Silas, but he didn't mind so much this time because the sweet flood of relief washed through him. She thought he looked like a character on some Netflix show, that was all.

"I don't see it," Franco said. "I, on the other hand, have been told I remind people of the Cowardly Lion from *The Wizard of Oz*. Only less cowardly and, you know, less gay."

"I don't know," Kris said. "I think you'd fit right in with the Bears out at Club 29 South."

Franco shook his head. "Stop trying to convert me. Silas, you should know that the only reason Kris is with you is because his attempts to get me to switch teams have been unsuccessful."

Silas laughed louder and longer than the joke warranted, but he felt almost giddy now that he knew his secret was still safe.

After saying their goodbyes, Silas and Kris left the bar, stepping out onto the busy street. Downtown Greenville on a Saturday night was a hub of activity, throngs packing the sidewalk, cars coasting slowly as drivers tried to locate parking spaces. Smoke wafted by, as did laughter and even shouts. The air smelled of tobacco, booze, and sweat. Silas's natural tendency toward agoraphobia gave way under the buzzing atmosphere of excitement and celebration.

"I need to get out more," he murmured to himself.

Kris glanced at him. "We don't have to go back to campus right away. I think M. Judson is doing some kind of poetry reading tonight."

A frightened part of Silas did want to postpone being alone with Kris, but another part of him was ready. And that part was stronger.

"No," Silas said, taking Kris's hand. "Let's go back to your room."

CHAPTER TWELVE

Kris's dorm room seemed different. It was the same room Silas had been in before, but Pete's absence altered it somehow. As opposed to feeling bigger, the room felt smaller, more intimate, and anticipation crackled in the air like static electricity. Silas knew this was all in his mind, but knowing that didn't change his perception in the least.

They stood in the center of the room for a few minutes, fidgeting nervously, making brief eye contact before looking away. Finally, Kris said, "Want something to drink? I have soda, water, maybe some apple juice."

"Water would be great."

"Okay, have a seat."

As Kris went to the mini fridge in the corner, Silas considered his options. The room was equipped with two small wooden desks with padded chairs. Silas could sit at one of the desks, or he could sit on one of the beds. The latter seemed a bit presumptuous, but the former not presumptuous enough, as if they were just study buddies here to cram for a mid-term exam.

Decision made, Silas settled onto the foot of Kris's bed. Kris sat next to him, their knees touching, and handed Silas a bottled water. Kris himself sipped a can of Dr. Pepper.

"Want to watch a movie or something?" Kris asked.

Silas shook his head, thinking that if one of them didn't make the first move they would literally just sit here in awkward silence until the sun came up. This was all new to him, however, and he wasn't sure *how* to make the first move. Should he put a hand on Kris's thigh, or would that move seem obvious and lame? Perhaps he should simply lean over and plant a kiss on Kris's lips to get the ball rolling. Something—*anything*—to break the ice.

Kris cleared his throat, sat the soda can on his bedside table, then said, "Um, I'm going to hit the restroom. I'll be right back. Make yourself at home."

And then he was gone into the bathroom, the door closing behind him, leaving Silas alone in a room that no longer seemed so cramped.

After he downed half the water, he stood up and began to wander around, glancing at the décor. If one could call a few band posters and books and papers strewn about décor. He wondered if "make yourself at home" was code for get undressed and under the covers, and would Kris come out of the bathroom naked?

Jeez, life isn't a porn movie. Try to relax and get past the nerves or else nothing is going to happen here tonight.

Easier thought than done.

Between the two desks was a three-shelf bookcase. Silas paused here and squatted down to look at the titles that lined the first two shelves. Some Jim Butcher titles, Nick Cutter, George R.R. Martin, horror comics, and a surprising number of novels based on an old TV show. There were no books on the bottom shelf, however; instead, it held a collection of board and card games. One in particular caught Silas's eye, and he pulled it out to study the box.

The bathroom door opened, and Kris stepped back into the room, smiling at Silas crouched down by the bookshelf. "I see you've found Pete's stash of games. The man has a serious problem. You have no idea how many nights I've had to play Clue or Sorry or Risk."

"Are the *Buffy the Vampire Slayer* novels his, too?"

Kris's hesitation revealed the answer even before he said, "Actually, no. There, you know my darkest secret. I'm a closet *Buffy* fan."

With a laugh, Silas held up the box for a card game called Truth. "Speaking of darkest secrets...how's this game work?"

"That's not a game; it's a torture device designed to embarrass and humiliate. You take turns drawing cards with these personal questions on them, and the first person to refuse to answer a question loses."

"Wanna play?"

Kris's smile faltered, twisting downward slightly. "Are you serious?"

"Yeah, sounds fun."

While that wasn't entirely the truth, Silas thought it could lead to fun. Or at least lead to them getting past their collective anxiety so they could just be natural with one another again. He'd been hoping for an icebreaker, and this could get them laughing, and nothing broke the ice better than shared laughter.

Oh, the irony of you wanting to play a game called Truth.

"Okay," Kris said with a bemused smile. "Let's have at it."

After removing their shoes, they settled on the bed facing one another, Kris at the headboard and Silas at the foot with the box between them. Kris removed a stack of cards, shuffled them for a bit, then placed the stack on top of the box. "We don't draw our own questions," he said. "I pick one and ask the question to you, then you pick one and ask the question to me."

Silas nodded. "Got it. Give it your best shot."

Kris picked up the first card from the stack, stared at it for a moment without saying anything, drawing out the suspense before asking the question. "What is your biggest fear?"

"Damn," Silas said. "Not starting out with anything light, like what's your favorite color, huh?"

"You have to answer honestly. Those are the rules."

Silas didn't answer right away, even though an answer immediately came to mind. It seemed too mortifying to voice. Then again, as Kris had pointed out, that was sort of the point of the game, and it had been Silas's idea to play. He couldn't chicken out on the very first question. So he took a deep breath and said, "Being alone. You know, that I'll live my entire life and never form any meaningful relationships."

Kris didn't offer any platitudes or assurances, he merely reached out and squeezed Silas's hand. That silent show of support was somehow so much more powerful than any empty words could ever have been.

"Your turn," Silas said, drawing a card. "Okay, here's a personal one. How old were you the first time you masturbated?"

Kris clamped a hand over his eyes, shaking his head. "Oh

God, are you making that up? Does it really say that on the card?"

"Am I about to win already?"

"No," Kris said, lowering his hand. "I guess I was about ten."

"*Ten*? Seriously? Talk about an early bloomer."

"What can I say, I'm gifted. I don't know, I was in bed, and I got...you know, a boner. I just started rubbing it against the mattress and it felt so good that I kept doing it. When I came, I had no idea what was happening. I thought I'd wet my pants. This is too much information, isn't it? The card only asked my age, and here I am volunteering all the messy details."

"You can share anything with me you want," Silas said, placing the card on the bottom of the deck. "I'm glad you feel comfortable enough with me to be this open."

"Yeah, well, you put me at ease," Kris said then took the next card. "A two-parter. Have you ever stolen anything, and if so, what?"

"No, never." Silas reached for the cards but then paused. "Oh wait..."

Kris smiled. "There's something, I can tell. What'd you steal, you little klepto?"

"Nothing major, sorry to disappoint. No grand theft auto or anything like that. However, when I was a kid, probably around the same time you were discovering the joy of making love to your mattress, I used to go to this convenience store near my house, make a beeline to the candy aisle, and if no one was around, I'd eat some of the Hersey's Kisses right there and then leave. I guess I tried to convince myself it wasn't stealing because I wasn't actually leaving the store with candy in my pockets or anything."

"No, just in your stomach," Kris said. "You're a wild one, the infamous Hersey's Kisses Bandit of legend."

Silas laughed. "Yeah, that's me. Bad to the bone!"

"I always wanted to date a rebel. I feel like Natalie Wood to your James Dean."

"Chocolate candies aren't safe in my presence," Silas said then drew the next card. "Let's see, this one should be illuminating. What are you most ashamed of?"

The smile on Kris's face froze then slowly wilted. Silas felt the immediate change in the room's atmosphere, almost like one of those unexplainable "cold spots" that paranormal investigators were always running into. "I can pick another card," he said, placing the offending one on the bottom of the pile.

Kris reached out and stayed his hand. "No, I want you to know me. That means everything, even the darker stuff."

"Darker than stealing Hersey's Kisses?" Silas said, hoping to lighten the mood.

Kris's attempt at a smile failed before it even got started. "I want to share this with you, because if you can hear it and still like me then maybe we have a shot at something real."

Silas took the cards and dumped them back in the box, moving it to the side. Obviously, game time was over. He moved up the bed and leaned against the headboard. He said nothing, simply waited.

Kris situated himself next to Silas and took his hand, but he kept his gaze focused on his lap. "When I was a sophomore in high school, I wasn't out yet. At that point in my life, I couldn't even conceive of a time when I'd be open about my sexual orientation. In fact, I was terrified of people finding out. I joined the basketball team not because I had any actual interest in the game, and I certainly had no particular aptitude, but I just wanted to do something stereotypically 'manly,' and sports seemed the best route. I briefly dated a girl, but it lasted only a month then she broke up with me after she asked why I rarely kissed her and the only answer I could give was that it didn't often occur to me. I talked a good game with the guys in the locker room, but I'd never even gotten to second base with a girl and didn't want to. I might have kept up this charade all the way through high school if Andy Crichton hadn't transferred in halfway through the year."

Kris hesitated, and Silas resisted the impulse to urge him to continue. Earlier, Kris had remained silent when Silas needed silence, and now Silas returned the favor.

After a moment, Kris took a deep breath and closed his eyes, continuing the rest of the story that way, as if his past were going to unfold in front of him like a play and he didn't want to have to see it.

"Andy was one of those really quiet, withdrawn kids. Didn't talk much, kept to himself, almost like he wanted to blend into the background like a chameleon and become invisible. Except in high school that kind of behavior has the exact opposite effect. Makes you stand out like a sore thumb.

"Wasn't just because he was quiet, but he was also super smart, always had a book with him, and he had a certain...*way* about him. Nothing obvious, he wasn't a flamer or anything, but there was something a little effeminate about him. His voice maybe an octave too high, carried his books against his chest instead of down at his side, that sort of thing. You know what I mean?"

Silas knew, he knew all too well.

"Anyway, the guys zeroed in on him pretty quick. At first, it was just murmurs of 'fag' as he walked down the halls, laughing behind his back. That's when I probably should have spoken up, but I couldn't. I wasn't exactly what you would call Mr. Popularity, but my being on the basketball team meant most people knew my name and I was pretty well liked. I didn't want to give that up and become one of the school's pariahs. So I kept my mouth shut, even joined in the laughter sometimes. You know, to keep up appearances. I was hoping it would stop there."

Silas found himself shaking his head. Of course, it didn't stop there. Once cruelty starts, it builds its own momentum, a few loose pebbles quickly becoming a rock slide.

"Pretty soon they were calling him 'fag' and 'queer' to his face. My bud Spence thought it would be funny to start calling him Angie instead of Andy, and that stuck. I even heard a couple of the teachers referring to him as Angie when they thought no one was around. Somebody even carved 'Angie' into the front of his locker. It got to the point that he couldn't go down the halls without having names hurled at him like rocks, people threw spitballs at the back of his head in class, and things got so bad in the cafeteria that he stopped eating lunch and would spend the hour in the library every day.

"I didn't actively participate in the name-calling, but I did laugh along with everyone else like a good little lemming. Part of me couldn't believe it. These were people I thought of as friends, people I'd known most of my life, people who had always seemed chill. I never suspected they could be this vicious. And it definitely reinforced my conviction that I could never come out to them. If not for the grace of passing, I could be Andy. I didn't want that, and so I laughed when they called him names and threw things at him. I felt like utter shit, but I laughed anyway."

"That's understandable," Silas said. "Sad to say, but it's human nature to want to deflect that kind of attention off ourselves. And society has put such a stigma on being gay that it makes it so hard for us to just be ourselves. I'm not saying what you did was right, but it is understandable."

Kris held up a silencing hand. "That's not...you haven't heard the worst of it yet."

Silas pressed his lips together, silently chastising himself for interrupting. Kris's pain was palpable, and Silas wanted nothing more than to provide some balm for it. He reminded himself that sometimes unburdening was in itself a balm.

Kris released a shaky breath before continuing. "I ran into Andy in the restroom one day. It was this small restroom up near the principal's office that people rarely used because it was sort of out of the way. My homeroom teacher had sent me to the office to turn in some attendance sheets, and I ducked into the restroom before the bell for first period. As soon as I pushed through the door, I heard the sound of someone crying. I turned the corner and there was Andy, leaning on the wall next to the sinks, sobbing. He had his hands in his hair, twisting, and his head was down. I froze, not sure what to do. I had just decided to back out quietly when Andy's head snapped up and he spotted me in the mirror.

"He whirled around, and I expected to see embarrassment in his eyes at being caught crying in the bathroom. And maybe there was a little of that, but mostly what I saw in his eyes was fear. *Of me.* I have to tell you, I felt about two feet tall and suddenly I was the one embarrassed. And ashamed. So fucking ashamed.

"I slowly started toward him, and he actually cringed back against the wall and told me he didn't want any trouble. I held up my hands and backed away. The first bell rang, and he jumped like a firecracker had gone off by his ear. Looked like he was going to bolt, but then he just sort of slumped down and let himself slide down to the floor. He looked up at me, and he was crying again. He said, 'Why won't you guys leave me alone?'

"I felt horrible, lower than dog shit someone has scraped off their shoe. I think in some ways I had worked to dehumanize Andy in mind, so that I wouldn't have to really dwell on his pain. But having him there in front of me, tears flowing down his cheeks, hearing the pleading tone in his voice...there was no way to hide from it. I couldn't help but see Andy as a real person, a real person who just wanted some peace and happiness, who was suffering over something that he couldn't control. In that moment, I saw myself in Andy.

"I suddenly found myself wanting to help him, wanting to be his friend, wanting to help take some of his pain away. I opened my mouth, and to this day I'm not entirely sure what I planned to say to him, but I never got the chance. The door opened behind me, and I turned around to find Spencer and two other guys from the basketball team walking in. Spencer seemed surprised to see me, asked what I was doing there since he knew I didn't smoke. Found out later they liked to duck into that particular restroom to take a few drags precisely because it wasn't used much. Before I could answer Spence, he spotted Andy crumpled up on the floor crying and started to laugh, said something about me having cornered a queer.

"At first I felt paralyzed, not able to move or speak. I had been thinking that I could see myself in Andy, and suddenly I could see myself living Andy's life. The daily taunting and torment, the constant ridicule and loneliness. I could see it, and I desperately didn't want it, so in that moment I made a choice. The easy choice, the selfish choice. I made the *wrong* choice.

"I said to Spence, 'I came in here and found him this way, just bawling like a little baby.' The other guys got a good laugh at that, and Spence sort of squatted down in front of Andy and said something like, 'What's wrong, Angie? Did your boyfriend break up with you or did they discontinue your favorite shade of lipstick?'

"The other two really cracked up over that one, but I have to admit that I was laughing louder than either of them. One of the guys snatched up Andy's backpack and upended it, so that all the books came raining down on Andy's head. The other turned on one of the sinks, pooled some water in his cupped hands, then flung the water at Andy's crotch, asking him if he'd wet his pants or creamed his jeans.

"During all this, Andy just sat there on the floor. Taking it, enduring it, but he kept his eyes on me. I saw a pleading there, a questioning, and I may have been reading into it, but I swear I saw recognition there, too. Like he knew I was a kindred spirit, so to speak, and wondered how I could turn on my own.

"I became afraid the other guys would see that look and know what it meant, so I had to assert myself and my machoism. I told the other guys I was glad they'd come along, I'd have hated to be trapped alone in the bathroom with a sniveling little queer, I could have caught fag and come to school the next day dressed as RuPaul. We all laughed, and I saw that pleading in Andy's eyes turn to...I don't know how to describe it. Wasn't quite anger or disappointment, it was more like resignation. Like I could see the moment where he truly gave up.

"Anyway, we continued taunting him for another minute or so then headed out when the bell rang for the start of first period. I felt horrible about myself, but the worst part is that I also felt a little proud. I had successfully maintained my disguise, and the guys still thought I was one of them. I had the nerve to be proud of that."

Silas felt the urge to say something, to offer some hollow assurances, but he sensed that Kris wasn't done, and he wouldn't interrupt again. When lancing a wound, it was important to get all the poison out if you wanted to make a full recovery. Silas braced himself for what would come next, but still wasn't prepared.

"Andy killed himself less than two weeks later," Kris said, his body going rigid and quivering. "Took a whole bunch of sleeping pills right before bed, and his parents found him the next morning, the bottle on his nightstand. He didn't leave a note or anything like that, but I don't think anyone at school was left wondering why he did it. We all knew, we were all responsible, even if not everyone accepted that responsibility.

"Spence was actually hit pretty hard. Guilt and shame, but not all the guys who participated in Andy's torment felt that way. At least they wouldn't admit to it. A lot of, 'He made his choice, not us,' and 'It's not my fault if he wasn't man enough to take some good-natured jabs.' It got a little bit of national attention, but quickly buried because it seemed every other week there was another gay teen committing suicide. Some celebrities would say 'It gets better' then everyone would forget. But not me, I couldn't forget. I'd played a hand in stuffing those pills down his throat.

"So I came out. Maybe as some kind of weird tribute to Andy, but also I think as a form of atonement. I figured the guys on the basketball team would be particularly hard on me. You know, since I infiltrated their ranks and all that. And truthfully, a part of me wanted that. Felt I deserved it.

"Anyway, I came out to my parents first. They reacted with awkward acceptance. After everything that had just gone down with Andy's suicide, I suspect they felt they had no other choice. Then I told my friends."

Another pause, this one longer. Silas felt that it would be okay to speak now. He squeezed Kris's hand and said, "Was it awful?"

Kris lifted one shoulder in a dispirited shrug. "Not as awful as I was expecting, to be quite honest. Like with my parents, I think people were shaken by what had happened with Andy. Even the guys who felt like he brought it on himself didn't want to give me their wrath full force. In a weird way, you could say that Andy shielded me from the worst of it. I mean, there was some hassling, some name-calling, a few spitballs, but nothing like what I'd feared. Nothing like what Andy had endured. Spence was actually really great, though; stuck by me. Andy's suicide seemed to affect him as much as it did me. He actually worked to get a gay-straight student alliance group started at the school. Of which there were three members. Me, Spence, and some freshman girl who was too shy to say more than two words at a time.

"For my part, I decided never to lie about who I am again and never to allow myself to fall sway to mob mentality again either. So...um...that's my long-winded answer to what I am most ashamed of."

A few tears leaked silently down Kris's cheeks, and Silas felt tears of his own caught in his eyelashes like wet cobwebs. He placed his fingers under Kris's chin and turned his head, forcing their eyes to meet.

"I'm not going to tell you that you shouldn't feel shame or that what you did wasn't bad, but this proves to me that you are a good person. That's why you feel shame, that's why it hurts so much. If you weren't a good person, it wouldn't hit you this hard."

Kris managed a weak smile and swiped at his eyes. "I get what you're saying, but I can't stop thinking about Andy crouched on that restroom floor. Needing someone to stick up for him, needing someone to lend him a hand. That could have been me, and then maybe he'd still be here. Maybe he'd be in college, have a boyfriend, friends, a bright future ahead of him. Knowing that my feeling bad about what happened makes me a good person is little consolation."

"I know, I just hate seeing you in so much pain."

Kris reached up and tugged gently on one of Silas's earlobes. "That's what makes you so special," Kris said. "You see someone in pain, and you don't hesitate to try to make them feel better."

Silas opened his mouth to respond, but Kris stopped him with a kiss. A kiss of passion and urgency, and Silas's body responded instantly. They reclined on the bed, arms entangling, Kris crushing his weight on top of Silas, but Silas didn't mind at all. He welcomed the press of Kris's body. When Kris's hand snaked down and his fingers probed into the waistband of Silas's jeans, Silas did not protest. Instead, he moaned softly into Kris's mouth. A part of him had known this might happen, had *hoped* this might happen.

Their shirts came off, somehow being shed with barely a pause in the kissing, a neat magic trick. Silas could feel Kris's erection pressing into his thigh, and Silas placed a hand against Kris's surprisingly furry chest. Not to stop the proceedings, but merely a time-out.

"Wait," Silas said, his breath coming in heaving gasps. "I should probably tell you, I've never done this before."

Kris took a half-moment to get his own breathing under control before answering. "We don't have to do anything you don't want to."

"I want to. Believe me, I want to, I just thought you should know."

"It's okay. I'm not exactly Mr. Experience myself. I've only been with one other person, but this is the first time I've been with someone I love."

The word hit Silas like a karate chop to the windpipe, snatching away his breath. Kris stared down at him, his expression a mixture of desperate need and excruciating fear. Probably afraid Silas wouldn't say it back.

And Silas hesitated. Not because he didn't want to say it back, and not because he didn't feel it. But because he recognized that this simple four-letter word, even more than sex, had the potential to change everything. That was exciting, but also terrifying.

"I love you, too," Silas said, taking the plunge.

The relief that shuddered through Kris vibrated through Silas's body as well, and this time when they kissed, Silas imagined their lips created sparks like stone on flint.

Kris swiped out and found the bedside lamp, extinguishing the light.

CHAPTER THIRTEEN

Silas's body sat in English Comp, but his mind was elsewhere. His mind had been elsewhere since Saturday night. His mind had never left Kris's dorm room, luxuriating in the small room filled with heat and sweat and panting breaths.

As Silas doodled in the margins of his textbook, a succession of tight spiral pinwheels, he felt the smile stretching his lips. A smile that had been a permanent fixture on his face for the past three days. Along with an unfamiliar sense of euphoria that made him feel as if his body was filled with helium and he may float up like one of those balloons in the Macy's Thanksgiving Day Parade. His father had certainly noticed the uncharacteristic giddiness, and Silas suspected his father was smart enough to surmise the source from which this newfound happiness sprang, but Silas wasn't yet ready to talk about it. It was so new, he wanted to keep it to himself for a bit longer, marveling over it.

Silas was in love, with someone who loved him back. He'd never experienced this level of intoxicating joy before.

Of course, there was that nagging voice in the back of his mind that reminded him this happiness was built on a lie, that the man Kris thought he loved didn't technically exist.

In his current mood, Silas had no trouble stuffing a gag in that voice's mouth. Kris knew Silas, all the important bits, and the bits that weren't true...well, Silas would work on making them true.

Of course, an important component of this plan was making sure he finished out Fall semester with an impressive GPA. If he were to stay on track, he supposed paying attention in class might be sort of a prerequisite.

Silas turned away from his rather hypnotic spirals and focused again on Mr. Henry, talking about imagery and symbolism. Silas made it about ten minutes before his thoughts began to drift again, like metal shavings to a magnet, to Saturday night. The feel of Kris's hot hands on him, the minty flavor of his kisses (suggesting his trip to the bathroom that night had included brushing his teeth and gargling mouthwash, a preparation that Silas considered more endearing than presumptuous).

He found himself staring out the window. The day was overcast and chilly, but he still wished he was outside, off campus, at Furman with Kris. They were meeting for an early dinner tonight, but that seemed an eternity away. And now that Pete was back in town, there would be no alone time. Regardless, just being near Kris was good enough.

So this is what love is, broken down to its simplest terms? Being happier with someone than apart?

Silas became aware that the guy sitting next to him was doodling as well, scribbling furiously into a notebook. A cursory glance at the page grabbed Silas's attention. No simple spirals for this fellow, but a rather elaborate and detailed drawing of a dragon, steam leaking from its nostrils. Impressive skill.

Mr. Henry finally managed to win Silas's attention again when he dismissed the class with a final reminder that he expected the assignment completed and ready to turn in on Wednesday.

The assignment? Silas must have missed that part of the lecture, and he couldn't very well ask Mr. Henry about it without revealing himself for the academic flop he really was. As Silas closed his textbook and stowed it in his backpack, he began looking around at the departing students rather desperately, trying to decide who to ask.

"A one-page essay," the guy from the seat next to him said. The dragon-drawer. "Any subject, but you have to use imagery and symbolism to reinforce your point."

Silas laughed. "Was it that obvious I was lost?"

"Don't worry about it. I'm an expert at zoning out. Luckily, I have the knack of completely spacing and still managing to retain what's going on around me through some kind of peripheral focus. My name's Finn, by the way."

Silas hated to admit he'd been sitting beside the guy all semester and had never even wondered what his name was. "Nice to meet you. I'm Silas."

The two left the classroom and started down the hall to the exit. They pushed through the doors, and Silas zipped up his jacket against the chilly breeze that buffeted him. For the first time this fall, he could really feel winter's promise announcing itself.

"Where you headed now?" Finn asked.

"University Transfer Building."

"Cool. Engineering Technologies here, we can walk together."

They fell in step up the walkway, and Silas took a moment to marvel at the ease with which he chatted with this young man who despite his persistent proximity in class was still a stranger. At the beginning of the semester, such a thing would have been impossible. Spending time with the Furman gang had really helped Silas in overcoming his inherent self-consciousness, making him more comfortable in social situations. Almost like free therapy.

Well, not exactly free. The cost is only your integrity.

Silas shook his head, as if to dislodge that nagging voice, then said to Finn, "I saw the dragon you were drawing in class."

Finn laughed then shrugged awkwardly. "I was just messing around."

"It looked pretty damn good to me. You draw a lot?"

"Yeah, I guess you could say that's my *thing*. Dave McKean is my god."

"Is that a painter?" Silas asked.

Finn gave him a look as if Silas had admitted to having never heard of Santa Claus. "Dave McKean...only one of the best artists working in comics today."

"Sorry, I don't really read a lot of comics."

"You seem like a nice enough guy, so I'll forgive you. There's a lot more going on in comics than just guys flying around in tights. A lot of cool stuff. Sci-fi, gothic, high fantasy. Some people have this pre-conceived notion about comics, like that jack-off pothead Bill Maher, but they don't really know what they're talking about. Dig a little deeper, and you'll find some really complex stuff."

Silas only caught bits and pieces of this dissertation on the value of comics, because he found himself scanning the students they passed, searching the faces, afraid of running into Katie. Greenville Tech wasn't exactly a massive campus, so chances were they'd passed each other perhaps dozens of times since the semester started but never noticed.

However, things were different now. They'd officially "met" Saturday at Smiley's, she had spent some time analyzing his face because she thought he looked like someone from a TV show, so if they passed each other now, she would definitely notice which would lead only to disaster. He had to be on guard and prepared to dive behind a bush like a character in some screwball comedy if necessary.

He became aware that Finn had stopped speaking, and when he glanced at the young man, the perplexed but expectant gaze alerted Silas to the fact that he had been asked a question. No way out of this but through honesty.

Not your strong suit these days, my friend.

"I'm sorry, what did you say?"

Finn laughed. "Dude, you really do need to work on this peripheral focus thing. I just asked if you were an artist."

"Oh no. I mean, not a *visual* artist, at least. I write a little."

"Really?" Finn said with a certain eagerness in his voice. "What kind of stuff?"

"Slice-of-life mostly," Silas said, realizing he'd answered this same question to the Furman gang, meaning he'd told more people about his writing in the past month than he had in all the years leading up to it.

"Ever do any genre work?"

"Not usually, though I have done a few pieces that could be considered ghost stories I guess."

"I'm always looking for writers."

"Why?" Silas asked.

"I'm halfway decent at drawing, but I suck royally at putting together a cohesive story. If I can find an interested writer to plot the stories, I can do the drawings, and we can maybe work on our own comic together."

"Oh. I don't know if I'd be the right—"

"Hey, I know you!"

Silas froze, thinking, *It's Katie. I let my guard down for a minute and she spotted me.*

Which was ridiculous, because the voice was clearly male. Silas turned his head slowly, imagining he could hear his neck creak like something rusty and in need of oil, and spotted the older man. He definitely looked familiar but at first Silas couldn't place him. He was dressed in jeans, but a button-up shirt and blazer, carrying a leather satchel. Definitely looked more professor than student.

And then it hit Silas, like a cartoon anvil to the head.

"Dr. Flem."

"You're … " The professor paused a moment, snapping his fingers while he tried to place Silas, just long enough for Silas to hope he would be unsuccessful. "Silas, right? You hang with Gus's group."

Silas scrambled for a response, finding his mind a complete blank, but then Finn nudged him gently and said, "Hey, I need to get to Bio, but I'll see you in class Wednesday. We can continue the collaboration discussion then."

Silas watched Finn walk off, wishing he could follow, but instead he stood his ground and turned back to Dr. Flem. Who was frowning at him.

"You're a student here?" the professor asked. "I'm sorry, I assumed you went to Furman like the rest of that group."

Silas employed the oldest of stalling tricks; he answered a question with a question. "What are you doing here?"

"Greenville Tech sometimes invites me to do guest lectures. I've published a few books, so I seem more impressive than I really am."

Silas recognized this as self-deprecating humor, but his entire body was clenched with the stress of the moment, and he didn't have it in him to offer even a polite chuckle. His mind whirred, a jumble of chaotic thoughts, as he tried to figure a way out of this.

"Are you going to do a lecture now?" he asked.

"Just finished one actually."

"Do you have a few minutes to talk?"

Dr. Flem hesitated, and Silas couldn't blame him. Silas was a stranger to him; someone he barely knew who wasn't even a student of his. However, the hesitation only lasted half a minute then he said, "Sure
. I don't have to be back at Furman for another hour."

They sat on a bench down from the TRC building, which housed the school's bookstore and auditorium. Silas hadn't been sure what he'd planned to tell the professor, but in the end he'd ended up spewing forth the whole ugly truth. He wasn't sure why exactly. Dr. Flem seemed like a trustworthy enough fellow, but he was in fact a stranger. Silas suspected it had less to do with Dr. Flem himself and more to do with the fact that Silas simply had to unburden before the secret completely poisoned him. Emotional ipecac.

Silence stretched out for more than a minute after Silas finished his story. Dr. Flem's expression remained impassive, but his gaze was intense and did not waver. Silas looked away, the loser in this staring contest. Finally, he said, "I'm sorry," not sure who exactly he was apologizing to and for what. To Dr. Flem for taking up his time; to his new friends by proxy for lying to them; to the universe itself for being such a shitty excuse for a human being.

When Dr. Flem spoke, his voice was firm but not harsh. Actually, rather gentle. "Young man, I don't envy you."

Silas closed his eyes and felt like crying. Hearing compassion in Dr. Flem's voice seemed to somehow be worse than anger. "No one would want to be in my shoes."

"I have to ask you a few questions."

Silas nodded.

"First, have you ever snuck into a Furman class to sell your story of being a student?"

"No, sir."

"Have you ever masqueraded as a student in the dining hall to get a free meal?"

"Of course not. I've never even been in the dining hall."

"Ever presented yourself as a student to get into plays or recitals or any other on-campus event?"

Silas shook his head.

"Okay then. You haven't committed any offenses that would require me to report you to the administration."

Silas looked up suddenly, his stomach muscles clenching in panic. He hadn't even considered that possibility, being reported to the Furman administration as an imposter.

"That doesn't mean what you're doing isn't wrong," Dr. Flem was quick to say. "It simply means that from a legal standpoint, you haven't crossed the line into criminality."

"Are you going to tell Gus and the gang?"

Dr. Flem didn't answer right away, which made Silas nervous, especially since the man's stare only seemed to intensify. Finally, Dr. Flem sighed and said, "You seem like a decent young man. If you weren't, you wouldn't be in such turmoil over the situation."

"Thanks, but that doesn't answer my question. Are you going to tell them?"

"No...but you are."

"Or else, right?"

"I can't make you tell them," Dr. Flem said. "But I don't believe you'll be able to continue living with yourself if you don't. You're a man under pressure, anyone can see that, and the only way to relieve that pressure is to come clean."

"But what if I am able to get into Furman next year? It's a long shot, but that could solve all my problems."

"Let's say you do get into Furman next year; doesn't change the fact that you'll have spent this entire year lying to your friends. And what if things really work out for you and Kris, you get married and build a future together? You're willing to go the rest of your life carrying the fact that your relationship started on a foundation of deception?"

Silas felt tears slipping down his cheeks, but he didn't care that he was crying in public. The emotion was too raw to keep bottled inside. "But I've never had what I have with this group before, and I honestly never thought I would. I can't give it up now, I just can't. If I went back to being the friendless loser I was before I met them, it would be so much worse because now I would know exactly what I was missing."

"I wish I could tell you that Gus and Kris and the rest would be understanding and forgiving," Dr. Flem said, his voice patient and calm, like that of a therapist. "But I can't. They are all decent young people as well, but I don't think anyone could predict how they'll react to finding out that you've been lying to them all this time."

"I don't want to lose them."

"I know it's a hard decision, but I do believe you'll eventually come to realize it's the only decision you can make if you don't want to completely destroy yourself."

Silas took a shuddering breath and swiped at his eyes. "I never meant for any of this happen."

"I know," Dr. Flem said, placing a hand on his shoulder. "And if you need to talk, my office is in Furman Hall."

"I appreciate that, and I'm sorry I threw all this at you out of the blue. You must think I'm completely insane."

Dr. Flem laughed. "Not at all. You're just young...which I guess in some ways is the same thing."

CHAPTER FOURTEEN

"All I'm saying is that everyone has the same opportunities here at Furman," Gus said.

The group sat in the grass near the amphitheater, in their usual loose circle. Silas and Kris were side by side, Kris's hand casually but meaningfully resting on Silas's knee. Silas found himself both excited by the contact but also oddly embarrassed. Public displays of affection were new to him, but then again, so were private displays of affection.

Sheila laughed at Gus. "You can't really believe that, can you?"

"Of course I do. Any student who attends Furman has equal opportunity to participate in the programs like my internship or Semester Abroad."

"Really?" Paige said. "I bet if we looked up statistics on those programs, we'd find that the more affluent students participate at a much higher rate than, say, scholarship students."

"If that's the case," Gus said, "it would only be because they aren't applying for the programs. That doesn't make it elitism."

Today's discussion had been prompted by an editorial that appeared in the latest issue of the *Paladin*, the school's newspaper, suggesting that Furman was an elitist school that provided a much different experience for students from lower socioeconomic backgrounds. Thus far, Silas had stayed out of the conversation, not really having anything to add. However, he realized now that maybe he did.

"You know," he said tentatively, "we're overlooking one thing. A school like Furman isn't a possibility for everyone, so there are a lot of people shut out from those opportunities simply by virtue of not being able to go here."

"There's absolutely nothing wrong with a school being competitive," Gus said. "I mean, you can't let everyone in so there have to be some academic standards."

Silas conceded the point. "True, but some people can't go here not because they aren't smart enough but because they aren't financially able and even financial aid isn't enough."

"That's why some people believe undergraduate colleges and universities should be free," Kris said, squeezing Silas's knee. "So that it really can level the playing field and provide people from all kinds of backgrounds the same opportunities."

"Well, thank you Bernie Sanders," Gus said. "Furman is expensive, but it offers all kinds of scholarships and grants, not to mention all the loans you can get."

"Yeah and be in crazy debt the rest of your life," Franco said. "Don't get me started on the crooked college loan industry. Almost as big a racket as the insanely inflated prices of our textbooks."

Gus rolled his eyes. "My point is that yes, Furman is an expensive school, but it's not out of reach for anyone who wants to matriculate here, as long as you've got the brains and the drive."

I hope that's true, Silas thought. *God, I hope that's true.*

"Don't forget about the Work Study program," Philip said. "If it wasn't for the ability to work on campus as part of my financial aid, I wouldn't be here. Speaking of which, I need to hustle to the Enrollment Office or I'm going to be late."

After Philip departed, the conversation turned to less controversial subjects. Franco talked about his progress with his stand-up night; the event had been moved to February, and so far three other students had signed up to participate with sets of their own, with Franco himself being the "headliner." Gus talked about his upcoming internship for a prominent congresswoman who had made an unsuccessful bid for President a few years ago. Paige talked about a new poem she was working on, in which she was attempting to capture in words the magical quality of sunset.

"What about you?" Paige asked Silas. "You working on anything new?"

Mark Allan Gunnells

"Oh, um, I just finished a new short story called 'Time Shift.'"

"I read it," Kris said. "It's incredible."

Silas felt himself blushing. Normally no one read his stories, except for a select few he'd let his father read, so it had been quite the act of trust to send this one to Kris.

"What's it about?" Gus asked.

Silas opened his mouth to answer...but found no answer forthcoming. Since his writing had always been such a solitary act, he'd never been in a position where he had to talk about it or even think too deeply about what his stories were *about*.

"Well, it's kind of hard to explain. It's just a little flash piece, about a man revisiting his home town after years away, and he goes to the arcade where he spent much of his youth, and it's been turned into a crafting store. Most of the story is him wandering the aisles, trying to reminisce but unable to do so because there are just too many changes."

"Ah," Gus said. "So working with themes of nostalgia, progress, mid-life crises, lost youth."

Silas laughed. "I guess. Honestly, I don't put a lot of thought into things like theme when I'm writing. I get an idea and I just *go*, see where it leads me. I don't know, for me writing seems less like an act of creation and more an act of discovery."

The last statement seemed much too overblown and melodramatic as soon as it left his mouth, but the group took it in stride. Gus even nodded his approval and said, "An instinctual writer, I like that."

"You should read us the story," Paige said, and everyone else chimed in their agreement.

The prospect terrified Silas, froze him as if a bucket of ice water had been poured over his head like in those ALS challenge videos that had been so popular online a few years ago. "I don't think, I mean I couldn't," he stammered. "I don't even have a copy of the story on me."

"I can pull up the attachment on my phone," Kris said, already tapping away at the screen. For an instant, Silas felt angry, as if Kris had betrayed him, but then Kris redeemed himself by adding, "I'll read it, if that's okay with you, Silas."

Silas nodded silently, thinking, *He gets me. He wants to challenge me but understands he can't push too hard too fast. He really knows me.*

Kris began to read the story, while Silas stared at a honeybee flitting from flower to flower, focusing on the small insect so he didn't have to focus on hearing his own words projected out to the group. Only when Kris reached the final line, "With that, he stepped out of the door and back into a present that seemed just a little bit darker than before," did Silas look up. His teeth were clenched and his posture rigid, as if bracing himself for a punch.

At first, only silence. Silas wasn't sure if that was a good or a bad sign, and no one's expression gave any hints. Finally, Paige leaned to the side and put a hand over his. "That was simply beautiful."

"Absolutely," Gus agreed. "I'm not a literary expert or anything, but it was impressive how much you could accomplish in such a short story. I mean, it felt like a fully realized world and character."

Sheila and Franco started talking at the same time, both offering their own compliments.

"If I had one constructive criticism to make," Gus said, "it would be that sometimes I felt you were telling the reader what to feel instead of trusting that the story itself will pull those emotions from the reader."

Silas nodded. "I know what you mean, and I sometimes do a little too much 'telling,' like I'm not confident enough that I'm getting the point across that I want to make."

"You don't have anything to worry about," Paige said. "You managed to create a story that was full of emotion without being overly schmaltzy."

"Thank you," Silas muttered, staring off to the side, searching for his little bee friend. His cheeks filled with heat, not sure how to take the praise. It wasn't something he had much practice with.

"Told you the story was exceptional," Kris said, bumping Silas with his shoulder.

"You should submit it to *The Echo*," Paige said.

Silas frowned. "The what?"

"*The Echo.* You know, Furman's literary magazine."

"Oh yeah, of course."

"Seriously, I know the girl who's editing it this year," Paige said. "I've already submitted a few of my poems. You should submit this story. I predict Grace would accept it in a heartbeat."

Silas began shaking his head, a little too vigorously. "Oh no, no, I couldn't do that."

"Why not?" Kris asked. "Your stuff is great, and the magazine is open to all students and faculty of Furman."

Panic erupted in Silas's chest like a mad bird beating against the bars of its cage. All he could think about was Dr. Flem's warning that masquerading as a student in any type of official manner could take this charade over the line from dishonest to downright criminal. "No, really, I don't want to. I'm, um, I'm just not ready for that kind of public scrutiny of my work yet."

"Hey, I understand stage fright," Franco said. "But you have to push through it. I mean, if you're serious about becoming a writer, eventually you'll have to reconcile yourself with the idea of large numbers of people laying eyes on your stuff."

"Yeah, eventually, but not now. I'm not ready now."

Kris put a steadying arm around him and pulled him close. "It's okay. If you're not ready, you're not ready. No one's going to force you. Right, Paige?"

This last was delivered a little pointedly, and Paige rolled her eyes. "I'm not trying to be all stage mother or anything, merely wanted to be encouraging."

"And I appreciate it," Silas said. "I really do, but I'd really rather not."

Paige reached over and touched his hand again. "I understand, and I apologize. My enthusiasm can be a bit overbearing at times. I won't say another word about it."

"Let's talk about Halloween," Gus said, and Silas could have kissed the man for the subject change. "We're going out, yes?"

"I heard about this really awesome haunted trail up in Hendersonville called The Haunted Farm," Franco said. "I think we should check it out."

Sheila looked skeptical and a bit bored. "A haunted trail?

If we're going to do something so pedestrian, surely there are places right here in Greenville."

"Yeah," Franco said, "but I know some guys from the theater department who are participating in this one and it's supposed to be something special. They even released this video online like a movie trailer."

He pulled it up on his phone and everyone watched, and the video was impressive. A professional looking trailer that made it seem the trail had an actual storyline and everything.

"Looks pretty cool," Gus said. "Let's take a vote. Everyone in favor of The Haunted Farm, raise your hand."

Everyone raised their hands, even Sheila albeit a little reluctantly.

"Of course," Gus added, "if we're doing it, we're doing it right. We all have to wear a costume."

Sheila groaned. "Do we get to vote on that one, too?"

Gus shook his head. "No, executive decision."

Silas found himself rather excited. He'd always loved Halloween, but since he got too old for trick-or-treating, he'd never had anything to do on the holiday. No one invited him to Halloween parties and going to haunted trails and spook houses was no fun alone. He usually spent the evening at home, watching horror movies with his father, and he hadn't dressed up in costume since he was twelve years old.

With a glance at his phone, Silas cursed softly when he saw the time. "I didn't realize how late it was getting," he said. "I really need to get home. I have a ton of studying to do."

Which was true. If he had any hope of getting accepted into Furman as a transfer student next year, he had to ensure he raised his GPA as much as possible.

"I'll walk you to your car," Kris said, standing and holding out a hand to Silas.

The group said their goodbyes and Silas and Kris wandered down to the lake then toward the parking lot, hand-in-hand. Silas still thrilled at the contact, which in a weird way felt as intimate as when they made love.

"So I was thinking," Kris said as they passed by the Trone Student Center. "I think it's time I met your father."

The bird began to beat at the bars of its cage in Silas's chest again, but he tried not to show it. "You do?"

"Yes. I mean, I'm crazy about you, and we have moved beyond casual dating, so it seems the next logical step is to meet the family. Mine isn't exactly close, but I would like you to meet them the next time they visit. And I'd like to meet your father, let him know I'm serious about you."

Silas had known this subject was likely to come up again, and he'd prepared an answer, but now that the time was here, he found himself having second thoughts. Nevertheless, he could think of no other alternatives.

"I don't think my dad wants to meet you," Silas said.

Kris stopped abruptly, causing a group of girls behind them to have to veer around. "What do you mean, he doesn't want to meet me?"

Silas gazed out at the lake, not wanting to look at the expression of disappointment and heartbreak on Kris's face. A flock of ducks in V formation swam away from them, as if fleeing Silas's cruel deception. He didn't want to go through with this, but he felt he had no choice. He was painted into a corner, and he held the paint brush.

"My dad isn't dealing very well with the fact that I have a boyfriend," Silas said.

"I thought your father was okay with the fact that you're gay."

"He was, when it was all theoretical and in the abstract. Now that I'm actually dating someone, it's a different story. He told me what I do with my private life is my business, but he doesn't want to hear about it and doesn't want me throwing it in his face."

Each word passed through Silas's lips like broken glass, making him feel progressively more torn up. His father had never been anything but supportive and lovely; saying such things about him felt like a betrayal.

"Sweetie, I'm so sorry you have to go through that," Kris said and wrapped Silas in an embrace meant to be comforting but which only made Silas feel like an even bigger shit. "People who are cool with gay people as long as we stay neutered are almost as bad as the outright, in-your-face bigots. Just know that it has nothing to do with you; it's your father's problem. You're wonderful, Silas. You're perfect."

Silas started to cry.

Kris thinks I'm wonderful and perfect. I take back what I thought before. He doesn't know me at all. He's dating a stranger.

CHAPTER FIFTEEN

"How do I look?" Silas asked, standing in the living room. His father, sitting on the sofa, looked him up and down. "You look fine, but…"

"But what? You can be honest."

"I don't know who you're supposed to be dressed up as."

Silas sighed, having feared that no one would be able to identify his costume. He'd glued on a fake, inverted-V mustache and was wearing a dark black suit and a white ruffled shirt with a high collar that he had found at a thrift store. On the right shoulder of the suit jacket, he'd sewn a stuffed black bird; the thing flopped around because he couldn't get it to stand up straight.

"I'm Edgar Allan Poe," Silas said with a shrug, causing the bird to bounce.

His father nodded. "Oh, I see. And that's…a raven?"

"Actually, I think it's a crow, but it was the closest I could find."

"Well, I think it's very imaginative."

"It's stupid," Silas said, dropping down next to his father. "I'm going to spend all night having to explain who I am. Maybe I shouldn't go. I'll call Kris and tell him I've got a stomach bug then we can have a horror movie marathon like usual."

"What makes you think I don't have plans?" his father asked.

Silas smiled. "I'm sorry for assuming. So what are your big plans?"

"I'm going trick-or-treating as the world's tallest child. I'll tell everyone I have that disease Robin Williams had in that movie *Jack*."

"Oh, well, I certainly wouldn't want to horn in on those plans."

"I'm getting to be a big boy," his father said. "I need my space to explore and grow as a person."

Silas laughed then glanced at the jack-o'lantern shaped bowl full of mini-candy bars sitting on the coffee table. A sign of unfulfilled hope. They lived outside the city limits at the terminus of a dead-end street. They never got any trick-or-treaters. Parents tended to take their kinds downtown and to the more affluent neighborhoods. And yet Silas's father insisted on having a supply of candy at the ready. "Just in case," he always said, though the two of them always ended up eating the candy themselves over the next couple of weeks.

"So what is Kris dressing up as?" his father asked.

"I don't actually know. He said he wanted it to be a surprise."

"And I suppose he is coming to pick you up like a proper gentleman?"

"I already told you, I'm meeting them all on campus and we're going together as a group."

"Oh yeah," his father said then leaned forward to pluck a mini-Snickers from the bowl. He unwrapped it and popped it in his mouth before continuing. And Silas knew he was going to continue. "I want to run something by you, son."

Something about his tone and his use of the word "son" instantly put Silas on edge. "Okay, shoot."

"I know it's about a month away, but I was thinking you could invite Kris over for Thanksgiving dinner."

Silas read in novels how when people are stunned, they simply blink. He never believed that really happened, but at his father's out-of-the-blue request, Silas blinked. He hadn't been sure what his father wanted to run by him, but this certainly hadn't been it.

"Dad, he has his own family in Texas. He'll be going home for the holidays to be with them."

"You can always ask. You never know, he might want to stick around."

"Sure, Dad, I'll ask," Silas said, thinking, *No way.*

"And you know, son," his father said in that alarming,

serious tone again, "it doesn't have to be a holiday for him to have dinner with us. We could all go out somewhere, maybe a restaurant in downtown Greenville or something."

Silas swallowed past the lump that suddenly felt lodged in his throat like a piece of dry bread. He realized his father's suggestion of a restaurant meant that he thought Silas was ashamed of bringing Kris to the mobile home in which they lived. Which wasn't without a certain amount of truth, but it wasn't the main reason. Of course, he couldn't tell his father the main reason.

His father reached over and put a hand on Silas's crow-less shoulder. "Look, I see the way you light up when you talk about this boy. I know things are getting serious."

Sex. He's talking about sex.

Silas shrugged off his father's hand. "We're just dating. It's not like we're picking out china patterns and planning to adopt a Vietnamese baby or anything."

"I know," his father said, holding up his hands in surrender. "I'm not trying to pry. Simply saying that if this continues to evolve, eventually Kris will have to meet the old man."

Silas knew this was true but had no idea how he'd handle it when the time came. Even if he managed somehow to get into Furman as a transfer student next year, how could he ever be confident that his father wouldn't bring up Silas's start at Tech? For that matter, his father thought that Kris went to Tech.

I'll cross that bridge when I come to it. For now, it's hard enough managing one double life.

Silas kissed his father on the cheek, something he hadn't done since he was a kid, and said, "You'll meet, I just don't want to rush things. You know, scare him off by asking him to meet my dad too early."

"You're a wonderful young man. If he has any sense, nothing can scare him off."

God, I hope you're right.

"I need to run or I'm going to be late."

"Okay," his father said, grabbing a mini-Baby Ruth. "You be safe and have fun, Edgar."

The parking lot for the Haunted Farm was just a large empty field. Several workers were stationed throughout, directing traffic and keeping chaos at bay. When the group arrived at a little past 9:30, they found the place packed and had to park at the far end of the field, about a half mile away from the actual entrance to the trail.

After they piled out of the two vehicles they'd come in, Shelia said, "I knew we should have come earlier." She wore a nurse costume, but not the sexy kind. Her light blue scrubs were ripped and stained with fake blood, her hair a disheveled mess.

Franco, dressed as Frankenstein's Monster, put an arm around her shoulders. "It's Halloween. The later, the better."

"I'm just saying we'll probably be in line longer than it will actually take us to go down the trail, and I still have class tomorrow."

"Don't worry," Franco said then held his arms stiffly out in front of him and began to shamble forward. *"Frank keep you entertained."*

Sheila's lips twitched with a barely repressed smile as she followed behind him.

Paige, looking dour as Emily Dickinson in her white dress and severely parted wig with the tight bun in the back (Gus had taken a look at her and Silas and dubbed them the Literary Twins for the night), wrecked the illusion with a bright smile of her own. "When those two realize they love each other, it's going to be a great shock to both of them."

Gus, done up in a traditional pirate costume complete with eyepatch and a plastic parrot on his shoulder (causing Franco to dub him and Silas the Bird Brains for the night), said, "Ah Emily, for all your gothic pretensions, you are a romantic at heart."

"Well, Gothic literature is part of the Romantic Movement."

The two started off after Franco and Shelia, and Philip trailed behind, casting a glance back at Silas and Kris. Philip was the only one not in costume, claiming that between classes, homework, and work study, he simply hadn't found the time to come up with anything.

Kris, however, was looking hotter than ever in tight jeans, a satin red buttoned-up shirt over which he wore a long leather jacket that hung down to his ankles (faux-leather, he'd assured animal rights activist Sheila), and a pair of plastic vampire fangs rounded out the outfit. He'd been a little disappointed when Silas didn't realize he was supposed to be some character from the *Buffy the Vampire Slayer* TV show, but what Silas did realize was that his boyfriend was oozing pure sex tonight, and he wished they were alone together somewhere instead of at a crowded haunted trail.

"Mind out of the gutter," Kris said, the fangs causing his words to be slightly garbled.

"What? I wasn't...I mean, how did you..."

"You were staring at my package," Kris said, leaning forward and talking softly into Silas's ear. "Which is fine, but I'm more than a piece of meat. I have a mind, you know."

"Yes, but your costume isn't accentuating your mind tonight."

"Touché. I guess these pants are sort of package-focused."

Laughing, the two linked hands, something which had become second nature as of late, and started after their friends. The night air held a pleasant crispness to it, and the clear sky sparkled with stars like glitter spread on a black carpet. Silas's nose twitched as the distant scent of smoke reached him; somewhere someone must be having a bonfire or burning leaves. The whole scene was so quintessentially autumnal that it could have been captured for the October page of a calendar.

Up ahead, Philip glanced back again and even in the gloom, Silas could sense the hurt and disappointment in the young man. It wafted off him like palpable wind, buffeting Silas right in the face.

"He still has it bad," Silas said.

"*Who* has *what* bad?"

Silas tilted his head and gave Kris his full "are you shitting me?" glare. "Don't play dumb."

Kris shrugged and stared up at the sky. "I don't know what to do about it. He knows I'm with you. I figure there's nothing to be done except give him time to get over it. Eventually he'll find a new crush, hopefully one that will reciprocate the crush, and then his feelings for me will become a distant memory."

"You're right, but I still feel bad for him. I know what it's like to be him."

"Have I mentioned that your empathy is incredibly sexy?"

"You're insane, but if you weren't, you probably wouldn't be with me, so I guess that works out in my favor."

The walk across the field/parking lot was a trek through a labyrinth of cars, passing by fellow travelers in an array of costumes. Some ghastly, some silly, some sexy to the point of trashiness. Everyone Silas saw was laughing and goofing around, some people chasing each other, an atmosphere of revelry touching everyone.

Silas's spirits dropped slightly as they got closer to the entrance of the trail, and he saw how dauntingly long the line really was. At least a hundred people, if he had to make a rough guesstimate, twisting around like a snake made of human bodies, contained in switchback rows created by wooden stakes and rope. Silas and Kris joined the rest of the group at the end of the line.

"Told you," Sheila said, her arms crossed and her trademark smirk tilting her lips like a seesaw. "Nothing worse than being at the end of a long line."

"Hemorrhoids right before a plane trip to Australia?" Gus said.

"Diarrhea on a first date?" Franco said.

"Laryngitis before a big speech?" Paige said.

"Calling out the wrong name during an intimate moment?" Kris said.

Silas hesitated, though a response had immediately sprung to mind. A wickedly inappropriate response, but in the end he felt comfortable enough around this group of friends to be inappropriate. "Being at the front of a short line at Auschwitz?"

First silence, and Silas wondered if he'd miscalculated, but then reluctant laughter erupted from the others. Even Philip.

"Dude, that was twisted," Gus said with a grin. "I like it. You win that round."

Perhaps, Silas thought, the testament to true friendship was the ability to tell politically incorrect jokes and get laughs.

Well, in your case the testament to true friendship certainly isn't honesty.

To squelch that nagging inner voice, Silas said to Gus, "Too bad Katie couldn't make it tonight."

Gus shrugged, trying to affect an air of ambivalent nonchalance and not entirely succeeding. "She had to work the evening shift. We're getting together tomorrow night to watch a scary movie, sort of a belated holiday celebration."

"So are you guys officially dating now or what?" Franco asked.

"We're just hanging out."

"Hanging out naked?" Shelia said, poking Gus in the side.

"I will not confirm that there has been at least some making out, but I will not deny it either."

"That as far as it has gone?" Kris asked. "The hypothetical smooching?"

"I don't kiss and tell," Gus said.

"Except you kinda did," Paige said.

"No, I neither confirmed nor denied."

Sheila shook her head. "Guys are such creeps. If you like her, and she likes you, and you're swapping spit, why can't you simply be dating instead of 'just hanging out'?"

"You know, I'm heading to D.C. after Christmas break and graduating in the spring. It isn't the right time to get into anything serious."

Franco tilted his head and gave Gus a surveying look. "She shot you down, didn't she?"

"She told me she wants to keep things very casual; she isn't looking to be anyone's girlfriend right now."

"Good for her," Shelia said, and she and Paige exchanged a high five.

"Hey," Gus said, "when you thought it was me who wanted to keep it casual, you called me a creep."

"No, actually I called all guys creeps, and it's different when a woman makes that decision."

"How?"

"That kind of role reversal is called progress."

"Some might call it a double standard," Franco said.

Sheila smiled up at him. "Not if they wanted to stay in my good graces."

Before Franco could respond to that, screams arose from those in line. Silas glanced around and noticed that three people dressed in psycho-clown outfits had materialized from somewhere, lunging toward and taunting those waiting. They seemed to focus especially on young women in line, eliciting high-pitched screams from some and laughter from others.

"I hate it when they come out into the crowd," Paige said with a sigh. "Like, save it for the actual trail."

"At least they don't have chainsaws," Shelia said. "That shit is not scary, just loud and annoying."

As if on cue, a demented clown came out of a nearby shed and revved up a chainsaw, minus the chain, and started waving it above his head Leatherface style. Shelia groaned and put her hands over her ears.

Gus said something but his words were lost under the roar of the chainsaw. Silas spotted yet another clown, this one cleverly dressed as a zombie version of Ronald McDonald, sneaking up behind Shelia. When the undead Ronald saw that Silas had spotted him, he at first held a finger up to his bloody mouth then turned his attention back to Shelia.

Only to freeze and quickly move his gaze to Silas again. His painted smile curled up grotesquely. "Hey!" the clown shouted, surging forward. "Silas, my man, what are the chances of running into you here?"

The other six all also turned his way, making fourteen eyes total on Silas and he felt the weight like a collapsed wall.

"You know this clown, Silas?" Franco said, giggling at his own joke.

Silas searched the white-and-red streaked face, underneath an insane tangle of red hair like a blazing forest fire on the guy's head. "Um, do I?" he asked the clown.

The deranged Ronald laughed. "Sorry, believe it or not, after a while it's easy to forget I have all this crap on. It's me, Finn."

"Oh shit!" Silas exclaimed before he could stop himself. Despite feeling like the collapsed wall had become a collapsed building crushing down on him, he recovered quickly. "I mean, yeah, what a surprise. You work here?"

"For the past two Octobers. Me and some friends do it just for fun."

"And we happened to come to the very haunted trail where you work. That's just...incredible odds, wouldn't you say?" *Almost like the universe is trying to teach you a lesson.*

"So Finn, how do you and Silas know each other?" Kris asked when it became clear Silas wasn't going to introduce the clown to the rest of the group.

"We know each other from school," Finn said before Silas could think of a suitable answer.

"Oh," Gus said, "so you go to Furman, too? Didn't know Silas here had any other friends on campus besides us. Is he ashamed of you...or us?"

Everyone laughed, Silas a mite too loud, except for Finn. The painted smile remained upturned, but Silas noted the real lips inside turned down slightly. He looked at Silas with a million questions in his eyes, questions Silas couldn't possibly answer right now. He hoped Finn wouldn't say anything else incriminating, but those hopes were dashed with the clown's next words.

"No, I'm a Greenville Tech student."

"Finn and I went to high school together," Silas blurted, surprised by how quickly the lie came to him. "We know each other from our Riverside High days."

The confusion in Finn's eyes was evident to anyone who cared to look deeply, and Silas could only hope the others wouldn't look too deeply. Silas tried with his own eyes to convey a pleading entreaty for Finn to not give him away.

"Uh, yeah, Riverside High," Finn said, apparently getting the message and going along with it. For now, at least. "Go... Warriors?"

"It's nice to meet you," Kris said, holding out his hand. Finn shook but kept his gaze on Silas. "Silas has told us absolutely nothing about you."

"Well, you know Silas," Finn said. "He is a man of mystery."

"I'm Kris, by the way, since my boyfriend's manners seem to have flown completely away."

"I'm sorry," Silas said with a nervous titter, and he went down the line, introducing everyone to Finn.

"Nice to meet you all," Finn said. "I'd love to stay and chat, but we're not really supposed to break character and mingle with the victims. I'll be seeing you, Silas. We have a lot to catch up on, don't you think?"

"Definitely. We'll get together soon."

Finn dropped back and faded into the crowd. The line finally began to move as another group was ushered onto the trail.

"Was it my imagination," Sheila said, "or was that super awkward?"

Philip nodded. "For sure. I'm the King of Awkward, and that was definitely awkward with a capital AWK. A lot of tension there."

"Finn and I haven't seen each other in a while," Silas said, simultaneously impressed and sickened by how smoothly the lies were coming now. "After we graduated high school, I went off to Furman and he went off to Tech and we lost touch. Probably my fault, I didn't put in the effort, so he likely feels that I abandoned him for new friends or something."

"I don't remember you ever mentioning him," Kris said. "He's not an old flame, is he?"

"Definitely not. It's not like we were even particularly close friends. More acquaintances than anything. Really, in high school all I had were acquaintances."

"I think we can all relate to that," Paige said.

"Speak for yourself, I was very popular in high school," Franco said. "I was the class clown, and everyone loved me."

Sheila reached up and patted Franco's cheek. "Poor deluded bastard, they were laughing *at* you, not *with* you."

"Well, everyone's going to be laughing with me at the stand-up show come February. I'm developing some new material. Mind if I try a bit of it out on you guys?"

At that moment, Silas could have kissed Franco right on the mouth. He seamlessly changed the subject and got everyone's mind off Finn, directing everyone's attention toward himself. Silas reveled in the break, practicing some of that peripheral focus Finn had first told him about. He laughed at all the appropriate places while Franco did a bit about how bad South Carolinian drivers were, but inwardly all he could think about was Finn. It was cool that he didn't bust Silas right then and there, but there would be a reckoning.

Silas found himself dreading Mr. Henry's English Comp class even more than usual.

CHAPTER SIXTEEN

Finn was waiting for him outside the ITC building.

Silas had thought he was playing it smart, arriving five minutes late for class, thus no time for conversation before Mr. Henry began the day's lecture, and he planned to zip out of the room as soon as the class was dismissed.

But here Finn was, playing it smarter with an ambush.

"Hi, Finn," Silas said, trying to act as if everything were normal and Halloween night had never happened.

Finn approached him and took his arm. "Come on, we're skipping class today."

"What?"

"You and I are going to head across the street to Pita House, get some drinks, and have a little chat."

Silas looked longingly toward the building's door. "I don't know, I really shouldn't miss class."

"Why should it matter if a Furman student like yourself misses a Greenville Tech class?"

Silas sighed in defeat. "Okay, you're right. We do need to chat. I owe you that much for not busting me at the Haunted Farm."

"Your car or mine?"

They ended up taking Finn's decades-old Mitsubishi hatchback, making the quick jaunt over to Pita House, a popular Middle Eastern restaurant famous around town for its great authentic food and reasonable prices. Before the lunch rush, the place was mostly deserted, and Silas and Finn took a table near the small market area that consisted of four aisles, away from the few other customers. Finn had a coffee, Silas a lemonade, and they got a plate of stuffed grape leaves to share.

"So," Finn said when it became clear Silas wasn't going to initiate the conversation, "how about you tell me why your friends think you go to Furman."

"I will, but first I have a question of my own. I'm just curious, why didn't you give me away the other night?"

Finn shrugged. "I don't know, I guess I didn't want to embarrass you in front of them. Whatever's going on, it's your business and not my place to get involved in it. However, by covering for your lie, I inadvertently did get involved in it. So it's only fair that I know exactly what it is I'm involved in that I shouldn't be."

Silas nibbled on one of the grape leaves, considering how much he wanted to tell Finn, which parts of the story he might want to alter slightly or leave out altogether...then opened his mouth and spilled it all, the entire unvarnished truth. The second time recently he had told someone who was for all intents and purposes a total stranger the whole ugly story.

Yet you simply refuse to come clean to the people who really deserve the truth.

But Silas thought, most people if pressed would probably agree that it's easier to make unflattering confessions about yourself to people you didn't really know. The risk was not as great.

When Silas had spilled the story, a pregnant silence followed. Finn looked vaguely uncomfortable, as if suffering from gas pains, and he pushed the plate of two remaining grape leaves toward Silas's side of the table, as if he'd lost his appetite. Silas also noted that Finn avoided looking him in the eye.

"I know," Silas said. "I'm a terrible person."

"No, you're not," Finn said, though he continued to gaze at the tabletop. "I mean, I get it. You didn't mean to get yourself in this situation, and now that you're ensnared in it, you don't know how to get yourself out again without losing people who've become very important to you."

"That's it exactly."

"Of course, I don't agree with what you're doing," Finn said, finally raising his gaze to meet Silas's. "I definitely think you need to tell them before you get in any deeper, but I also can understand how this all happened and why it's so hard for you. You seem like a decent guy in a tough spot, caught between the proverbial rock and hard place. And because I do believe you're a decent guy, I know that eventually you're going to do the right thing, but the longer you wait to do it, the more devastating it's going to be. For everyone involved."

Silas heard Finn's words, and he recognized the wisdom of them, but his main takeaway from this was that his secret was still safe, and he allowed himself to relax.

You're fighting so hard to hold on to your lie. Maybe you're not as decent as Finn seems to think you are.

"The main reason I feel like I can't tell the truth is Kris," Silas said. "Don't get me wrong, I care about all of them, but Kris...what we have is something special and something I never expected to find. I don't see any way out of this without hurting him and destroying the best thing that has ever happened to me."

Finn thought this over a moment, sipping his coffee. "If you love him, you owe him honesty at the very least."

"I am honest with him...about all the important stuff, anyway. I mean, where I go to college shouldn't be that big a deal."

"Then why did you feel the need to lie about it in the first place?"

"Stop with all the logic and making sense, it isn't helpful to me," Silas said, and they shared a laugh.

Finn reached over, snatched up a grape leaf and gobbled it in two bites. "Can I make a confession that might make me sound like a terrible person?"

"Please, make me feel better about myself."

"I'm sort of jealous of you."

This revelation caught Silas by such surprise that he actually recoiled a bit and could only blink at Finn for a moment. "Jealous? Why on earth would you be jealous of *me*?"

"You're not the only one who had a miserable time in high school, you know. Not the only one who had trouble making friends."

Silas sat back, feeling appropriately chastised. Once again, he'd become so caught up in his own self-created drama that he failed to consider what other people were going through. "You didn't go to Riverside, did you?"

"No, I'm from Spartanburg actually, went to Dorman High."

"So can I take it that Dorman wasn't a utopic society of acceptance and diversity?"

Finn snorted a laugh. "No, it was your typical cliquish high school environment. My freshman year, I did have my own little group of like-minded nerds that would gather for Dungeons & Dragons almost every weekend. We were far from popular and took our share of teasing and sometimes outright bullying, but at least we had each other and our shared interests."

"What happened to them?" Silas asked.

"They outgrew those interests. By junior year, they considered D&D and sci-fi/fantasy conventions kids' stuff. I guess you could say they left me behind, sort of a painful reminder of their geeky past. They became interested in sports and cars and girls. Well, I'm interested in girls, too, but you don't meet a lot of them in comic book shops. Anyway, they started making fun of me, saying I was developmentally retarded, stuck in some sort of arrested development. I had always taken the ribbing and name calling at school in stride, but having my former friends join in...that was hard to take. My senior year was lonely and rough. So yeah, I totally get why you wouldn't want to do anything to ruin what you've found with this gang at Furman. I'd like to think if I were in your shoes I would tell them the truth. I'd like to think that, but I'm not a hundred percent certain."

"Hey," Silas said, "I don't know anything about Dungeons & Dragons except what I've seen on *Stranger Things*, and we already established I don't know much about comics, but I think you're a cool guy and I'd love to hang out sometime."

"And maybe work on a comic together?"

Silas rolled his eyes. "This isn't blackmail, is it?"

"Not at all. Actually, I was hoping you'd do it out of pity alone."

Silas thought about it for a minute. "How about this? I'll send you a few of my short stories, and if you see anything you like, you can take a whack at adapting it to comic form."

"Fair enough," Finn said, holding his hand out over the table.

Silas clasped his hand, and they shook, sealing the deal on the start of a friendship.

When Silas got home that afternoon, he was surprised to find his father lying on the sofa, staring at the flickering television.

"What are you doing home?" Silas asked. "I thought your shift at the store didn't end until eight tonight."

His father muted the television and sat up. "Yeah, but Mr. Dryer sent me home early."

Silas could sense that something was wrong. His father's expression tried too hard for casual to actually be casual, and Silas could sense a certain tension in the air. The kind of tension that was familiar on days his father sat down to pay the bills.

"You sick?" Silas asked, sitting next to his father.

"No, nothing like that. He over-scheduled, that's all, so he needed to send someone home."

"Doesn't sound like Mr. Dryer. What's going on?"

His father didn't answer at first, simply stared at the silenced television as if trying to read the cast of *Will & Grace*'s lips. Finally, he sighed heavily and said, "He's cutting me back to part-time."

"What? Why would he do that? You're the most experience worker he's got at the store. You've been with him almost as long as he's owned the place."

His father tried on a reassuring smile, but it looked as false as a plastic Halloween mask. "It's nothing personal, he's cutting most of his employees to part-time. Business isn't exactly booming these days. A mom-and-pop in a chain store world struggles to make a profit, and this year has been a bit more of a struggle than usual."

"Is this permanent?" Silas asked.

His father shrugged, a gesture so weary and defeated that it caused an ache in Silas's chest. "I hope not. Dryer thinks things will pick up during the Christmas season, and if they pick up enough, he says I can go back to full-time after the New Year."

Silas cast his gaze around the living room, at the worn furniture and dusty knickknacks. He and his father didn't exactly live a life of luxury, but they were at least comfortable. "Will we be able to stay afloat on a part-time salary?"

His father hesitated before answering, which was answer enough. "May take some juggling, but we'll be okay."

"I should get a job. I saw a 'Help Wanted' sign out at Barista Alley downtown."

"*No*," his father said with his usual vehemence at this subject. "While you're in school, that is your job and your *only* job. I'm not going to let anything interfere with that or split your focus. College is your ticket out of the trailer park."

Silas wondered if his father had caught him surveying the room and took it for criticism. "There's nothing wrong with where we live," he said quietly.

His father opened his mouth then closed it abruptly, but Silas imagined his held-back words were going to be something along the lines of, *Is that why you won't bring your boyfriend here?* Instead, his father said, "We're going to be fine. Remember my friend Kevin?"

"The one who runs his own handyman business?"

"That's the one. Anyway, he needs some help on a couple jobs. House painting, putting in cabinets, that sort of thing. He's going to let me pitch in and pay me under the table. That'll be enough to keep the lights on and food on the table. However..."

"No water?" Silas asked, trying to lighten the mood.

His father laughed and reached out to ruffle his hair like when Silas was a kid. "Don't get sick or have any accidents, kiddo. Part-time status at the hardware store means no health benefits. So it's our mission for the time being to stay fit and healthy. Got it?"

Silas sat up straight and raised his right hand to his forehead in a salute. "Sir, yes, sir."

"Good boy. Now get out of here. I think Jack and Karen are about to do something crazy and immature."

"So unlike them," Silas said. He hugged his father then stood and headed toward the hall.

"No plans with Kris tonight?" his father asked.

Silas turned back. "No, I really need to focus on homework tonight. You know, school is my job and all that."

"Again, good boy."

"You make me sound like a dog."

"Sit, Ubu, sit."

With a bemused laugh, Silas retired to his room and put his backpack on his desk. Honestly, he would rather be spending the evening with Kris, but what he'd told his father was the truth. He needed to hit the books. The temptation to spend all his time outside of class on the Furman campus was strong, but he had to resist if he ever hoped to be there as a legitimate Furman student. Of course, even if he got into Furman, that still left the insurmountable obstacle of paying the tuition, but he was willing to take out as many loans as needed even if it meant being in debt for the rest of his life.

Besides, his aspirations to transfer to Furman weren't totally selfish. A degree from a better college would mean better career prospects, which would help not only himself but also his father. It would be nice to be in a position to repay his father for all he'd done for him over the years.

Dress it up however you want, but what you're doing is still despicable.

Silas sat at the desk and rummaged his history book from the backpack. He had three new chapters to read for class tomorrow and was behind a few chapters he was supposed to have read already. He received a text from Finn which he ignored, a group text from the Furman gang which he ignored, and an individual text from Kris which he read.

Hey, I know it's study night and you are not to be disturbed, but I wanted to ask if you wanted to have joint study time tomorrow. Meet me at the lib around 4:30?

Silas responded, *"Fine, now leave me alone so I can absorb knowledge."*

He tried to concentrate on the reading, but his mind kept turning to a variety of other topics. The feel of Kris's hands on him; the guilt at lying to his friends; the fear that either Dr. Flem or Finn could still decide to rat him out; his father's new precarious financial situation. He felt like one of those plate spinners, trying to keep a dozen plates spinning on the ends of sticks.

If even one plate fell, all the rest would come crashing down in succession.

CHAPTER SEVENTEEN

The James Buchanan Duke Library was a large brick building with six massive columns out front. Stone steps led to an expansive porch, populated with round black tables and chairs. As Silas made his way up the steps, his phone buzzed with a new text. He paused on the top step and read the message from Kris.

Running late. Wait for me in those chairs to the left of the circulation desk. Should be there in 10.

Silas responded with a "K" and continued across the library's porch. He briefly considered waiting outside at one of the tables; he'd have a great view of the large pond with the jets that sent water shooting up in sprays. However, the weather was a bit too cold, even with a jacket. His breath misted from his lips like a ghost, and he shivered as he pushed through the glass doors and into the warm library.

To his immediate left was the circulation desk, and beyond that were a cluster of chairs, arranged in groups of four. A quartet of polka dotted chairs were empty, and Silas took a seat in the one with the best view of the entrance.

Silas had a deep affinity for libraries. Any time he entered one, he experienced an overwhelming sensation of coming home. He once joked to his father that if he survived the apocalypse, he would set up shop in the nearest library and live out the rest of his solitary existence reading his way through the stacks. His father had laughed and said, "Time enough at last," but Silas didn't get the reference. Greer had a lovely public library branch, and he could of course request anything from any of the Greenville County branches (not to mention all the digital loans he could access electronically), but he still liked to spend time in the main branch in downtown Greenville because it was just so big, a temple of books with texts surrounding him everywhere.

He thought the Duke Library at Furman was almost as big as that.

"Hey, Silas."

Silas started at the sound of his name and turned to see Paige approaching, arms full of books, Philip following behind as if on an invisible tether. Paige sank into the chair to Silas's left, putting her books down on the table. Philip hesitated before finally taking the chair across from Silas.

"What are you doing sitting here like you're waiting on a plane?" Paige asked.

"Waiting on Kris, actually," Silas said, cutting a quick glance at Philip. "We have sort of a study date planned."

Paige nodded. "Ah, Philip and I just finished up one. Of course, our study date is strictly platonic."

"Like all my relationships," Philip said with a weak laugh that did not mask the bitter tone.

Paige afforded a sympathetic smile Philip's way before turning back to Silas. "It's rather fortuitous that I ran into you, because I have some good news for you."

"I'm always open to hearing some good news."

"First, a disclaimer. I over-stepped my bounds, it's a habit of mine, and your first reaction might be to get angry, but this really is exciting news."

Silas's entire body seized up with tension. He had no idea where Paige was going with this, but an opener like that suggested it couldn't be anywhere good.

"So," Paige said, "I had Kris send me that story of yours, 'Time Shift.' I told him I liked it so much, I wanted to reread it."

Silas started to see some markers that indicated the destination to which this conversation was headed, and he braced himself for a fiery crash.

"I know you said you didn't want to submit it to the magazine," Paige continued, speaking in a rush. "But the story was too damn good not to. I showed the story to Janice, the editor, and she loved it. She said she would be happy to feature it in *The Echo*."

In his head, Silas heard the sound of squealing breaks, tires shredding on cement, then the rending noise of crumpling metal. "Please tell me you're joking," he said.

"Look, I get it. It's frightening to open yourself up to critique and judgement; all artists feel that trepidation. Way I see it, I did you a favor, took the issue out of your hands. And it paid off, your story was a hit. You should feel privileged; Janice is a tough editor. She once marked up a poem of mine with so much red ink I thought she'd cut her wrists and bled all over it. Let me tell you, that really—"

"I'm sorry, did you say I should feel privileged?" Silas interrupted, his tone so sharp that Paige instantly fell silent, and several people nearby looked his way. "You did me a favor, did you?"

"Calm down," Paige said with a nervous laugh. "I thought this would be good for you, force you to get past your fears."

"Oh, so it's like tossing me in the middle of a lake to get me over a fear of water, is that it? Well, aren't you the Good Samaritan."

One of the librarians behind the circulation desk made a pointed shushing sound, and Silas realized the volume of his voice had continued to rise.

Paige looked to Philip for help, but he was busy studying a loose thread on his sweater. "She loved your story," Paige said, as if that made everything all right.

Silas snorted a laugh devoid of humor. "You think that's the point? I specifically told you I didn't want to submit my story. You don't know my reasons or motivations, but you did know my feelings on the subject. And you ignored them. That's a pretty shitty thing to do. Now I want you to get in touch with this Janice and tell her I don't want my story in her little magazine."

Paige seemed at a loss for words, her mouth opening and closing like that of a puppet being manipulated by a mute. She swiped at her watering eyes, obviously near tears. Silas was surprised to find that this didn't elicit sympathy from him, but only served to make him angrier. He refused to relent or apologize.

When she finally found her voice, Paige said, "Okay, I'll

message her and tell her you are withdrawing your story," then gathered up her books and scurried away.

Silas watched her go, realizing that all murmur of conversation in the library had ceased and everyone had watched this little melodrama play out. As Paige pushed through the exit door, Silas felt his first pang of guilt, quickly followed by a sharp stab of shame.

He didn't entirely let Paige off the hook. She had no right to do what she did, to go behind his back and against his wishes. However, his reaction might have been a tad more apocalyptic than was necessarily called for, and he recognized that all the tension and pressure he'd been living under lately had made him snap. Tension and pressure of which he was the primary author, and yet instead of lashing out at himself, he'd lashed out at the most convenient target. Paige.

After a moment, those nearby turned back to their own business, and the hum of activity and chatter resumed. Only then did Silas realize that Philip hadn't left but was still sitting across from him.

"Some people just don't get it," Philip said with a shrug.

"Don't get what?"

"You know, that for some of us it's easier to stay invisible. Some people are naturally outgoing and want to put themselves on display, but then there are people like us who find that kind of scrutiny scary. It's better for the turtle to stay in its shell. Safer in there."

This was possibly the most Philip had ever spoken to him, and Silas found himself surprised to find that this quiet young man he'd always assumed hated him actually understood him. Perhaps better than anyone else in the group. In some ways, the two of them were almost kindred spirits.

"Yeah," Silas said. "It's like people think they're helping you by forcing you out of your shell before you're ready. They don't get that it's like shoving you out of a plane without a parachute."

"And you can't explain it to them. They think social anxiety is nothing more than a bad case of shyness and we should be able to get over it with a snap of the fingers. As if it's that easy, as if we don't want to be able to just go up to someone and start a conversation."

"They mean well," Silas said. "I know that, but you're right. If all we had to do to not be this way was not to be this way then we wouldn't be this way. If that convoluted sentence makes sense."

"I know what you mean. College is a great time to reinvent yourself, but it's a little harder for some of us than others."

Silence settled between them, but it was comfortable and companionable. After a moment, Philip glanced at his watch and said, "I need to go, or I'll be late for Work Study."

"It was nice talking to you."

Philip stood and started away, but he paused and glanced back. "I should probably say I'm sorry."

"For what?" Silas asked.

"We both know for what. When you came along and Kris took such an obvious interest in you, I got all possessive. Felt like you'd taken something away from me, even though it was never really mine in the first place."

Silas didn't know how to respond to this, so he merely smiled and nodded.

"Anyway," Philip said, "I just wanted to say sorry. You seem like a cool guy."

Philip headed for the exit again, passing Kris on his way in. They shared a brief hello, and Silas rose as Kris walked toward him.

"Got here as fast as I could," Kris said and kissed him. "Let's grab one of the study rooms. Cut down on the distractions."

Silas followed Kris to one of the small glassed-in rooms, thinking that Kris was all the distraction he needed. Once they were inside and settled at the table, Kris said, "Did you hear? Near the end of next month, just before Christmas break, the theater department is putting on a musical production of *A Christmas Carol*."

"No, I hadn't heard that."

"Want to go? A little play date?"

"That would be nice," Silas said. "Want me to spring for the tickets?"

"Why would we need tickets? Students get in for free, remember? Just have to show our IDs."

"Oh," Silas said, his stomach suddenly cramping. He sometimes worried he was going to give himself ulcers. "I actually lost my ID."

"No problem, just stop by the Enrollment Office to get a new one. Hell, Philip may even be able to get you one without having to pay the replacement fee."

"Yeah, I'll ask him."

Kris opened his American Government book and began reading. Silas opened his history book and stared at the pages, but he couldn't concentrate on the words.

Dr. Flem's office was easy enough to find. A quick search of Furman's website told Silas that the professor was located on the first floor of Furman Hall. Silas had no idea what Dr. Flem's office hours might be, but he showed up at half past five, having feigned not feeling well to cut out of his study date early. He found the door, wallpapered with comic strips cut out of the newspaper, and even as he approached it, the door opened and Dr. Flem stepped into the hallway, a worn leather satchel thrown over one shoulder.

"Oh, it's you," Dr. Flem said, gaze sweeping the nearly empty hall. "What are you doing here?"

"I didn't sneak into a class, if that's what you're thinking. I came to see you. You said I could. Do you have a few minutes?"

"I was just heading out, actually."

"Please," Silas said. "Five minutes, that's all I ask."

Dr. Flem scanned the hall again and Silas thought he might refuse, but finally the professor sighed and said, "Come in and have a seat, but we have to make it quick. I promised my wife I'd pick up dinner on my way home."

Silas walked into a cramped office. Actually, the room might have seemed spacious if every inch wasn't taken up with either furniture or books. A large desk covered in papers and folders occupied almost the entire back wall, two large, cushioned chairs on this side of it. An old sofa sat next to the door. The walls were lined with bookshelves, and more books stacked in precarious towers turned the remaining space into a literary labyrinth. Dr. Flem motioned toward the sofa then positioned himself on the edge of the desk, knocking over a sheaf of papers which he ignored.

Silas moved two large volumes to make room for him to sit on the sofa, noting they were both compilations of comic strips, *Peanuts* and *Calvin and Hobbes* respectively. "You're really into comics," Silas said as he sank into the cushions.

"I'm teaching a course in the Philosophy of Comic Strips this semester."

"Wow," Silas said. "They don't teach interesting classes like that at Greenville Tech."

"I doubt you stopped by to discuss my curriculum."

"I'm sorry. I don't want to waste your time, and I probably shouldn't be here at all. I don't know what I'm doing. And I mean that in regard to all aspects of my life, not just showing up at your office door."

"I've spotted you with Gus's group a few times recently," Dr. Flem said. "I take it you haven't told them the truth yet?"

Silas stared down at his lap and shook his head. "And living this double life thing is making me feel like a crazy person."

"You know I'm not a counselor or anything of the sort."

"I know, and it's really not my intention to use you like a therapist. It's just that I don't have many people I can talk to right now. Not about *this*."

"It has to be difficult keeping up this pretense," Dr. Flem said, but any judgement that might have been in his voice was eclipsed by a warm compassion. "I'd imagine you're quite mentally drained."

"It's a lot of work, I'll tell you that. You know, I actually got a hold of Furman's course list for this semester and came up with a fake schedule for myself so I could be sure of always being consistent, and I purposefully tried to make it so that all my classes were as far away from Kris's classes so that he wouldn't wonder why we never bumped into one another. I got these cheap paper book covers and put them on all my textbooks like a big dork so that no one would notice that my books aren't the ones used in Furman classes. I'm always having to make excuses for why I can never meet up between classes, why I never go to the dining hall. Now Kris wants to go to a play next month, thinking we'll both get in free being students and all. Except I'm not a student so I've got to figure out what I'm going to do about that. It seems like every day brings some new complication, some new stress, and I'm about to pull my hair out by the root."

Dr. Flem didn't say anything for a moment, but his expression said plenty. "There is something you could do to relieve all this stress and anxiety."

Silas snorted again. "Tell the truth?"

"Bingo. I know it will be hard, but it's not like living this lie is easy."

"I get what you're saying, but I'm scared. I have so much to lose."

"If what you have you attained through false pretenses, did it really belong to you to begin with?"

This reminded Silas of something Philip had said. *Felt like you'd taken something away from me, even though it was never really mine in the first place.* Thinking of his moment of connection with Philip only made Silas feel worse.

"Look," Dr. Flem said, standing and walking over to Silas, "I can't make you do anything, but I think you want to tell the truth. That's why you came here to talk to me, because you knew I'd tell you to do what you know in your heart you need to do. You're basically trying to psych yourself up to actually do it."

Silas chewed on that one, recognizing the validity of it, then said, "Maybe after the holidays."

Dr. Flem laughed. "Is that like saying you'll stop procrastinating next week? It's not going to be any easier after the holidays."

"No, but the holidays are notoriously a time for depression as it is, and if I go and wreck my life right before them then that will make it all the more depressing."

"I'm here if you need an ear," Dr. Flem said, and Silas thought he actually meant it.

"Thanks, and I really am sorry for taking up your time with my drama."

"No problem, I only wish I could help."

"You are."

"Glad to hear it. Now I really need to go. I can feel my phone buzzing in my pocket, undoubtedly the Mrs. wanting to know where her Thai food is."

They said their goodbyes and went in opposite directions. As Silas made his way across campus, keeping his head down and hoping he didn't run into any of his friends, he thought about what he'd said to Dr. Flem, about not wanting to wreck his life right before the holidays.

You can play pretend for a little while longer if you like, but you know good and well that you've pretty much wrecked your life already.

CHAPTER EIGHTEEN

Finn sent a text Thanksgiving morning.

Fam is driving me nuts. Gotta get outa here. Wanna hang for a bit?

Silas read the text standing in the kitchen. Pots bubbled and steamed on the stove, and his father currently had the turkey in a dented roasting pan, ramming stuffing inside it in a way that seemed grossly perverse.

"That your boyfriend?" his father asked with his hand inside the turkey.

"No, another friend from school, Finn."

"That the artist or the comedian?"

"The artist. Franco is the comedian."

His father turned to him, lips curling in a sly little smile.

"What?" Silas asked.

"Nothing. You've just become quite the social butterfly, that's all."

"Not so much. My circle of friends consists of a half dozen people."

"That's a half dozen more people than you hung around with in high school."

Silas nodded, conceding the point.

"This Finn isn't competition for Kris, is he?"

"God, no. Finn is strictly of the hetero persuasion."

"Ah, I see. What's he want?"

"To hang out for a bit."

"He's local?"

"Yeah."

"At least one of your friends is," his father said, giving the turkey his full attention once again. "I didn't realize Greenville

Tech attracted so many students from out of the area."

Silas responded with a noncommittal grunt, not wanting to delve into this subject too deeply. His life had become a terrain of quicksand into which he had to continually avoid sinking.

He started to text Finn back, and his father asked, "What are you telling him?"

"That I can't hang out right now because I'm helping you with dinner."

"I've got everything under control here. Go on, meet up with your friend."

"I can't leave you to do all this work by yourself."

"What work?" his father said. "It's mostly opening cans and pouring the contents into pots, and the turkey is all but ready to go in the oven. It's not exactly a gourmet meal I'm preparing for us."

"Still more trouble than you need to go to. I mean, we could just have burgers or something. No need to go to all this fuss when it's only the two of us."

"Have I instilled no sense of tradition in you, boy? There are certain holidays that require certain foods. Thanksgiving *requires* turkey, cranberry sauce, pumpkin or sweet potato pie. At the very minimum, other side dishes optional and variable."

"And that's why we're going to have turkey again at Christmas and then black-eyed peas and collard greens on New Year's, right?"

"Now you're getting it," his father said, washing his hands at the sink. "Seriously, though, I can handle this. Go be with your friend. Just be back no later than four, okay?"

"You sure?"

"Yes. Be gone."

Silas deleted the text he had started and composed a new one, asking Finn where he wanted to meet.

They arranged to meet at Falls Park, near the stage where Silas had gone to see *Waiting for Godot* with the Furman gang. The air had a chill to it but not unbearably so. Finn was already there when Silas arrived, sitting on the stone edge of the stage and flipping through a comic book. Silas sat next to him.

Finn looked up from his comic and smiled. "Nice having the place almost to ourselves, isn't it?"

Silas glanced around the park, noting that it was more deserted than usual. He could see a few people strolling across the suspension bridge and he heard some laughter and voices from the direction of the waterfall. Still, considering how packed the place could get, it did seem downright vacant today.

"Guess everyone is enjoying the warmth of hearth and home," Silas said.

"What the hell is a 'hearth'?"

"Beats me," Silas admitted with a laugh. "Just one of those old-timey words that give the impression of the kind of idealized past that probably never existed."

Finn nodded. "I know what you mean. On Thanksgiving and Christmas, if I'm out and about and see houses with the driveways and yards full of cars, I imagine these Rockwellian family gatherings where everyone's laughing and reminiscing and enjoying each other's company. Then the realist side of my brain reminds me that it's probably as much a dysfunctional shit storm as my own family get-togethers. Thus, my escape."

"What are you reading?" Silas asked.

Finn held up the comic, which was worn and tattered and sported an odd abstract cover featuring a pale man with dark tangled hair looking down on a lush green island. "*The Sandman*. It's an old comic Neil Gaiman used to do."

"Not familiar with it."

"It's really cool, full of history and mythology and literary references. Hmm, I realize that doesn't make it sound very cool, but trust me. This was the last issue of the original run, 'The Tempest.'"

"Like the Shakespeare play?"

"Yeah, Shakespeare is actually a character in this one, and there was an earlier issue called 'A Midsummer Night's Dream.'"

"I saw that play once, right here," Silas said. "My dad took me to see Shakespeare in the Park a couple of years back."

"Shakespeare has always been a little difficult for me. We studied *Hamlet* in high school, and I couldn't make heads or tails of it."

"It can be challenging, for sure. When we saw the play, my dad was completely lost and kept whispering to me, asking what was going on. It's like a certain rhythm your brain has to synch up to or something."

"I don't think my brain is capable of that rhythm," Finn said, putting the comic on top of a green folder next to him. "So is your place as crammed full of relatives as mine?"

"No, it's just me and my dad."

"Your folks divorced?"

"My mom passed away when I was little."

"Oh shit, I'm sorry," Finn said.

"It's okay. I mean, it was a long time ago."

"Still, it's got to hurt. Especially during these family holidays."

Desperate to change the subject, Silas pointed to the green folder and said, "What do you have there?"

"Ah, that is a surprise for you, my friend."

"Early Christmas present?"

"Something like that," Finn said, taking the folder and holding it out to Silas. "Hope you like it."

Silas opened the folder to find a stack of papers, each sheet divided into several panels with black-and-white drawings in them. He recognized the work as Finn's and realized it was a homemade comic, but when he looked more closely he realized something else.

The drawings were Finn's, but the story was Silas's.

True to his word, Finn had adapted one of the stories Silas had sent him to read. This one was "Unfinished Business", the tale of an avid reader who dies in the middle of reading a novel. He continues to haunt his wife until she finally reads the rest of the novel out loud so that her husband's spirit can rest.

"Wow," Silas said, flipping through the pages. "This is so... *cool.*"

The most surprising thing was how much he genuinely meant it. He'd sent the stories to Finn only to placate him, never really expecting anything to come of it and thinking he didn't care even if it did. And yet seeing his story brought to life in this way gave him a thrill he couldn't deny.

"All the stories you let me read were excellent," Finn said, "but this one really spoke to me."

"You did an outstanding job. The artwork is fantastic."

"I'm really proud of how it turned out. I was actually thinking of selling it, with your permission, of course."

Silas frowned. "Selling it? Where?"

"There's this place up in Asheville called Downtown News and Books. They actually let artists and writers sell their hand-made underground comics through the store, sort of on consignment. I figured I could do a whole series based off your stories, and you'd get half of anything we made."

"Oh," Silas said, looking back down at the pages. "I, um, I don't know about that. I'll need to give it a little more thought."

"Think away. In the meantime, is it okay if I do a few more of your stories?"

"Absolutely, I'd love to see them."

Silas tried to hand the folder back, but Finn said, "That's yours. I made a few copies. Don't worry, I haven't shown anyone else yet. I wouldn't do that without getting your permission first."

Well, he gets this whole friendship thing better than Paige does.

Oh please, like you haven't done much worse to her.

"So how goes your double life?" Finn asked.

Silas smiled but couldn't hold it, the sides of his mouth trembling. "Not great, honestly. I really don't think I can keep this up much longer."

"No doubt. Have you decided what you're going to do yet?"

"I've given it a lot of thought," Silas said. "I mean, it's all I *can* think about, and I feel like there's only one realistic course of action."

"Which is?" Finn asked when Silas wasn't forthcoming.

"I know what I'm doing is dishonest and wrong, but I can't risk losing Kris. Can't risk losing any of them. I'm going to stick with my plan. Try to get into Furman for Fall semester next year."

Finn nodded, rubbing his hands on his thighs. He obviously had a lot to say, but he waited a moment before speaking and then only said, "What happens if you don't get in?"

"I have a contingency plan. I'm going to say that I found the Furman curriculum too overwhelming, and I'll drop out and enroll in Greenville Tech instead."

Another pause before Finn responded. "Do you really think that's the best thing to do?"

"Probably not, but like I said, I feel like it's my only real option."

Finn nodded. "You're my friend, and I'm not going to judge you, but I do sincerely hope this doesn't all blow up in your face."

"So do I," Silas said. "So do I."

CHAPTER NINETEEN

As Silas got dressed for school the first day after Thanksgiving break, he received a text from Kris that sent him into a frenzy of panic.

Hey, I skipped English Lit this morning to surprise you outside your History class, was going to try to tempt you into skipping with me, but you weren't there. Everything okay?

Even as Silas cursed his bad luck, he also recognized there was some good luck at play as well. Because his first Greenville Tech class started an hour and a half after the fake Furman schedule he'd concocted, he had time to fix this. If he'd already been in class, he might not have even read the text until irreparable damage had been done.

He could only hope his good luck held and that Kris hadn't asked any of the students or God forbid the professor if they knew where Silas might be. However, if that had happened, surely he would have received a much different text than the one that only expressed concerned. He sat for a moment on the edge of his bed, one shoe on and the other foot still bare, and took a few deep breaths to calm himself before responding.

Shit overslept this morning, about to head out the door now.

The three little dots appeared to let Silas know Kris was composing a reply, and Silas sent out a silent prayer for Kris to buy that explanation to all the gods and goddesses that had ever been worshipped, hoping at least one of them would hear and take pity on him.

None of us wanted to be back today. Want to just swing by my room when you get here?

With a sigh, Silas responded with a thumbs up and heart emoji.

After squeezing his foot into the other shoe, he grabbed his keys and headed out, throwing a quick goodbye his father's way. He carried his backpack even though he knew he wouldn't be going to school today. Missing an entire day of classes, especially this close to finals, wasn't exactly the best way for him to improve his GPA, but he didn't see any way around it. He had to make sure Kris didn't get suspicious. How had his life gotten so out of control and complicated?

You made your own bed, dug your own hole, built your own prison.

The drive to Furman took half an hour, and Silas spent that time debating with himself about the prudence of his decision to keep up the ruse at least until summer of next year. He didn't know if he had the stamina to keep this up, not to mention that on top of the mental exhaustion, the continual deception left him feeling like the lowest of slime.

Then again, if he came clean his life might be easier, but would it be *better*? Would honesty be its own reward if he lost everything?

After parking near the dining hall (DH, he reminded himself), he sent a text to Kris and then met him outside the dorm. Kris waited with a huge grin, enveloping Silas in a tight bear hug and kissing him with a passion that robbed Silas of his breath.

"I know it has only been a few days, but I missed you like crazy," Kris said. "I wanted to come see you last night, but I got in so late."

"I missed you, too. I enjoyed the running commentary of your Thanksgiving dinner."

"Yeah, hope your father didn't mind me texting you so much, but in a way it made me feel like we were spending Thanksgiving together. I'll probably do the same thing over Christmas break."

"I don't even want to think about it," Silas said, leaning his forehead on Kris's chest. "Almost two weeks apart."

Kris took his hand and led him inside the dorm. "I know, but we can FaceTime every day."

Kris's room was on the second floor, and as they walked down the hall he said, "Pete is in class. I requested he make himself scarce until after lunch so we could be alone for a while."

Silas's body immediately reacted to this prospect, rising to the occasion as it were.

As soon as they were in the room, they were on each other. Groping and kissing and panting. To an outside observer, they would probably seem like Siamese twins trying to devour one another, meld until they were no longer two beings joined but only one being entirely.

They made their way slowly toward the bed, barely managing to stay upright. As Silas's legs hit the edge of the mattress, Kris abruptly pulled back, his face flushed. "I swear, I didn't invite you here just for this. I'm not an animal, but I really fucking missed you."

"You don't hear me complaining," Silas said.

"Okay but hold on a minute. I got you a gift."

Silas groaned as Kris crossed the room, bent and started digging through a duffle bag by his desk. A buzzing against Silas's thigh alerted him to an incoming text. He pulled out his phone and glanced absently at the screen, but what he saw there killed his libido instantly and made him feel as if he'd been dunked in a vat of black ink.

A text from Philip. Two sentences, eight words total, but enough to bring Silas's world crashing down around him.

Meet me at the bookstore NOW. I know.

"Here you go," Kris said, coming back across the room and placing a box in Silas's hands.

Silas found it hard to concentrate, and he stared down at the box in his hands for almost a full minute before his mind could make sense of what he held. A DVD box set of all seven seasons of the show *Buffy the Vampire Slayer*.

"You know it's my favorite old show," Kris said. "I thought maybe we could watch together, from beginning to end."

"I have to go," Silas said.

"Oh, well, we don't have to watch it if you don't want."

"No, it's not that. My father sent me a text, he fell and hurt himself. I'm going to go take him to urgent care."

"Oh shit, is he okay?" Kris said, placing a hand on Silas's shoulder.

"He doesn't think it's anything serious, nothing broken, but he's in some pain. I have to get to him."

"Want me to come with you?"

"No!" Silas said, too quickly and too vehemently. "I'll call or text when I know something, okay?"

Before Kris could argue, Silas kissed him then fled.

The walk from Kris's dorm to the bookstore was a short one, but Silas took his time. To delay, he turned into the rose garden and paced a circuitous route among the paved paths. At this time of year, no blossoms exploded with color and filled the space with their heady perfume, but he wouldn't have notice even if they had, his focus turned completely inward. He tried to convince himself that Philip's cryptic message didn't necessarily signal disaster.

You don't know that he knows you're not a Furman student. His text could be about something else entirely, something totally innocuous. Like maybe he knows you skipped class, and he's just teasing you.

But then why ask me to meet him at the bookstore? No, not even ask. DEMAND! Why DEMAND I meet him at the bookstore?

A good question, and the only way to discover the answer was to get to the bookstore and find out. Of course, he could always text back and tell Philip he couldn't make it right now, see what kind of response that garnered.

Before Silas could decide on whether or not to take that course of action, Philip beat him to the punch with another text.

I know you're on campus at Kris's. I'm only waiting five more minutes then everyone will know.

This message made it harder for Silas to kid himself that Philip didn't know his big secret, but he didn't want to completely give up hope. Still, he left the rose garden and jogged the rest of the way to the bookstore, entering by the café. Walking to the center of the store, Silas scanned the area for Philip, spotting him up near the bargain books and Nike apparel. Philip spotted him as well, jerking his head to the side in a gesture to follow him.

At this time of year, the cafe was the only part of the store that did a brisk business, and Philip led Silas over to the children's section, a deserted area that afforded them a bit more privacy.

"What's up?" Silas asked, trying to keep his voice light despite the dread that wrapped around him like slimy black tentacles.

Philip bothered with no such pretense. He stood with his arms folded tightly across his chest, his mouth puckered into a tight button. Silas figured it could be his imagination, but he seemed to feel an almost palpable disdain wafting from Philip.

"What took you so long?" Philip said. "I know you were just over at Kris's room. He messaged me a little while ago to say you two were skipping classes to spend the morning together."

"Really? He told you that?"

Philip laughed, though it came out more like a cough. Perhaps the first time Silas had ever actually heard someone *scoff*. "We messaged a lot over break. I apologized for the way I had been treating the two of you, you in particular, and told him I wished only the best for you both. God, I was a fool. I was actually starting to like you, to think you were a good guy and that maybe we could be friends. The rest of the gang can be a little trusting, but I consider myself the more skeptical one, but you had me snowed as much as the rest. You're a good actor, I'll give you that much."

"I don't know what you're talking about," Silas said, not quite ready to give up the charade, foolishly clinging to the thinnest strand of hope like someone falling off a cliff and reaching for a single blade of grass to stop his descent.

"Oh, I think you do. You're not a student at Furman. Never have been."

The blade came loose, and Silas felt himself plummeting to the rocks below. Still, he tried to bluff, not sure if Philip really *knew* or merely suspected. "Why would you say that?"

"Kris asked me to do a little favor for him, to see if I could get you a new student ID."

Silas closed his eyes in defeat. To think, Kris's inspiring kindness was the very thing bringing about Silas's downfall.

"I was going to wait until I went to do my Work Study this afternoon," Philip continued, "but since my first class wasn't until 10 today I decided to run by and take care of it first thing.

I'm sure I don't have to tell you what I discovered. Or what I *didn't* discover, I should say. No records of a Silas Granger as a registered student at this school. Funny, huh? I figured it must be some mistake, that I was spelling your name wrong or something, but then I really started to think. You don't have any classes with a single one of us, we never see you around campus during the day when classes are going on, you don't have a student ID. Suddenly a lot of pieces started to fall into place."

"Philip, please, I can explain if you'll just let—"

"I don't need explanations," Philip said, his voice more forceful and confident than Silas had ever heard it. "What I need is the answer to one simple question. Are you a student at Furman University?"

With a trembling breath, Silas accepted his defeat. "No, I'm not."

Philip reacted with a laugh. Not the kind of laugh one gives at hearing a hilarious joke, but the kind one gives at hearing something almost too ridiculous to believe. Like dinosaurs evolved into birds or Cardi B wanted to run for political office.

"This is insane," Philip said. "What are you, some kind of attention-seeking pathological liar like that crazy lady that went around claiming she was a survivor of 9/11 attacks when she wasn't even in the country at the time?"

"It's not like that; *I'm* not like that. If you'll hear me out, I think you might understand how it all happened."

"I don't want to hear you out. I don't want to hear anything from you. At this point, I wouldn't believe a single word that came out of your mouth anyway. God, just looking at you makes me feel physically ill. You've got to be the sickest person I've ever actually met."

The words stung Silas like poisoned darts, even more so because he knew he deserved them. He felt tears begin trickling down his cheeks.

"Save your crocodile tears for someone who doesn't know you're full of shit," Philip said with a derisive grunt.

Silas wiped at his eyes, a sinkhole opening in his gut and swallowing him from the inside out. When he spoke, the pathetic whine of his own voice disgusted him. "What are you going to do?"

"You mean, am I going to tell everybody what a psychotic fraud you are? No, I'm not going to have to, because you're going to disappear."

Silas frowned. "What do you mean, *disappear*?"

"You're going to drop completely out of our lives. Like you were never even here."

"I can't do that. I'm… "

"You're what? Part of the group? You weaseled your way into our circle with a lie, so you can weasel your way out with another."

Silas shook his head, not understanding.

With a roll of his eyes, Philip said, "It's not that hard. Say you and your father had to move across the country to live with relatives or something. Then change your number, deactivate your social media accounts, and *poof*, you're a memory."

"Please don't do this to me."

"So now you're the victim? Interesting. I'm not doing anything to you, you're doing this to yourself. I'm being generous here."

"You call this generous?"

"Extremely. I could blow your cover right here, right now. Instead, I'm giving you the chance to bow out gracefully. Not because I give a damn about you, but because I don't want my friends hurt any more than necessary. The benefit to you is a side-effect."

"What benefit? I'm going to lose Kris."

"You're going to lose him one way or the other," Philip said matter-of-factly. "Either through the truth or through a lie. With the lie, he'll at least continue to think of you fondly as opposed to knowing you're the slimy piece of shit you actually are."

The tears began to fall again, and this time Silas made no move to wipe them away.

Philip's expression softened, but only for a few seconds, and then steely resolve tightened his features again. "Like I said, I'm being remarkably generous. I'm giving you until Christmas break."

"What?"

"It'll be easier that way. We'll all be at our respective homes; Kris can't go running to you when you send out the message. By the time we get back to school, you'll be in California or Arizona or Alaska or wherever the hell you decide to say you had to go. If you don't sever ties that way, I'm telling everyone the truth. So I suggest you enjoy the next couple of weeks and say your goodbyes as best you can, because come hell or high water, by the New Year you will be out of our lives."

Silas shook his head again, this time not because he didn't understand but because he didn't want to understand. He wanted to go back in time to before this conversation started and find some way to prevent it. Or back to when he first met the group by the bell tower and make himself clear up the misunderstanding when he was mistaken for a Furman student. Or maybe even back to when his father met his mother at the Bloom grocery store, somehow sabotaging their relationship so that he would never even be conceived.

Without another word, Philip walked away, not even sparing a glance back over his shoulders. A sob escaped Silas's mouth like a belch, and he leaned against a rack of purple T-shirts to keep from collapsing.

"Are you okay?"

Silas started at the sound of the gentle voice, and he turned to find a lovely young woman in a floral peasant dress approaching him. Behind her glasses, her eyes were kind and concerned. The nametag she wore (*Crystal J.*) identified her as the store manager.

He couldn't take anyone's sympathy right now, that would only grate like sandpaper against his wounds. He tried to tell her he was fine, but his voice failed him, and he merely turned and fled from the store, leaving Crystal J. to watch after him.

CHAPTER TWENTY

Silas could have gone to Greenville Tech and made the rest of the day's classes, but he was in no kind of shape for that. He couldn't go home either; his father had the day off and there would be questions if Silas returned so early.

He drove aimlessly for close to an hour before making his way back down Wade Hampton Boulevard to Greer. With no particular destination in mind, he found himself at Greer City Park. The day was cold and overcast, the threat of rain casting a pall over everything, almost like a meteorological manifestation of Silas's mood. He parked near City Hall and walked down to the pond, making his way around to the gazebo. A light sprinkle began to spit down from the gray clouds, so he sat under the shelter and thought about what a mess everything had become. All because of damn Philip.

So you're going to blame him and not yourself? Think about it, if this were a movie, you'd be the villain here, not Philip. Philip would be the one you were cheering for. He'd be the Harry, and you'd be the Voldemort.

Silas felt his phone buzzing in his pocket. He pulled it out saw he had several texts. One from Gus sent out to the whole group, suggesting they get together at the P-Den around four; one from Finn, asking if he was at school today; and three from Kris, inquiring about his father. Even as Silas stared at the screen, the phone began to ring. An incoming call from Kris. Silas let it go to voicemail and stared out at the rippling surface of the pond. The rain came down harder now, causing the water to churn like a boiling pot. A chill wind sent drops under the gazebo, striking Silas's face like spittle. He didn't move to wipe away the moisture, letting it mingle with his own tears.

So many lies, an elaborate yet precarious house of cards he'd built, stupidly thinking it would remain standing even in a tempest. He laughed bitterly at his own foolish belief that he could somehow pull this ruse off and there would be no consequences. One didn't have to be Buddhist to believe in the concept of karma, what goes around comes around, and Silas figured he was getting what he deserved. No matter what justifications he provided to help himself sleep at night, at the bottom of it all, he wasn't a good person. Good people didn't lie to all the people they claimed to care about the most.

His phone began to ring again, and without giving it a moment's thought, Silas tossed the cell out into the pond. It broke the surface with a faint *plop* and quickly sank. Almost instantly, he regretted his rashness. How would he explain the loss of the phone to his father? Another lie, he supposed, one more to add to the mountainous pile that threatened to tumble down and crush him like an avalanche.

He pushed himself to his feet and left the gazebo, walking slowly, heedless of the rain that soaked him within seconds, freezing him to the marrow. Why not look like a drowned rat? He was a rat, after all, and drowning would be a worthy penance for his crimes. Although, on second thought, perhaps too merciful.

In no particular hurry, he walked up Cannon Street, past the Episcopal Church and the Spinning Jenny Music Hall. At the corner of Cannon and Poinsett, he stopped and took a seat on a low brick wall next to one of the pipe sculptures that had been placed throughout downtown. This one was a series of red pipes twisted to look like a man in a fishing hat sitting on the wall, one hand raised in a wave or awaiting a high five that would never come. Silas couldn't remember exactly how it had started, but he and his father had taken to calling this particular sculpture Edgar.

"Howdy, Edgar," Silas said, feeling more than a little silly sitting in the rain talking to an inanimate object, but it wasn't as if anyone else was around to hear him. "How's life been treating you? I mean, I assume not too good since your ass is bolted to the wall and you can't even get in out of the rain. Then again,

I *can* get in out of the rain and am choosing not to, so you're at least less pathetic than me."

The rain began to fall more heavily, beating down on Edgar to create a pinging percussion. To Silas's ear, it sounded like the pounding drums of apocalypse. Of course, he realized his current state of mind may be tainting his perception. Normally he loved the rhythm of the falling rain; then again, normally he was listening warm and dry inside, not right in the middle of the deluge.

"Giving me the silent treatment, huh?" Silas said to the sculpture, trying for a bit of humor but falling flat even in his own estimation. This wasn't a scene in a movie where the plucky hero talks to himself for the amusement of the audience at home; this was a sad sack letting himself get drenched because his life was about to be ruined and he knew he had no one to blame but himself.

With a sigh, Silas stood, reaching out to lightly slap his palm against the sculpture's raised hand. "Stay cool, Edgar. I'll probably come back by to visit, as pretty soon you may be the only friend I've got, and then only because you're incapable of running away from me."

Silas started walking down the paved path toward the park's multi-tiered fountain that looked somewhat like a wedding cake, his feet splashing through puddles, the water running into his shoes to saturate his socks. He began to shiver so much that his teeth chattered together, creating a cacophony in his head louder even than the rain. When he reached his car, he climbed inside, starting the engine and turning the heater on full blast.

He didn't pull out right away, instead sat there for several minutes, playing the last several months back in his head, thinking of all the many things he could have done differently, all the better choices he could have made. A pointless endeavor, of course. He couldn't go back in time and undo what was done, right what was wrong. All he succeeded in doing was making himself feel worse, sinking into a hole of sticky tar from which he could never hope to extricate himself.

"It's where I belong," he muttered to himself, finally putting the car into reverse and backing out of the parking space. He headed for home, where he would have to tell his father that he'd lost his phone.

The first of many conversations he didn't want to have.

CHAPTER TWENTY-ONE

Silas paused outside Plyer Hall. Kris continued a few more steps before realizing his date had stopped. Turning back, Kris said, "Is something wrong?"

Loaded question, Silas thought. *Can any particular something be wrong when absolutely* everything *is wrong? If wrong is the new normal then maybe something would have to be right to be wrong.*

"Guess I'm a little distracted," Silas said. "My mind's kind of scattered right now."

Kris walked over to him and took his hand, squeezing his fingers. "Still worried about your dad? You said his arm wasn't broken, right? Just a sprained wrist?"

"Yeah, but you know, that's still giving him trouble. A lot of stuff he can't do with one hand in a brace."

Silas had taken the time to do some online research on sprained wrists. Would it require a cast? No, most sites agreed, just a brace and daily icing to reduce swelling. How long did it take to recover from a sprained wrist? For minor sprains that didn't require surgery, the recovery period could be as short as one to two weeks. A person could tell they had crossed a line when his lies required research.

Maybe Philip is doing you a favor in the long run.

"I know you had a scare," Kris said. "It could have been worse, but it wasn't. Your dad is going to be fine. He can survive for a couple hours while we watch Gus get his debate on."

Silas nodded and tried to force a smile, though he doubted the effort was very successful. He had promised to attend this debate before Philip's ultimatum, and he had since considered weaseling out of it. However, in the end the selfish part of him reasoned that if he had limited time left with Kris and his friends then why not maximize that time?

Of course, it wasn't as if he were enjoying himself, being around them in fact only served to make him more miserable, so what was the point? Unless that was the point, some sort of punishment, penance, self-flagellation.

The two entered the building and walked past the large glass windows, more like window-walls. As they neared the Patrick Lecture Theater, Silas slowed. "Are you sure they don't require a student ID to get in?" he asked.

Kris shook his head. "No, it's open to the public. I can't believe Philip hasn't gotten you a new ID yet. He promised me."

"Maybe he's been too busy."

Now it was Kris who stopped, right outside the double doors leading into the lecture theater. "I'm afraid he's still jealous. I thought he was coming around, but the last couple of days he's been acting super weird again. I was thinking I should have a talk with him."

"No!" Silas said, too loud and too strident, causing a couple of girls passing them to look his way, frown, then giggle. "I just don't want to cause any more tension. Drop it, please. If he doesn't get me a new ID then I'll just pay for a replacement, which is what I should have done in the first place."

"Are you sure?"

"Positive. Now let's get in there before they run out of seats."

Kris laughed. "I doubt that's going to be a problem."

Silas realized what he meant when they walked into the lecture theater. *Theater* was the correct word for it, a massive space with auditorium-style seating. They entered on the top level, rows of seats cascading down to the lowest level, where two podiums were set up, behind which six students sat in folding chairs, Gus being one of them. The illustrious Furman debate team. Dr. Flem stood at the end, talking to one of the debaters, a cute young man with a headful of tight curls.

As for the actual audience, including Kris and Silas there were also six in attendance. Exact amount as the debate team itself. The actual debate didn't begin for another five minutes, but things didn't look promising for a stellar turnout. Silas spotted Sheila and Franco down near the front, which meant the majority of the audience were made up of Gus's friends. The other two were the girls that had passed Silas and Kris out in the hallway, sitting near the very back and giggling over some TikTok video they watched on one of their phones.

Pinkies linked, Silas and Kris started down the steps toward the front. Sheila and Franco had left the two seats closest to the aisle open for them.

"Here are our little lost babes," Sheila said with the smirk that seemed as permanent a feature of her face as her nose. "We thought maybe you'd lost your way in the woods, like Little Red Riding Hood."

"Little Red Riding Hood didn't get lost," Kris said, dropping into the seat next to Sheila, leaving the aisle seat for Silas. "She went straight to Grandma's house. Think you're thinking of *Hansel & Gretel* maybe."

"Whatever. In any case, we were getting ready to send out a search party."

Franco nudged her with his elbow. "Give the two lovebirds a break. They probably stopped somewhere on the way to make out."

Silas and Kris exchange a glance then started to laugh, because in fact they had stopped at the fountain by the Milford Mall and made out for a bit.

"Public displays of affection should be outlawed like public nudity," Sheila said, but she laughed as well.

"So," Silas said in an effort to change the subject, "how's Paige doing?"

Silas hadn't talked to Paige much since the incident in the library, though she had sent him a lengthy apology text for submitting his story without his consent and assured him it had been pulled from the magazine.

"She's still sick," Shelia said, "but it's not nearly as bad as she's making it out to be. Nothing but the common cold, but she's acting like she's got Bubonic Plague or something. Creative types, they can be such drama queens."

Silas reached across Kris and swatted her on the arm. "Watch it now. Remember, I'm a writer."

"I stand corrected. Creative types tend to fall into one of two categories. Drama queens like Paige, or emotionally crippled introverts like you."

"Damn straight," Silas said and all four of them shared another laugh.

I'm going to miss this. How can I be expected to give this up?

The reason Silas's whole world was about to crumble wasn't present, but no one asked about Philip. He'd sent a group text earlier, stating he couldn't make it because he needed to cram for finals. Gus had given him a hard time, but Philip had wished him well while insisting he was too busy to attend the debate.

That suited Silas fine, though it was small consolation. The deadline Philip had given him hung over Silas's head like that deadly pendulum in the Poe story. He could hear a ticking clock inside his head that never stopped its countdown toward devastation, the timer on a bomb set to detonate sometime over Christmas break and leave his life in a shamble of rubble.

Four more students showed up at the last minute, meaning that the audience at least outnumbered the debaters. Franco scribbled something on a piece of notebook paper, snickered over it, then passed the paper down the line. When it got to Silas on the end, he saw that Franco had written in his sloppy scrawl, "The Furman team should change their name to the Mass Debaters."

Crude and childish, but Silas still laughed, and Kris laughed along with him. Sheila only shook her head and gave Franco a weary smile that seemed to both patronize and humor, like a mother whose son thinks farting is the height of hilarity. Still, Silas could spot the affection in the smile. The more time he spent around Sheila and Franco, the more he thought they made a perfect pair. An unlikely pair, but those were often the most perfect kind. Improbable matches rarely got bored, challenging and surprising one another. Silas and Kris were an unlikely pair.

Yes, he's decent and honest and you're—

Silas cut the thought off and passed the note back.

"You sure you're okay?" Kris asked, whispering directly into Silas's ear so that his breath ticked the fine hairs around the auricle.

Silas nodded then put a finger to his lips as Dr. Flem walked over to stand between the two podiums. The debate was about to begin.

"Thank you all for being here," the professor said, addressing the sparse crowd without aid of a microphone. He didn't need one, his voice ringing clear and loud throughout the theater. "If anyone doesn't already know, I'm Dr. Flemming. I'm the faculty sponsor for the Furman Debate team."

Franco looked down the row and mouthed the words, "Mass debaters," cracking himself up again. Sheila elbowed him in the side.

"I ask that everyone be respectful to the debaters and keep quiet," Dr. Flem said pointedly, though his lips curled at the edges. "That also means silencing all electronic devices. Even if you think you've already done that, take a second to double check." He gave them all the proposed second to check before continuing. "Tonight's debate will be a Lincoln Douglas, one on one. The first topic tonight is going to be Free College Tuition: Should Two-and-Four Year Undergraduate Degrees Be Accessible to All? The two debaters who will be discussing this topic are August Monroe, taking the pro side, and JohnPaul Sleiman, taking the con side."

Dr. Flem walked down to the front row, and before taking a seat, he glanced over and made eye contact with Silas. Silas couldn't be sure, but he thought he detected a slight frown, an expression that seemed to say, *Still keeping up with the charade, huh?*

Silas turned his gaze back to the front, where Gus took the podium on the left and his opponent the one on the right. JohnPaul was the student with the curly hair Dr. Flem had been speaking with when Silas and Kris first arrived. Gus wore a suit and looked quite dapper. From an inside pocket, he pulled a small stack of note cards.

"Hello everyone," Gus said into his podium's microphone. "I see that our audience tonight is comprised solely of Furman students. We lucky few, and I do mean lucky. These days a college education has become so astronomically expensive as to render it practically inaccessible to all those but the most elite.

And I don't mean only tuition costs, but a single semester's books can cost five hundred to a thousand dollars, depending on the course load. Add in various other fees and dues, and you effectively close out a large section of the population from seeing college as a realistic option."

Gus paused and glanced at JohnPaul, waiting for him to make his counterpoint. Silas found this odd. His only real experience with debates were when the presidential candidates held them in the months leading up to an election, and they all interrupted and insulted and talked over each other, no sense of decorum or organization. Because of this, he had always associated debate with chaos and yelling. Here he received a taste of what it was meant to be.

"A college education has always been expensive," JohnPaul said. "If you take into account inflation, college costs no more than it did in 1950. And there are many options for prospective students who don't have the capital to pay outright. Academic and athletic scholarships, need-based grants, government and private loans. Students can choose to go to tech schools or community colleges, which are more economical, and State schools offer deals for residents. Not everyone has to go to college all the way across the country. And if push comes to shove, there are people who work their way through college."

"You and I both know that there is no job a college student could get that would fully pay for tuition, not even to a community college. I'm going to dismiss the idea of loans, because all that does is leave you with crippling debt at the end of four years that you may not be able to pay off in your lifetime. However, you are right that there are scholarships and grants, but if you are brought up in a low-income family where college is never presented as a possibility, how motivated might you be to seek those things out? It is more likely you will have ingrained in you a form of helpless resignation that makes you think it's impossible, so you don't even try. And while there's nothing wrong with tech schools and community colleges, those degrees don't hold as much weight in the work force, and often people go there only because they can't go to the schools they truly want to go to. Basically, what you are saying to people with big dreams is to lower their expectations and take what they can get instead of what they really want."

Silas squirmed in his seat, the topic making him uncomfortable. It hit a little too close to home, hit like a sledgehammer to the forehead in fact. The group had discussed this very topic once out at the amphitheater, ironically with Gus taking the opposite stance as he did on the stage, but Gus had told him once that the debaters were often randomly assigned a position on an issue even if it was contrary to their personal one and were expected to argue passionately and logically, nonetheless.

"Fact of the matter," JohnPaul said, "is that college isn't meant for everyone. It does and should weed out certain people. Not everyone is designed for a career that requires higher learning. Where would we be without janitors and waiters and fast-food workers and—"

"That's some truly ignorant and elitist talk right there!"

"August," Dr. Flem admonished. "No talking out of turn. JohnPaul was not finished."

"Thank you," JohnPaul said. "As I was going to say, making two- and four-year degrees free and available to all would also throw the job market into a tailspin. Once upon a time, a high school diploma was all one really needed to succeed, but times changed, and now the more skilled jobs require two- or four-year degrees. If suddenly everyone had one of those, the market would adjust, and you'd find that now the skilled jobs were requiring graduate degrees, Masters and PhDs."

Gus laughed and shook his head. "I'm sorry, but that theory doesn't hold water. Whether you pay for it, or it is free, the education and training you receive are the same."

"Exactly," JohnPaul said. "Which could lead to potentially one of the most massive civil lawsuits in history."

Gus frowned. "How do you figure?"

"If tomorrow you made college free, how do you think that would make all the people who had to pay for their degrees feel? Might they not feel cheated, and like they were owed compensation? They could sue the federal government and crash the economy, all because some kids who should be happy with tech school feel they are entitled to a four-year degree."

Silas could stand it no longer. He leaned toward Kris and whispered, "I've got to get out of here."

"What's wrong? Are you sick?"

"I just can't be here right now. I need to go."

"I'll come with you. We can head back to my room."

Silas didn't wait. As Kris bent toward Sheila and Franco, Silas bolted from his seat and moved at a crouch up the steps and toward the exit.

CHAPTER TWENTY-TWO

By the time they made it to the dorm, Silas was crying. Kris asked what was wrong, seemed near tears himself, but Silas couldn't answer. The sobs shook through him like seizures, and any attempt to speak came out as an unintelligible jumble of sounds that only remotely resembled words. Kris, who looked like he was torn between holding Silas and calling 911, hurried him into the dorm and up to his room.

Pete was sitting in his bed, a thick textbook open on his lap. "You're home earlier than I—" His words cut off abruptly when he looked up and saw Silas's hysterical state. "Jesus Christ, what happened? Did someone die?"

Kris led Silas over to his desk and eased him down into the chair. "Pete, I hate to ask, but could we have the room for a bit?"

"Oh sure," Pete said, grabbing his shoes from under the bed and fumbling them on. "I'll go study in the library." He gathered up his books, and at the door turned back. "Is he okay?"

Kris answered only with a shrug.

Pete left the room, and Kris knelt next to Silas. He didn't speak, merely held Silas's hand and waited for the tears to pass. Patient, understanding, exactly what Silas needed at the moment.

And exactly what he didn't deserve.

After a few minutes, the weeping subsided. At least the worst of it. Silas wiped his streaming eyes and nose on his sleeves. Gross, he knew, but he was beyond the point of keeping up appearances. "I shouldn't be here," he said in a shaky voice.

Kris squeezed his hand. "It's okay. You can stay here as long as you need, all night if you want. Pete won't mind."

Silas laughed, though the sound held no mirth. "I'm not

talking about your room. I'm talking about this school, Furman. I don't belong here."

"We all feel that way our freshman year, fish-out-of-water syndrome I call it."

Silas forced himself to raise his head and look Kris in the eyes. To do otherwise would be cowardly, and for the first time in a long time he was determined to be brave. "You're not listening to me, or at least not comprehending, which isn't your fault. I'm saying I literally don't belong here. This isn't my school."

"Are you flunking out or something? Is that what this is about?"

"You can't flunk out of a school you don't go to," Silas said. "I'm not a Furman student. I'm a Greenville Tech student."

It was Kris's turn to laugh. "What kind of a joke is this? Of course, you're a Furman student."

"This is no joke. I don't attend this school; I never did."

Silas could see a war waging in Kris's eyes. Realization was dawning, but he fought it. He fought it because the truth was too ugly to face. "You're crazy. Of course, you go to Furman, you're here all the time."

"I'm on the campus, but have you ever seen me go into a class? You know I don't have a student ID. Think it about it and you'll see that it's glaring."

"So … what? You've been running around campus pretending all these months?"

Silas felt the tears coming again but he refused to give in. Now that he'd started this, he had to see it through to the end. Whatever that end might be.

"Yes, that's exactly what I've been doing."

Kris stood suddenly, banging his hip into the side of the desk as he backed away. "Why would you do that? I don't understand."

"I didn't mean to, at least not at first anyway. I've always liked to hang out on campus, and the day I met you guys, everyone just assumed I was a student here, then Gus made a derogatory comment about community college, so I was embarrassed and didn't correct the assumption. I figured it was a harmless lie of omission to a group of strangers. I had no way of knowing then how important you all would become to me; how important you in particular would become to me. Then it all began to snowball out of control, and I felt trapped. I guess I trapped myself. I never intended for it to go this far, you have to believe me, but I didn't see a way out."

"And suddenly after all this time you started feeling confessional?"

Kris looked down at Silas with a grimace of distain, like he was observing something slimy and scaly that had slithered out of a sewer. Silas found himself regretting coming clean this way, but things had progressed too far to stop the avalanche of truth. He should have planned this better or planned it at all. The confession had simply slipped out, and he couldn't take it back now.

"I couldn't live with the deception anymore," Silas said, tears cascading again. "Every minute it felt like I was being poked with red-hot needles. Something had to give, but I couldn't just disappear without a word like Philip wanted, so I—"

"Wait, what?" Kris shouted. "You're saying that Philip knows?"

"He found out when he tried to get me a new student ID. He confronted me the other day and told me I needed to get lost, drop out of your lives. I thought maybe I could do that but then I realized I couldn't, so that's why I'm telling you the truth now."

Kris stumbled over to his bed and sank onto the mattress. "Oh yeah, real easy to be honest when you're pretty much given no choice. Tell me, if Philip hadn't found out, would we be having this conversation, or would you have just kept up the lie?"

Silas wanted to answer that he still would have confessed, but in good conscience he couldn't so he said nothing instead.

Kris buried his hands in his hair and began tugging at his curls. "I don't believe this. I don't even know who you are."

"Yes, you do," Silas said, jumping to his feet and approaching the bed. Kris cringed back against the headboard and Silas stopped halfway across the room. "I'm still *me*, I'm still the guy you fell in love with."

"That guy isn't real. You made him up, like one of your stories. I fell in love with a fiction, which means that wasn't real either."

"Don't say that. It is real, how I feel is real."

"Sure, you love me so much that you've lied to me on a daily basis since the moment we first met. Real testament to your affection."

"Please, I know you're angry and you have every right to be, what I did was inexcusable—"

"But here's the part where you try to explain why I should excuse it, right?"

Silas felt himself sinking into a hole, as if the floor had opened up into a swirling vortex that would suck him under. He flailed desperately, trying to find any handhold to keep him afloat.

"Everything important you know about me is the truth," he said. "You know the real me, the deep-down-nitty-gritty me. The only part that was a lie is where I'm enrolled at school, and in the grand scheme of things that seems like a pretty trivial thing."

Kris said nothing for a moment, merely gazing at him with a stare so cold that it actually made Silas shiver. "What was your end game?" Kris finally asked. "I mean, were you going to try to make it all four years without us finding out that you don't even go to Furman?"

"I plan to apply as a transfer student for fall semester next year."

Another of those incredulous laughs. "That would make everything all right, wouldn't it? Doesn't matter if you lie as long as you have a plan get away with it. That your reasoning?"

"No, it's just that ... hell, I didn't have any reasoning. The whole thing is a clusterfuck, I realize that. All I ask is that you hear me out, try to understand why I did what I did. You don't have to forgive me, but I want you to understand at least that none of this was malicious. I never wanted to hurt you."

Kris closed his eyes and took several deep breaths before standing. He appeared calmer, and the coldness in his eyes dissipated. What replaced it wasn't exactly warmth, but Silas dared to hope that perhaps it was curiosity.

"You need to go," Kris said. He didn't yell, and his words held no aggression or anger, but they were firm.

"Please, give me five minutes."

"I've given you more than enough time," Kris said, still speaking with that eerie composure that was somehow worse than rage. "I think I'm done listening to you. I'm asking you to leave, and the least you owe me is to respect that."

Silas wanted to plead, he wanted to beg, he wanted to entreaty, but in the end he merely shuffled toward the door. As he reached for the knob, he said without looking back at Kris, "Don't hate me."

"I don't hate you. I don't feel anything toward you. You're basically a stranger to me."

Silas's sweaty hands fumbled with the knob for several seconds before he got the door open and fled weeping. No chance of a dignified exit here. He rushed down the hall toward the stairs. He passed a common area with vending machines and realized a handful of students stood watching his retreat, but he didn't care if they stared. He couldn't really see them clearly through his veil of tears.

When he made his way outside, he was struck by the frigidity of the air. He hadn't really noticed on the walk over from Plyer Hall, too lost inside his own head, but now the cold bit into his flesh like teeth made of icicles. Inside his coat, he shivered and ducked his head down into the collar like a turtle.

Though he had parked up by the auditorium, he began walking in the opposite direction, toward the lake. The sun sank over the western horizon, but the usual fiery display of reds and oranges was muted by a thick cloud cover like a down comforter blanketing the earth. He followed the path around the lake to the Asian garden, walking past the pond and taking a seat inside a small bamboo enclosure barely larger than an old-time phone booth with two benches facing one another; a pergola, he thought it was called. A light rain began to drizzle down as Silas huddled on one of the benches.

For several minutes, he gave in unabashedly to his grief, crying with an intensity that caused his entire body to heave.

And grief was the correct word for what he felt, like something precious had died and he was currently attending its funeral. The fact that he was the one who had murdered it only heighted the grief, concentrated it until he worried the tears may never end, a bottomless well of mourning that would consume him until he was nothing but a dried husk that someone would one day find in this structure like a mummy in a sarcophagus.

Eventually, however, the tears did taper, though the feeling of loss remained. Hunched over and hugging himself as shivers ran though his body like cold electrical currents, he became aware of a soft ticking sound and realized there was sleet mixed in with the rain, striking the top of the enclosure and bouncing off like small pebbles. He knew he should head home in case roads became icy, but he lingered for a few moments more, mustering the strength and motivation to simply get to his feet.

He walked briskly through the sleet and rain in the direction of his car, keeping his head down. This campus, which he had foolishly started to think of as a home-away-from-home, suddenly felt alien and dangerous, like he had been dropped into the middle of a jungle full of wild animals and savage natives. He wanted to get home, get to his room, bury himself under the covers like a bear hunkering down deep in a cave to hibernate.

As he approached his car, drenched with ice crystals forming in his hair, he realized that he couldn't hide from his problems. He was the problem, and he carried himself wherever he went.

CHAPTER TWENTY-THREE

Silas checked the clock. Nearly midnight, and he didn't feel remotely sleepy. Tired, yes, a sort of bone-weariness that was more mental than physical, but when he closed his eyes, he merely lay there in the dark, replaying the conversation in Kris's room, the cold indifference in his parting words. The memory haunted him like a nightmare, only even worse because he was wide awake and could not escape it. This was no fractured and fantastical storyline created by his subconscious and unconscious mind; this was his life.

With a sigh, he sat up in bed and turned on the lamp on the nightstand. His stomach grumbled at him, and he became aware of the gnawing hollowness in his gut. His father had made hot dogs and fries for dinner, but Silas had eaten very little. In the same way that he was tired but not sleepy, he was hungry but had no appetite. Still, he knew his body needed fuel to keep functioning, and it was a bit melodramatic to starve himself because of an emotional upset.

He made his way to the trailer's kitchen, moving slowly and quietly so as not to wake his father. He didn't want to endure any probing questions. When he'd returned home so much earlier than expected, his father had made a few inquiries but dropped it when he realized that Silas didn't want to talk. Still, if his father found him up this late, he might not be so willing to let the subject drop.

Silas turned on the bar light over the sink, shedding a sickly yellow glow over the room that seemed to accentuate shadows as opposed to vanquish them. Rummaging items out of the fridge, he hastily threw together a ham sandwich and took it and a can of generic soda back to his room. Looking down at the sorry snack, he felt no desire to eat it, but he forced himself. Going through the motions, not really tasting the bread or the meat or even the spicy mustard he'd slathered onto it.

He glanced over to his cell, resting on the nightstand. The new cell his father had bought for him after Silas lied and said he'd accidentally dropped his old one down a sewer grate. As irresponsible as that made him sound, it was better than the truth, that he'd impulsively but purposefully tossed the phone into the pond at Greer City Park. His father hadn't seemed angry so much as disappointed, and he'd spent money he could ill afford to replace the lost phone. Nothing fancy, the cheapest pre-paid thing he could get, but still an expense he shouldn't have had to deal with.

Putting his sandwich aside after three bites, he reached over and picked up the phone. Shortly after leaving the Furman campus, it had begun to buzz with incoming calls and messages. He'd merely turned the phone off, and it had stayed off ever since. Going with the old adage of out of sight, out of mind. If he didn't read the messages or listen to any voicemails, he could pretend that nothing had changed.

Of course, self-delusion could only last so long.

He powered the phone on, waiting with hands that trembled. The phone buzzed and vibrated as all the notifications began to pop up. Over a dozen text messages, and two voicemails.

None of the messages were from Kris, but everyone else in the gang had sent texts. He glanced at a few.

From Franco: *Dude its not true is it?*

From Sheila: *Why would you do this to us?*

From Paige: *You're a sick person. Guess I was getting a glimpse of the real you at the library that day.*

From Gus: *I cant believ youd do thes to us when we tok you n as 1 of our own*

From Philip: *You ratted me out you sonofabitch, I hope you rot in hell.*

There were more, all becoming increasingly angrier and more insulting, especially from Philip. The only one that refrained from calling him names was Franco. His messages seemed more disbelieving and shocked than heated. They all carried with them a sense of betrayal, and Silas reminded himself that such a feeling was justified.

He'd missed calls from Franco, Paige, Philip, and Gus, but only two had left voicemails. Silas wasn't sure he wanted to listen to them and considered deleting them unplayed, but in the end he decided any road through this had to start with owning up to what he'd done, the havoc he'd wreaked.

The first voicemail was from Philip, his voice so loud and furious that Silas feared even through the phone it may wake his father. The rage was so intense that Silas had trouble reconciling it against the quiet young man he'd come to know these past few months.

"What the fuck is wrong with you, dude? I gave you a chance to bow out with a little dignity, to walk away without exposing yourself as the piece of shit liar you are, but not only didn't you take that chance, but you fucked me over in the process. Everybody's mad at me now for not telling them, treating me like I'm as bad as you are or something. Did you do this just to ruin me? Is that your game plan? I swear, I better never see your face again. I'm not a violent person, but the way I feel right now, I'm not sure what might happen."

After that unfocused threat, the message ended. Philip had clearly been crying by the end of his short diatribe, the pain in his words as sharp as a blade. Pain that Silas himself had caused.

He hadn't exactly meant to tell Kris that Philip knew and had used that knowledge to try to get him to disappear, that part had simply slipped out, but even then he hadn't paused to consider what kind of devastating effects that would have on Philip's relationship with the gang.

It was Philip's decision, he could have gone straight to the others and told them. He chose instead to blackmail you. And no matter how pure he thought his motives were, it was *blackmail. He will have to deal with the consequences of his own choices same as you.*

True, but it didn't stop Silas from feeling like he had the opposite of the Midas touch. Everything he touched turned to shit.

Before he could lose his nerve, he played the second voicemail.

This one was from Franco. Like his texts, his voicemail held less anger and more bewildered confusion.

"Hey, it's me. Franco. I just … I don't know what to say, which is stupid since I'm the one calling you, but … this is all too weird, and I can't quite wrap my head around it. Are you okay? I mean, I thought you were my friend. Was that all part of some game you were playing with us? If so, I don't understand what you were trying to accomplish. You seem like such a decent guy. Guess it goes to show that you never really know someone."

Are you okay? That was the part that really hit Silas hard and made his eyes burn with tears again. Franco was hurt and betrayed and yet in the midst of all that, he still somehow had concern for Silas.

He turned the phone off again and tossed it to the foot of the bed. He glanced at the sandwich but knew he could eat no more. His stomach churned, as if he might upheave what he'd already consumed. He returned to the kitchen, tossing the sandwich in the trash and pouring the soda out in the sink. Wasting food, which was wasting his father's money, on top of everything else.

Jesus, is there such a thing as guilt overload? What will you blame yourself for next, the Pulse nightclub shooting? The Ebola pandemic? The 2016 election?

No need, you have enough blame for the stuff that actually is your fault to last you a lifetime.

Back in his bedroom, he took his laptop and logged onto Facebook, needing to satisfy a curiosity. He tried to look up Kris's page but came up empty. Blocked. He must have blocked Silas. Not merely defriended him but blocked him altogether. A month ago, Silas had also created an Instagram account, though he'd posted only two photos since then, and he found that he'd been blocked on that platform as well. He tried the accounts of the rest of the gang and the only other one that had blocked him so far was Paige.

"I deserve it," he said to himself. He told himself admitting that wasn't a pity party, but merely taking responsibility for his actions. Hurt every bit as much, however.

He briefly considered flipping on the TV at a low volume

and finding something mindless to watch, but he dismissed the idea. Wouldn't be much to choose from since his father had cancelled the cable around Thanksgiving to save money. Silas hadn't minded much at the time, as he had been so busy with his suddenly active social life that he didn't spend nearly as much time at home. He could look up YouTube videos, he supposed, but he'd probably just end up playing depressing songs by Adele.

He switched off the lamp and crawled back into the covers. He closed his eyes, figuring he'd cry himself to sleep. He did cry, but he didn't sleep.

CHAPTER TWENTY-FOUR

Somehow Silas made it through his finals. He didn't think he'd flunked any, though he wouldn't know for sure until the grades were emailed, but he'd found it hard to concentrate on studying. His last exam was for English Comp, and he hoped Mr. Henry wouldn't realize he'd bullshitted through half the essay questions.

He didn't even finish the last essay, the two-hour time limit running out before he could finish scribbling his jumbled thoughts onto the page. He turned in his papers and scurried out of the building with the two other students who had worked right up until the end.

Outside, he was surprised to find Finn waiting for him.

"What are you doing here?" Silas asked. "You finished your exam at least an hour ago."

"I know, but I figured we could hang for a while."

Silas was touched, but also a little annoyed. "I don't need a babysitter. I'm not going to off myself or anything like that."

"I'm not trying to be your babysitter, man. Just your friend. I feel like you could really use one right now."

The annoyance fell away, leaving only a feeling of gratitude. Silas went to Finn and hugged him. Once upon a time he would have been self-conscious embracing anyone, let alone a straight guy, but it felt good to be close. Finn hugged him back.

"You had lunch yet?" Finn asked.

"No."

"That settles it. We're going to go grab a bite somewhere and talk. You've obviously been upset, even more so than usual, and whatever it is, you need to get it off your chest. I promise I won't judge you."

"They do say confession is good for the soul," Silas said with a laugh. "Where do you want to eat?"

They went downtown and ended up at Handi Indian for the lunch buffet. Silas had never had Indian food before, and he didn't know what anything was but merely took a sampling of whatever Finn piled on his plate. His first few bites were tentative, but the exotic spiciness of the food set off tiny explosions in his taste buds and soon he was wolfing everything down. While they ate, Silas told Finn all about the blackmail, as well as the subsequent confession and fall out.

"And you haven't heard from any of them since that night?" Finn asked.

Silas shook his head. "I've thought about calling Kris or sending a group text to the whole gang. Just, you know, to say I was sorry, but I figured that would be pretty lame and not actually accomplish anything. Probably make them angrier and certainly wouldn't make me feel any better."

"Well, it's all probably for the best."

Silas laughed. "If this is how the best feels, I'd hate to experience the worst."

"You know your situation was unsustainable, right? There was absolutely no scenario where the truth came out that people didn't get hurt. But I also believe there was no scenario where the truth didn't eventually come out. It's better that everything's in the open now. The damage has been done, and now the chips will fall where they may, and you can all go about trying to pick up the scraps and start piecing your lives back together. Won't look the same as it did before, but at least you'll have something whole again."

"I don't think there are any pieces worth salvaging. I've pretty much obliterated everything, nothing left but ash and soot. You'd be surprised how much damage can be done when you're a terrible person."

Finn set his fork down and gave Silas a look so serious and intense that it was unnerving. "I believe there aren't really any terrible people. Just people who make terrible choices."

"Sounds like semantics to me," Silas said. "What's the difference?"

"The difference is that when it's about choice, you can always *choose* something different. Did something terrible today? Well, tomorrow is a new chance to do something better. Doesn't change the past, doesn't mean you don't have to pay the consequences of yesterday's choices, but each day you can make a conscious commitment to choose better choices, to take a different path."

An unexpected and overwhelming love for Finn washed through Silas. "You know, your Pollyanna nature is kind of adorable."

"It's not Pollyanna; it's very realistic. Do you think I'm naturally this cool and wise? No, I make the choice to be. Every day."

The two shared a laugh and Silas said, "Well, my decision-making hasn't been so stellar thus far in my life."

"That's my point. You can change that. Nobody is destined to be only one thing his or her entire life. People are constantly redefining themselves. Some of the most kind and compassionate people you know may very well be compensating for some terrible choices they made in their pasts."

Silas found himself flashing on Kris's story of the bullied kid from high school, Andy, and the way Kris himself had participated in the bullying. And, of course, how Andy's suicide had affected Kris, caused him to reevaluate his life and make some changes. To make better choices.

But could it really be that simple?

Silas thought of the pain Kris had revealed when telling that story, and he realized that no, there was nothing simple about atonement, about rebuilding yourself from the ground up. It was a daily struggle, hard and maybe even sometimes agonizing ... but worth it?

"I don't know how I'd ever make amends to Kris, to the others," Silas said.

Finn shrugged, but his words were not dismissive. "Maybe you'll never be able to. It's not about that. It's about you, about forgiving yourself and letting this make you better, stronger. Your current choice is clear. You can sit around wallowing in self-pity, or you can dust yourself off and get on with living. Only one of those choices will actually get you anywhere."

Silas took a minute to think about what Finn said, to really consider it and absorb the words. "You really are wise," he said.

"What can I say? My mother watches a lot of Dr. Phil. Some of the man's wisdom was bound to rub off on me."

The two laughed again, and it felt good. A little voice in Silas's head suggested he should feel bad about feeling good, after all he'd done, but he squelched that voice.

He made the choice not to listen.

CHAPTER TWENTY-FIVE

Christmas Eve at the Granger household was full of traditions. First, the little artificial tree with its blinking red and green lights and shedding tensile, perched on the table by the window next to the front door. Considering that theirs was the last trailer at the end of a dead-end road, this little display was for no one's benefit, but Silas's father insisted that it was for the festive nature of the holiday.

Second, the red stockings with their names stenciled on them in gold glitter. His father had gotten those and applied the glitter himself when Silas was five, and they'd been hung up every year since. Of course, the trailer had no fireplace, so his father always hung them on either side of the front door. Tomorrow morning, they would be full of fruits, nuts, and candy canes.

Third, the meal of turkey, mashed potatoes, green beans, and sweet potato soufflé with the marshmallow topping. His father didn't buy a whole turkey like he did at Thanksgiving, but he'd get turkey breast and roast the slices in the oven.

Fourth, opening presents just after dinner. The gifts would be wrapped or bagged and tucked up under the table on which the tree sat. Simple gifts but heartfelt and appreciated. This year Silas gave his father a pocket knife and a DVD of a live production of *Company* starring Neil Patrick Harris and Patti LuPone. The DVD was out of print, and Silas had to do a lot of online searching to finally find a copy on eBay that was reasonably priced. His father got choked up at this gift, which made them both vaguely uncomfortable. Silas received a gift certificate to Mr. K's in Greenville and a nice hardcover edition of Ray Bradbury's *Zen in the Art of Writing* that was actually signed. The inscription was "To Jennifer," but it had Bradbury's signature scrawled there nonetheless which made it priceless to Silas.

Fifth, the Christmas movie marathon. Started at eight p.m. and lasted until … whenever one of them fell asleep on the sofa. They didn't watch any of the usual suspects during this marathon. No *A Christmas Carol*, *It's a Wonderful Life*, or *Miracle on 34th Street*. Silas and his father always started with *A Christmas Story*, followed by *National Lampoon's Christmas Vacation* and the obscure comedy *The Ref*. If they lasted past those three, they'd pull out *Die Hard* and *Gremlins*. One year they'd made it all the way through to dawn and had ended up watching a duo of early Tim Burton films, *Edward Scissorhands* and *Batman Returns*.

This year, halfway through *Christmas Vacation* Silas's father already fought sleep, his chin sliding down toward his chest before snapping back up. He seemed to be exhausted all the time these days. Silas couldn't blame him. 2018 had been a rough year for him, with the job woes and financial worries. Of course, Silas had his own stress that he hadn't been able to talk about.

Yet if he really meant to change his life, to make a fresh start and redefine himself as Finn had mentioned, then maybe the first step was being honest with all the people he loved.

"I'm going to apply to transfer to Furman in the fall," Silas said suddenly, as on the screen Clark Griswold fought with a vicious squirrel in a Christmas tree.

This woke his father right up, and he grabbed the remote to pause the movie. "Well, that's a big announcement to come falling down right out of the blue."

"It's not really out of the blue. It's something I've been contemplating for a while now. I've been afraid to bring it up."

"Afraid of what?" his father asked.

"I don't want you to worry. Even if I get in, I'll apply for every loan and grant I can to cover tuition. I know the reality of our financial situation."

Silas saw the pain in his father's face, the shame at not being able to provide for his son the way he wanted. "Son, I support you in whatever you want to do, but you do realize that Furman is a very competitive school, right?"

"Yes, and this may not even happen. I thought about not mentioning it to you until I knew one way or the other whether I could even get in, but it felt wrong keeping it from you. So there it is, I'm going to apply."

His father nodded, considered for a moment, fiddled with the remote without resuming the movie, then said, "Does this have anything to do with the fact that you haven't been hanging out with Kris lately?"

Silas tensed. His father had surely noticed that he'd been spending a lot more time at home and no longer mentioned spending time with anyone but Finn, and yet they hadn't talked about it. "What do you mean?" Silas asked, curious how much his father had surmised.

"Just that if you and Kris had a fight and broke up or something, maybe you want to run away from it. Like to another campus entirely."

"That wouldn't exactly work, since Kris goes to Furman."

His father frowned. "I thought he went to Greenville Tech with you and the rest of that little group."

"No, they all go to Furman. I've got to tell you something, Dad, and you're not going to like it, but I ask that you let me tell you the whole story before you say anything. Can you do that?"

A look of intense concern tightened his father's face and he sat up a little straighter. Silas could only imagine what was going through the man's mind—suicidal thoughts, STDs, infidelity, adolescent heartbreak—but surely he couldn't guess at what was actually coming. His father thought for a moment then nodded.

Silas took a deep breath and laid it all out on the table, from the misunderstanding upon his first meeting of the gang, the escalation of the lie, all the way to the inevitable implosion. The only slight fib he told was suggesting he'd come clean on his own. Not to make himself look better, but he didn't want to confuse things with Philip's blackmail. This story had only one true villain, and that was Silas. Best to own up to that.

It took only ten minutes to recount the whole sordid tale. Four months of deception, laughter, shame, love, friendship, tears … all boiled down to a ten-minute narrative. Kind of put things into perspective.

When Silas finished, he sat back and waited for his father's response. At first, none was forthcoming. Silence stretched out, as on the TV screen the Christmas tree remained frozen mid-topple. Silas had feared an immediate reaction of anger and recrimination, and while he was relieved not to have that outcome, this extended suspense felt almost as excruciating.

Finally, his father looked him in the eye and said, "You know I raised you better than to lie to people like that."

"I know, you did. This is all on me, I take full responsibility. I can't go back and change what I've already done, but I have to find some way to go forward."

"I can see you know you did wrong and that you feel bad about it, and that's good. That means the young man I raised to be a person of principle is still there. But, son, I don't know that you're thinking straight on the matter. How do you figure transferring to Furman is going to fix this?"

"It's not about fixing it," Silas said. "I may have very well broken this beyond repair, and that's something I'll have to live with. All I can do now is focus on me, make some changes in myself."

"And Furman is the first step?"

"You know I've always loved that school and wanted to go there. My senior year of high school when it was time to apply to colleges, I didn't even try to see if Furman might be a viable option. I dismissed it out of hand as a lost cause and only applied to Tech. Why did I do that? Because it was easy. Taking an objective look at myself, I think too often I go for what it easy. Like it was easy to let Kris and his friends assume I was a Furman student. If I want my life to get better, I need to stop doing what's easy just because I'm afraid of failing at something harder. So the first step is telling the truth, to Kris and to you and to myself. Second step is seeing if I have a chance to get into Furman, because it might be hard but it's what I want. It was what I wanted long before I ever met Kris and the gang."

Another beat of silence then his father nodded, said, "Okay," and resumed the movie.

"Wait, what?" Silas said. "That's it?"

His father paused the movie again and glanced at him with a smile. "I could scold you and give you a stern lecture, but I doubt I could tell you anything you don't already know. I suspect you've beaten yourself up over this enough, no need for me to add to that. If I thought you hadn't learned anything from this, it would be different. But it seems clear to me you've learned a hard lesson, a lesson that has the potential to make you stronger if you let it."

Silas started to speak but he got choked up and had to wait a few seconds, clear his throat, and wipe at his eyes before he tried again. "I love you, Dad. I'm lucky to have you."

"Love you, too, buddy," his father said, reaching over to pat Silas on the cheek. He fiddled with the remote some more, holding it in the middle and seesawing it back and forth.

"What?" Silas said, as his father clearly had more to say.

"Nothing. It's silly."

"Dad, I laid a lot on you tonight, I'm aware of that. If you have something you want to discuss or questions you want to ask, now's the time. I know you said you don't feel I need a scolding, but we both know I deserve one. Let me have it, I can take it."

"Nothing like that," his father said, leaning forward to toss the remote onto the coffee table, where it clinked against the glass. "Just a question."

"Shoot."

His father looked at Silas but then away, instead staring down at his hands folded on his lap. Almost as if he couldn't quite bring himself to meet his son's gaze. "Is this why you never wanted to bring Kris home to meet me? Wasn't because you were, you know, ashamed of your old man or anything?"

Silas felt his heart breaking, could almost imagine he heard a distinct *snap* somewhere in his chest. He had thought he'd already experienced the lowest low a human could reach but looking at his father now he sunk even lower. The full ramifications of all he'd wrought crashed on top of him like a falling tree, grinding him down into the mud.

His lie had caused pain to a lot of people who didn't deserve it, and he'd known his father's feelings were hurt by Silas's refusal to bring Kris home to meet him, but now Silas realized it went far deeper than hurt feelings. He had made his father feel inadequate and like a failure, all this coming as he was bumped down to part-time at the hardware store and forced to take odd handyman jobs just to pay the bills. Silas had been aware of all this in a peripheral sense, but he hadn't really focused on it directly. He hadn't wanted to, another of those choices that had gotten him in so much trouble. His father had merely been collateral damage in the mess he'd made.

Silas felt the tidal pool of self-recrimination again, but he swam away from it. Not because he didn't deserve it, but because it was useless and counterproductive.

"I could never be ashamed of you," Silas said, his voice coming with vehemence. "You're the strongest man I know, and if I could become half the man you are, I'd be extremely lucky. I would love for Kris to have known you. He'd have loved you, and I think you'd have loved him. I was the one standing in the way of that. Me and only me."

At this, his father looked up, and Silas saw tears glistening unshed in the man's eyes. "You're already every bit the man I ever was."

Silas laughed. "I'm not sure how you could say that after everything I've told you tonight."

"Hey, being a man doesn't mean you never make mistakes. It means that when you do make mistakes, you acknowledge them and do everything you can to keep from making the same mistakes in the future. You seem to have that covered."

Silas scooted across the sofa and wrapped his arms around his father. His father returned in kind, and they held each other tight. Though they had always been close, they had never really been huggers, but it felt good to be in his father's arms right now.

When they pulled apart, both swiping discreetly at their eyes, his father said, "Okay, let's get back to the movie. I love the part where Clark kidnaps his boss. I might just have to do that to Dryer if he doesn't put me back to fulltime next month."

WINTER 2019

CHAPTER TWENTY-SIX

Silas awoke on New Year's Day at half past nine, the sun streaming through his window highlighting dust motes that wafted through the air like smoke. After a feline stretch, Silas untangled himself from his sheets and swung his feet onto the floor. He'd slept in jogging pants, a sweatshirt, and thick socks, but still he shivered as he made his way to the bathroom to relieve his aching bladder.

His father had been turning the heat down at night for the past few weeks. They hadn't discussed it, but Silas knew it was to keep the power bill manageable, so he didn't make a fuss. He stopped at the thermostat and nudged it up a few degrees before shambling into the kitchen to fix himself some breakfast.

The hardware store was open today, and Silas knew his father had a four-hour shift from eight a.m. to noon. Still, his father had left a note stuck to the fridge with a Grumpy Cat magnet, reminding Silas of his hours and letting him know there were frozen waffles in the freezer and that he'd pick up burgers from Fuddruckers for lunch on his way home.

With a smile, Silas popped a couple of generic Eggos in the toaster for a couple of minutes then slathered them with margarine and syrup. He brought this nutritious breakfast along with a glass of milk back to his room and settled at his desk. After scarfing the food down, he sat the dishes aside and opened his laptop, bringing up the Furman website.

"New year, fresh start," he muttered as he navigated to the application for potential transfer students. He had to create an account and winced at the fifty-dollar application fee. He had just under a hundred in his bank account, which would seriously deplete his cash reserves, but he would have to bite the bullet. Nothing ventured, nothing gained as the old saying went. Of course, if he didn't get in, he'd have ventured and still gained nothing. He doubted Furman offered refunds of the application fee for the poor losers who didn't make the cut.

Silas scanned the requirements to complete the application. He would have to request both his transcripts from Greenville Tech and Riverside High, which would probably incur more fees. He also would need to provide two letters of recommendation, but he would worry about those later. The final part of the application process would be writing a five-hundred-word essay. As someone to whom the written word had always come easily, he wasn't overly worried about this part and therefore decided to do it first. There were five provided topics from which he could choose, and as he began to read these over, his phone buzzed with an incoming call.

He grabbed the cell, expecting the call to be from Finn or his father, but he nearly dropped the phone from the surprise of seeing Franco's name displayed on the screen.

Silas hadn't heard from any of the gang since the night of the debate, and he really didn't expect he would ever hear from them again. He considered not answering, simply let the call go to voicemail and see if Franco left a message.

But no, that would be the easy thing to do, and he had committed to stop doing that. He swiped the screen to answer the call. "Hello?"

A pause on the other end then, "Um, Silas?"

"It's me. How are you doing, Franco?"

"I'm okay. Have a good Christmas?"

"Can't complain. You?"

"Pretty good," Franco said. "My folks got me an old-time turntable and a few vinyl comedy albums by some guy named George Carlin. Apparently he was a big comedian back in the day."

"I think I've seen some clips on YouTube. Very cool of them."

"Yeah, guess they're pretty cool."

Silence played out as Silas sat up rigid in the chair, phone pressed to his ear. The whole conversation had a surreal quality to it, despite the mundane nature of the chitchat. In fact, it was that very mundane nature that made the conversation so surreal. As if they were picking up a banal dialogue they'd been having only moments ago; as if they hadn't been out of contact for over a month because of Silas's lies.

"So what can I do for you, Franco?" Silas finally asked, just to get the discussion moving along again.

"Well, I, um, thing is we settled on a definite date for the stand-up show. February sixteenth. It's a Saturday."

"That's great, Franco. I know you've been looking forward to it."

"I really am. I think it's going to be great, and I ... you see, I guess I wanted to invite you to come."

This rendered Silas as temporarily speechless as a sucker punch to the mouth. After a moment of stammering and stuttering, he said, "Why?"

"Because this wouldn't even be happening if you hadn't given me the nudge I needed to get the ball rolling. It wouldn't feel right if you weren't there."

"Do Kris and the others know you're inviting me?"

A pregnant pause that revealed the answer even before Franco said, "No. I haven't discussed it with anyone else."

"I doubt they'll be happy to find out you asked me to attend."

"Probably not, and I get that. To be honest, I'm pretty conflicted on the issue myself. I've gone back and forth about a gazillion times on whether or not I should call."

"What finally tipped the scales in favor of calling?" Silas asked.

"Like I said, you're partially responsible for this show even happening. It wouldn't be fair if I didn't at least extend the invitation."

Silas swallowed a sob. "So does everyone pretty much hate me?"

Another damning pause. "I can't speak for anyone other than myself. I don't hate you, Silas. There is hurt and anger and sadness, but no hate."

Silas took a shuddering breath. "Thank you for that."

"I don't want you to think this means we're friends again. That's not what this is. I do want you at the show, if you want to go, but I'm not saying I want you back as a part of my life."

"I get it," Silas said. "I don't expect anything."

"Okay, well, like I said, February sixteenth, show starts at seven."

"Thank you," Silas said, but Franco had already hung up.

Silas felt almost numb, giving him the sensation that he wasn't so much sitting in the chair as floating an inch above it. He realized he was shaking and crying, but his emotions were too deadened to know if he was sad or happy. He also didn't know if he'd actually go to the show. The idea of facing the gang scared him. Of course, if he really meant to transfer to Furman in the fall, he'd have to face the idea that he could very well run into them on campus.

Still, he didn't have to decide about the show right this second. Simply being invited meant something to him, and that was enough for now.

Glancing back at his laptop, his eyes zeroed in on the third suggested admissions essay topic. He actually laughed out loud at the appropriateness of the topic, almost as if it had been designed for him.

His fingers found the keyboard and began flying over the keys almost as if they had a collective mind of their own. He let the words flow, not really from his brain but from his heart. From his gut.

After all those months of deception, he let the truth pour out through his fingertips.

CHAPTER TWENTY-SEVEN

Silas returned to Greenville Tech for the new semester with renewed vigor and purpose. He'd used the holiday break to shake off most of his morose self-loathing, replacing it with a determination to do better, to *be better*. He was nearly ready to send off his Furman application, and then there would be nothing but the waiting. In the meantime, he had a lot of work to do on himself. He'd squeaked by the previous semester with a 3.0 GPA. Actually a small miracle he'd done that well with all his divided attention, but still lots of room for improvement. And he planned to do just that.

Silas and Finn had no classes together this semester, but they had agreed to meet for lunch at half past noon. However, in his second class of the day, Anatomy, he recognized a familiar face two rows over.

Katie from the Village Grind, Gus's crush.

He sat slumped over his desk with his head turned slightly away, hoping Katie wouldn't notice him. Unfortunately, the class wasn't that big, and halfway through class when he furtively cast a glance her way, he found her staring right back. And nothing remotely surreptitious about her stare.

After class, he gathered up his books and tried to make a break for it, but her seat was closer to the door and she was out of the room first, waiting for him in the hallway.

For the best. Remember, you were going to stop running away from things.

"Hey, Katie," he said. "Fancy meeting you here."

"Tell me about it. Guess it's a good thing your secret already came out or else this would have really blown your cover."

Silas surprised himself and Katie by laughing. "Never

thought of it that way. Small blessings and all."

Katie seemed slightly thrown off by Silas's good-natured response. Clearly this conversation wasn't going the way she'd envisioned, and it left her off-kilter. "So, have you talked to any of the guys from Furman since it all went down?"

Of course, Silas flashed on the phone call from Franco, but he didn't think it would do any good to reveal that, so he shook his head.

"Other than Gus, I haven't talked to the others much myself," Katie said.

"Gus already in Washington?"

She nodded. "Left last week. He texts me like three dozen times a day. I'm thinking of telling him to cool it. I'm not that into the whole long-distance thing."

"Gus is a really nice guy. The whole long-distance thing might be worth it."

Katie tilted her head and gave him an appraising look. "What would you know about being a nice guy?"

The words stung, but Silas shrugged them off with a literal shrug. "Touché. But you don't have to be a thing to recognize it."

He walked past her toward the stairs, but after only a few steps she called to him, "I get it."

He stopped and looked back at her. "Get what?"

"Why you did it."

Silas didn't want to be late for his next class, but he walked back to Katie, intrigued. "What do you mean?"

Now she shrugged. "I don't want you to get me wrong. Gus is great. They're all great."

"But?" Silas prompted.

"But sometimes there is this vague snobbishness that comes through. Nothing intentional, nothing malicious. Just this sense that they don't really get what it's like for people like you and me, people with fewer opportunities available to us. Not that they look down at us Tech students, but I don't think they fully see us as one of them either. That was why I made it clear when I first met them that my plan was to get some prereqs at Tech then transfer into Furman. To make me seem a little less alien and give me some cred with them."

"At least you were honest with them from the get-go and didn't start lying immediately."

"Yeah, that was pretty shitty," Katie said, but her words held no venom. "But like I said, I get it."

"I appreciate that. Have you applied to Furman for fall?"

"Not yet, but I plan to get that done by the end of the month. I'm nervous as hell."

"Good luck."

Katie reached out and briefly squeezed his arm. "Yeah, you, too."

Silas and Finn sat at a picnic table near the STAT Center, eating their pre-packaged lunches. Silas looked over three new comics Finn had made from Silas's short stories.

"So you must be feeling pretty good," Finn said before taking a big bite out of his sandwich.

Silas glanced up from the page. "Why do you say that?"

It took Finn a minute to chew and swallow before answering. "Come on. First the invite from Franco, and now that barista girl shows a little understanding."

"One, the barista girl has a name. Katie."

"Katie what?" Finn asked with a lopsided smile.

Ignoring him, Silas continued. "Two, I'm not caring about that right now. Does it feel good? Of course, but that's not my objective. I'm not looking for forgiveness. I don't deserve forgiveness, and I'm cool with that."

"You know, you don't forgive someone because they deserve it or because they earn it. Forgiveness is an act of mercy."

"Maybe so, but I don't have any control over whether or not someone shows me that mercy."

"True."

"So there's no use dwelling on it," Silas said. "I royally fucked up those friendships, in all likelihood for good. Still hurts, but I'm making peace with it."

"On the upside, you still got me. And let's face it, what do you need with other friends when you have Fennimore Jameson on your side?"

Silas laughed. "You got me there."

Finn sipped at his soda, his mood becoming more serious. "Although you are trying to abandon me here all by my lonesome for the greener pastures of Furman."

"It's not like that and you know it. Even if by some miracle I got into Furman and could get enough financial aid to go, a string of longshots, we'd still be friends. Hell, you're the best friend I've got."

"I'm the *only* friend you've got."

"That's not true. I've got my dad."

"I guess I can't compete with that."

"Seriously though," Silas said, "I wouldn't be getting through this without you. I want you to know how much I appreciate your friendship."

"Dude, don't get all sappy on me. You know I don't swing that way. Okay, maybe we'll get to first base someday, but absolutely no tongue."

"You're a sick individual."

"So I've been told. On numerous occasions by countless people. Sometimes strangers on the street."

"I probably won't get into Furman anyway," Silas said.

"No self-defeatism here. It's a rule."

"Self-defeatism or realism? Pretty much a tomato/tomahtoe situation. I was wondering if you'd want to read my admission essay, though."

"When you planning to submit the application?"

"Soon. I already got one letter of recommendation from Dr. Frost, my advisor. I just have one more to get then I'll be ready. I thought a second pair of eyes on my essay might be a good idea."

Finn shook his head. "I'll read it after you submit your application."

"What? Why?"

"Because you shouldn't be second guessing yourself on this. My opinion might make you tinker around with it. I say go with your first instinct."

"As a writer, I do believe in the power of editing."

"Yeah, but you can also edit the life right out of something so that it loses whatever magic it originally had. I am a firm believer in the initial creative spark of creation."

"Well, speaking of creative spark," Silas said, gesturing to the comics, "these are fantastic."

"Thanks. I've been having a lot of fun adapting your stuff."

Making a decision, Silas slapped his hands down on the top of the table. "What are you doing this weekend?"

Finn shrugged. "No definite plans. Some homework, maybe play some World of Warcraft, watch some porn."

"Sounds scintillating, but if I can pull you away from Pornhub for a few hours on Saturday, what do you say we take a little road trip?"

"I'm down. Where to?"

"Asheville. Let's see about selling these comics through that bookstore you told me about."

"Really?" Finn asked, excitement glinting in his eyes. "You sure?"

Silas looked back down at the comics. His words, Finn's art. A perfect marriage.

"I'm sure," he said. "Let's do it."

CHAPTER TWENTY-EIGHT

Silas sat in the hallway, his back against the office door with his knees bent and pulled up toward his chest. While he waited, he read over his notes for his Romantic Authors class. He'd been there for twenty minutes when he looked up and saw Dr. Flem coming down the hall toward him.

Stowing his notes into his backpack, he got to his feet to greet the professor. "Dr. Flem, hi. You have a minute?"

Dr. Flem stopped, a slight frown tugging at the corners of his lips. "What are you doing here, Silas?"

"Just need to talk to you, ask a little favor actually. Won't take but a minute, I swear."

Dr. Flem seemed to think it over then unlocked his office door and stepped inside, turning back to say, "Come on in, but I have a student conference in ten minutes, so you'll have to make it quick."

Once inside the office, Silas decided not to sit. Sitting indicated an expectation of settling in, and he wanted to make it clear he was indeed going to be brief.

"I heard about what happened with you and the others," Dr. Flem said, dropping into the chair behind his desk.

"Yeah, everyone's pretty mad at me."

"They aren't too pleased with me either."

"Oh, I didn't tell them you knew," Silas said.

"No, I did."

Silas nodded. "Right, complete honesty. I'm working on that."

"I'm not sure what you want from me," Dr. Flem. "The whole thing is a mess, and I wish I'd never gotten tangled up in it. Whatever you think, I can't help you out here."

"This isn't about all that."

Dr. Flem's frown deepened. "Then what exactly is this about?"

"I was wondering if you'd write me a letter of recommendation."

Dr. Flem actually shook his head as if recovering from a blow. "You're still applying to Furman?"

"Yes, sir. I need one more letter of recommendation, and I was hoping it would come from you."

"Silas, I don't even really know you."

"In some ways, you know me better than anyone else."

"I really don't think it would be a good idea. This isn't going to win you any points with Gus and his group."

"I told you this isn't about that, and I mean that sincerely. This is something I want, so I'm going to go for it."

"If that's how you feel then I wish you well," Dr. Flem said. "But I don't think I can write you a letter of recommendation."

"You once told me you thought I was a decent guy, despite everything. Do you still believe that?"

"That's not important."

"It's important to me."

Dr. Flem took a moment before replying. "Yes, Silas. I believe you are a decent guy who got in way over his head."

"And now I'm paying the consequences, and I'm okay with that. Not okay in that it doesn't still feel like I'm being stabbed in the gut, but I also recognize it's my hands holding the knife. That doesn't mean I have to spend the rest of my life punishing myself."

"I agree."

"So all I'm asking is that I get a shot at a brighter future. Furman is one step on that journey, I think. A letter of recommendation from you could go a long way. I won't beg, though I realize that's sort of what it sounds like I'm doing, but I am asking that you at least think about it. If you ultimately decide you can't, I'll have to respect that. If, on the other hand, you decide you can, email me."

Silas pulled a scrap of paper from his pocket on which he'd neatly printed his email address and placed it on the professor's desk.

Dr. Flem took the paper and stared at it for a few seconds.

"I'll think it over, but I can't make you any promises."

"That's fair," Silas said. "Now I'll go. Thank you for hearing me out."

"Sure thing. You take care."

Silas started from the room but paused at the door. "I'm sorry I got you all tangled up in my mess."

Dr. Flem didn't say anything, but Silas didn't expect any kind of answer or absolution. He left the office and headed for the nearest exit.

Once outside, Silas paused in the covered walkway that ran the length of the building. This was the first time he'd been on the Furman campus since before the Christmas break, and he felt the temptation to wander around a bit. The sun was beginning to set, and he thought it might be nice to meander down to the lake and watch the fiery reds and oranges reflected on the water.

But no, that would increase the likelihood he might run into Kris or some of the others and he wasn't ready for that. Not yet. He'd told himself on the drive over that he would get in and out, quick and painless. He'd parked out behind Daniel Chapel, across the Furman Mall from this building, to minimize his time on campus.

As he made his way around toward the chapel, he began to think of a backup strategy. He still hoped that Dr. Flem would come around and write a letter of recommendation—he figured a letter from an actual Furman faculty member would hold a lot of weight—but if he didn't, Silas needed a plan B. Few of the professors at Greenville Tech knew him all that well, and he couldn't use his father because family members weren't allowed to write letters of recommendation. Maybe Mrs. Conner who taught him senior English back in high school. She'd always been very complimentary about his writing.

Lost deep in this contemplation, he at first didn't hear his name being called until he was right in front of the chapel. He recognized the voice and that cowardly part of him wanted to make a mad dash for the parking lot behind Daniel, but instead he held his ground and turned to see Philip approaching. Silas braced himself.

"What the hell are you doing here?" Philip said, stopping a few feet from Silas as if not wanting to get too close lest he catch some contagion.

Silas hesitated a moment, deciding he would tell just enough of the truth not to further entangle Dr. Flem in any of this. "I had a meeting with someone. I'm applying to transfer here in the fall."

Philip laughed, but it wasn't a pleasant sound. "Jesus, you never give up, do you? Furman doesn't want you."

"*You* don't want me here, I get it, but that's not the same as the university not wanting me. I mean, maybe they won't, that remains to be seen, but I have to at least try."

Philip didn't answer right away, and Silas had time to really examine the young man. Noting the bags under his eyes, the wrinkled shirt underneath his coat, the chapped lips. He didn't look good. In fact, he looked more miserable than Silas had ever seen him, and he'd seen Philip look pretty miserable before.

"You doing okay?" Silas asked.

Another laugh. "Peachy, other than the fact that I have no friends now."

"What?"

"Everybody's pissed at me, because I didn't tell them about you as soon as I found out. Kris went off on me and called me names I don't care to repeat, and now no one's talking to me."

More collateral damage. Your father, Dr. Flem, Philip. A lot of bodies in your wake.

"I'm sorry," Silas said. "I guess that's my fault."

"Not really," Philip said begrudgingly, the words squeezed out between his teeth. "You're definitely a piece of shit, but they're right. I should have told them; I shouldn't have tried blackmailing you into doing a disappearing act. That was my choice, so that's on me."

Silas found himself a bit taken aback by Philip's seeming fair-mindedness and willingness to accept a little culpability. So taken aback in fact that Silas felt the need to try to lift that weight from his shoulders.

"You wouldn't even be in this situation if I hadn't lied."

"True," Philip said quickly. "You're not off the hook, but

when I found out, I should have told everyone. I can't blame you for that."

"Well, you were trying to show me a little mercy."

"That's not why I did it," Philip said so softly that Silas had to strain to hear him. "It had nothing to do with you. My motives for giving you the chance to sneak out without anyone finding out the truth were entirely selfish."

Silas frowned. "How? I don't see what you could possibly have gotten out of that scenario."

Philip shifted from one foot to the other, glanced around as if to check they were alone, then said, "Think about it. Kris finds out you've been lying to him since the second you met, his primary emotion is anger. Outrage. And when people are angry, it tends to spread beyond the initial source of that anger. Angry people often push everybody away, and in that case I'd be shut out. However, if you were to have simply broken up with Kris then disappeared from his life, his primary emotion would likely be heartbreak, sorrow. Heartbroken people often need comfort, and that would give me the chance to get closer to him. Maybe even be the one to get him through it, which would make him see me in a different light. That makes me a pretty shitty friend, all things considered."

Silas was surprised by how much thought Philip had put into this, and equally surprised the young man had the guts to admit to it now. Perhaps Silas wasn't the only one recognizing his questionable behavior and wanting to be better.

"They'll forgive you," Silas said. "I'm the one they're really mad at, and you're right. Angry people lash out at anyone tangentially related to what they're angry about. They'll cool down and realize that you don't deserve their rage. Just me."

Philip blinked away tears, and Silas mused that he had spent so much time lately around people who were crying.

"I shouldn't have done that to you," Philip said. "I mean, you certainly shouldn't have done what you did, and you needed to be exposed, but the sadistic way I handled the situation, using my knowledge like a weapon against you. Wasn't something a decent person does, and it makes me no better than you."

Makes me no better than you. That hurt but was also fair.

"Don't beat yourself up, Philip. Sometimes decent people make really indecent choices."

Philip nodded. "You know, what I said before wasn't entirely accurate."

"Which part?"

"When I said no one was talking to me. Actually, I heard from Franco. He invited me to the comedy show. Said he invited you, too."

"He did."

"You going?" Philip asked.

"Still considering."

"If you do decide to come, maybe we'll see each other there. Might be nice to have someone to sit with."

Before Silas could respond, Philip turned and walked quickly away, back toward the auditorium.

More than the phone call from Franco or the conversation with Katie, this encounter felt the most bizarre to Silas. Philip was the puppet master of the shambles his life had become (*No, that's you.*) and here he was actually apologizing and seeming to offer a modicum of sympathy.

Then again, it made a certain sense considering how events played out. Perhaps Philip had gained some insight into how people could do things out of character that hurt those they cared about the most, including themselves. And how no amount of regret could take it back or change the past.

As Silas walked around the chapel to the parking lot, he thought about Philip's parting statement. *Might be nice to have someone to sit with.* It might, indeed.

So Franco, Katie, even Philip ... they all seemed to have at least some feelings of compassion toward Silas. Why not Kris?

Because Kris was the one closest to you, and therefore the one most devastated by your deception. The one taking it the most personally.

Sitting behind the wheel of his car, Silas let sorrow wash over him. It wasn't self-pity, because this had nothing to do with him. This sorrow was for Kris. He no doubt felt alone and used and like a fool. Silas hated to think that this experience had left such a beautiful young man even less sure of himself and more afraid to trust. First his experience with Brandon telling him he wasn't good enough to be "boyfriend material," and now Silas's elaborate ruse. Kris didn't deserve that.

What he did deserve was a real apology. It wouldn't change anything, and maybe he wouldn't even want to hear it, but he definitely deserved it. And not in the form of text or email, but a face-to-face apology. Maybe not right away, let some more time pass first, but there was a reason step nine of the recovery process was making amends.

And what was Silas if not a recovering liar?

As he drove off campus, he muttered the Serenity Prayer under his breath.

CHAPTER TWENTY-NINE

"Thank you for coming with me," Silas said. "I don't think I'd have had the nerve to come by myself."

Finn offered him a rather pained smile. "You've thanked me about a hundred times, and so for the hundredth time, you're welcome. Of course, my coming with you is an empty gesture if we never actually go in."

The two sat in Silas's car near the back of the parking lot behind McAlister. Fifteen minutes had passed since Silas had first pulled into the spot and killed the engine, and the inside of the car had turned quite frigid without the heater blowing.

"Do you think this is a good idea?" he asked, his breath puffing out like vaporous word bubbles from one of Finn's comic books.

"You were invited, weren't you?"

"Yeah, but as far as I know the rest of the gang doesn't know that. Could be a scene if we bump into them."

"You mean we might have to have to a rumble?" Finn said with a laugh.

"I know I'm being silly, but it is a possibility that worries me."

"Silas, if you are serious about wanting to transfer here, you are going to have to face them sooner or later."

"I just want to be sure I'm ready for it when it happens."

"You're ready," Finn said with finality. "I'm declaring it. Do you believe me?"

Silas held up a hand and tilted it back and forth in a seesaw motion.

"Well, I believe me," Finn said. "So let my confidence carry you through. And if there's any trouble, I'll start stripping while

I sing 'Call Me Maybe' at the top of my lungs as a distraction."

"That would be pretty distracting, for sure."

"So we going in?"

Silas chewed on his lower lip and glanced at the dashboard clock. "Five more minutes."

"The show starts in ten minutes."

"That's the point," Silas said. "I'd rather wait until the last minute. Sort of reduces the risk of anyone seeing me."

"Let me guess, you're the type who peels the Band-Aid off one excruciating hair at a time instead of ripping it straight off, right?"

"What about a compromise? Two more minutes?"

"Fine, I'm nothing if not fair, but we are staying through the whole show. No ducking out early."

"Deal."

They shook on it then Finn took out his phone and began scrolling through TikTok. Silas didn't really understand that app. While he had no account of his own, he'd seen enough of it that it seemed to be comprised mostly of short clips of people dancing lethargically to annoyingly upbeat pop music.

With Finn ignoring him, it felt silly to be sitting in the cold car instead of the warm auditorium. Of course, it had always been silly, Finn was right about that.

"Okay, let's go," Silas said, popping open his door.

Finn smiled and opened his own door. They walked across the parking lot to the front of the McAlister Auditorium. As they reached the bottom of the steps that led up to the ticket window and entrance, Silas spotted Philip approaching from the opposite direction.

"So you made it after all," Philip said.

"You, too, and I guess we both decided to use the same last-minute tactic of non-detection."

"And you brought back-up," Philip said, glancing at Finn.

"Oh, I'm sorry. Finn, Philip. Philip, this is Finn. We go to school together … only *really*."

Philip actually laughed at this. "Since serendipity has us all converging here at the same time, want to sit together?"

Silas hesitated. It still seemed bizarre to have Philip of all people acting friendly toward him, and it left him unbalanced. Finn stepped in and said, "That's cool."

Silas threw him a grateful smile and they all walked up the steps together. At the window, Silas and Finn bought tickets and Philip flashed his student ID. Silas wanted seats near the back, but the show was nearly sold out and the only three they could find together were middle of the house on the far-right side.

They had barely gotten settled before the lights went down, a single spot from above revealing a mic stand and lone stool on the stage. Dr. Wells, a young professor in tasteful brown slacks and a crème blouse, took the stage to a smattering of applause.

"Welcome everybody," she said into the mic, "to Laugh Riot, Furman University's first ever stand-up comedy extravaganza. If tonight's show is a success, who know? This may just become an annual event."

More applause, this time with a bit more enthusiasm and even a few wolf-whistles and catcalls. Dr. Wells continued with the usual preliminaries urging people to silence cell phones and other electronic devices, letting everyone know the locations of the emergency exits. As she went on, Silas found himself scanning the auditorium, searching for signs of Kris or Paige or Shelia. The darkness, however, shrouded the space, turning everyone into silhouettes and shadow-people. He could barely make out the people on his own row, much less those farther away.

The bright side of this, of course, was that if it was impossible to identify them in a crowd, they wouldn't be able to spot him either.

Finn sat to Silas's left, Philip to his right, sandwiching him in. This created a slight sensation of confinement and claustrophobia, making a speedy escape more difficult should the need arise.

Jesus, drama queen much? It's not like an angry mob is coming after you with pitchforks and torches.

Finn glanced over at him and nudged his arm with an elbow. "You doing okay?" he asked in a whisper.

Silas nodded, trying to will himself to relax. He closed his eyes for a moment and took several deep yogi breaths, practicing some meditation techniques he'd read about. It did seem to calm him down, at least a little bit, and when he opened his eyes, he found Philip smiling at him.

"What?" Silas said.

"And I thought I was a nervous wreck. By comparison, I'm on a pretty even keel."

The two laughed, and again Silas marveled at the fact that he was sitting here next to this young man, sharing a certain camaraderie after everything that had passed between them. Not only was it surprising that Philip didn't hate Silas, shouldn't Silas be angrier at Philip? Yet searching deep inside revealed no lasting, lingering animosity. Silas had made his choices, Philip had made his, and now they both were living with the aftermath of those choices. And if Silas wanted the chance to start fresh and reinvent himself, shouldn't he extend that same opportunity to Philip?

On stage, Dr. Wells finished her remarks and introduced the first performer, a freshman named Kelly Fowler.

The set started out shaky, the girl obviously nervous and lacking in confidence. However, after a few of her jokes landed and got laughs, she began to loosen up and deliver her punchlines with more self-assurance. Silas laughed along with the crowd, which helped to loosen him up as well.

The lineup consisted of six students and one professor. Some were better than others, the professor turned out to be surprisingly funny, but no one outright bombed. The final performer of the night was Franco himself. Unlike the others, who got around fifteen minutes each, Franco ended the show with a thirty-minute set. Made sense, this whole project had been his baby so he should be the star.

And not only was his set the longest, it also garnered the most raucous reaction from the audience. Franco was smart in that he tailored his act around Furman life, poking fun at specific professors, the food at the DH, campus housing. His funniest bit had to do with the frat tradition of throwing freshmen pledges into the bacteria-infested lake, crafting a scenario where a student mutated into a deformed, pulsating creature which got revenge on the frat boys who did this to him. It was grotesque, sometimes raunchy, but absolutely hilarious. Listening to his extended bit, Silas realized that though the medium might be different, Franco was also a storyteller.

When Franco ended his set, he received a much-deserved standing ovation. *Standing up for a stand-up,* Silas thought, cheering along with the rest of the crowd as the lights came up in the auditorium. He was so caught up, in fact, he had forgotten his plan to dart out of the place the second the show ended. It wasn't until some others from further down their row asked to get by that he realized people were beginning to file out.

"Shit, let's get out of here," he mumbled, nudging Finn out into the aisle.

The three of them got caught up in a traffic jam near the doors into the lobby as people stopped to chat and catch up and have family reunions or whatever the hell they were doing that prevented Silas from making a quick departure. He cursed under his breath and kept his head down, staring at the scuff marks on his shoes.

After what felt like an hour but was probably no more than five minutes, the trio finally made it into the lobby. Without checking to see if Finn and Philip were keeping up, Silas began winding through the crowd for the exit. Five steps from the door, he heard his name called. The temptation to continue on was strong, but instead he stopped and said hello to Dr. Flem.

"I didn't expect to see you here," the professor said.

Silas shrugged. "Yeah, well, I'm nothing if not unpredictable."

Finn and Philip caught up then, and Philip said, "Hey, Dr. Flem."

The professor blinked, visibly taken aback, looking from Philip to Silas then back to Philip. "Did you two come together?"

"Not exactly," Silas said.

Philip continued, "We sort of bumped into each other and sat together during the show."

"Oh, that's ... nice. Franco was certainly on fire tonight, wasn't he?"

Silas chuckled. "I'll be looking over my shoulder for that mutated pledge all the way to the car."

Dr. Flem nodded, fidgeted a bit, then said, "Anyway, I saw

you and wanted to apologize face-to-face. I know how much you wanted me to write you a letter of recommendation, but I simply didn't think it would be appropriate."

"It was inappropriate of me to even ask," Silas said. "Please, don't worry about it. I got one of my high school teachers to do it, and I sent in my application a couple of days ago."

"The essay he wrote is excellent," Finn added.

Dr. Flem smiled. "I'm glad to hear it, and I wish you all the—"

"What the holy fuck do we have here?"

Silas stiffened. He recognized the voice, but the disdain and fury that dripped from it was unfamiliar to him. In the past, that voice had been lilting and sweet, never so harsh and hard.

"I can't believe you'd dare show your face here," Paige said, stalking up to Silas.

"We just came to see the show," Philip said.

Paige seemed to notice Philip for the first time and her eyes practically bulged out. "And you, too? What is this, a convention of lowlifes?"

"Paige, perhaps this isn't the best time—" Dr. Flem started, but Paige cut him off.

"You stay out of this, Dr. Flem. I'm not exactly excluding you from that convention."

The words visibly stung the professor, and he stammered a moment before saying, "Paige, that isn't fair."

"None of this is fair," Paige said, her voice loud and sharp, causing those around them to stop mid-conversation and turn their way. From the crowd came Kris, Shelia, and Katie, completing a circle of judgment with Paige.

This was it, the confrontation Silas had been dreading for months. What surprised him was that he greeted the moment with a certain degree of ... expectation wasn't exactly the right word, but a sort of eager relief. The worst would now happen, and he would no longer have to imagine in, fear it, have nightmares about it. He could face it, endure it, and put it behind him.

The tension permeated the air like static electricity. Wanting to play the part of peacemaker, Dr. Flem tried to deescalate it, like human fabric softener. "Let's all take a minute before we start talking."

"I've got this," Silas said to the professor. "You go on."

Dr. Flem looked at him with doubt but also a little gratitude. "Are you sure?"

"Positive. I can handle it."

The professor still looked uncertain, but he also looked wounded, and he scurried off. Silas watched him go then turned back to face his accusers. It gave him a small comfort to have Finn and even Philip next to him, but this gauntlet was his alone.

"You're some piece of work, you know that?" Kris said, gaze drilling into Silas. He sounded like a character in some 80s teen flick, and under other circumstances it might have been humorous. But there was nothing funny about this. "You throw all our lives into chaos and then actually show up here tonight like nothing happened. Who does that?"

"I'm not pretending nothing happened," Silas said. "And I didn't come here to cause any further chaos. I wanted to show my support to Franco, that's all."

Kris sneered. "Oh, isn't that sweet? You've got to be the most thoughtful compulsive liar around."

Sheila tugged at Kris's sleeve. "Come on, let's just go. We were having a great night, why ruin it?"

"He's the one who fucking ruined everything!" Paige said. The gentle poet he'd known was gone, burned away by fiery rage. Everyone left in the lobby seemed to have stopped to observe this scene playing out before them. An unexpected second show for the night, this one the tragedy to go with the comedy from earlier.

Next to Silas, Philip took a step back as if in retreat. This attracted Kris's attention, and he seemed about to speak, but then he didn't, as if Philip wasn't worth his time. Instead, his eyes moved over to Finn. "Found someone new already, I see. What did he tell you, that he was a government spy?"

Finn looked around as if unsure he was the one being addressed. "Who, me? I'm a boring, run-of-the-mill breeder, but don't hold that against me. I'm only here for moral support."

Another sneer twisted Kris's normally generous mouth. *"Moral* support. That's a joke. Trust me, there's nothing *moral* about this one."

Silas thought he now had an idea what it felt like in the old days when someone convicted of some shameful crime would be sentence to public humiliation, forced to stand in the town square while the populace pelted him or her with ridicule and recrimination. Although, unlike those criminals of old, no pillory held Silas in place. Only his own sense of justice.

"Guys, it's getting late, and I need to go," Katie said softly then made a hasty exit. Sheila looked after her, as if she wanted to do the same.

"Look," Silas said, "I realize there's nothing I can say, no apology I can offer, that will make any of this better."

"Damn right," Kris said. "So don't waste your breath. The very sight of you makes me feel sick. Did you even think of how it would make me feel seeing you here? Or did you not give me a single thought, just did whatever you wanted to do regardless of how it might impact others? You know, your usual m.o."

"What are you even doing here?" Paige said. "Same goes for you, Philip."

"They're here because I invited them," Franco said, coming through the crowd to join them.

"What?" Kris and Paige exclaimed simultaneously.

"You heard me. I can't simply cut them completely out of my life. I wanted them to be here, so I invited them. Sue me, but it was my decision."

Sheila took Franco's hand and leaned her head against his shoulder, and Silas realized in the months since he'd been separated from the group, the relationship between the two had grown in the direction he'd thought it was headed.

"I can't believe this," Kris said, his face crumpling in misery. "It's like I don't know anybody anymore."

He barreled past Silas and burst through the exit. Paige quickly followed him.

Franco and Sheila remained a moment longer, though neither seemed to have anything to say. Finally, Franco muttered, "Hope you enjoyed the show," and the two of them left as well.

Which left Silas, Finn, and Philip as the center of attention for the curious crowd. Finn suddenly bent at the waist in an elaborate bow and said, "Thank you, folks. We're workshopping our new original one-act play, *College Drama for the Masses.*"

A few uncertain titters rippled through the crowd as the three pushed through the exit and hurried down the steps like a trio of Cinderellas fleeing midnight.

At the bottom of the steps, Philip said, "I should get back to the dorm."

He started to go but Silas reached out and stayed him with a hand to his arm. "I'm really sorry, man. I know that doesn't mean much, but I am truly sorry. For everything. You don't deserve this."

For a few seconds Philip didn't move then he lunged forward so suddenly that at first Silas thought he was going to be attacked. Instead, he was pulled into a brief and loose hug. "I'm sorry, too," Philip said directly into his ear then hurried off toward the main part of campus.

The weight of the night crashed onto Silas, and he began to shake so violently that he worried his legs might not support him. Finn took him by the elbow and led him toward the parking lot. He didn't say anything, perhaps sensing words were not what Silas needed right now.

The inevitable confrontation had finally happened, and it was as bad as Silas had suspected it would be. He had thought he would feel better getting it over with. And he did.

But only a little.

CHAPTER THIRTY

Silas lay in bed, covers pulled up around him. He stretched out on his side, head propped up on one hand, staring blankly at the laptop open next to him. A succession of live Kelly Clarkson performances played. Sometimes he sang along with a few snatches of lyrics, other times he was barely aware of the music. Mostly, he had his brain shut off and unplugged, receiving no signals or stimuli. A closed circuit.

He responded slowly to the knock at his bedroom door, pausing Kelly in the middle of a rousing rendition of "Whole Lotta Woman" and mumbling, "Come in."

His father opened the door a crack and stuck his head through the gap. "I'm about to head out. Got some errands to run before I head in to the store."

"Have a good day. I'm really glad you're back to full time."

"Me too, buddy."

Silas started the video back but after another run of the chorus realized his father hadn't left. Pausing the video again, he said, "You need something?"

"You doing anything with Finn later?" his father asked.

"No, not today."

"Gonna go out to Mr. K's maybe, finally use that gift card?"

"I don't think so."

Still his father remained in place. Silas didn't have the energy to do anything but wait him out. Finally, his father walked fully into the room and said, "You doing okay, son?"

"Yeah, why?"

"It's nearly noon and other than a trip to the bathroom and to the kitchen for a bowl of cereal, you haven't left that bed."

Silas shrugged though he wasn't sure if the gesture translated from beneath the covers. "It's Saturday. We're all entitled to a do-nothing, recuperation day now and then, aren't we?"

His father bent over the bed and kissed him on the temple in a way he hadn't done since Silas was a small boy. "I know you're under a lot of stress right now, and I worry about you. It's a father's prerogative."

"I appreciate that, Dad. And you're right, the stress has been kind of wearing me out. That's why I'm resting today. I need to chill and decompress."

"Fair enough. I'm off at eight tonight. How about I bring us home a pizza?"

"Sounds good," Silas said then patted the bed. "You know where I'll be."

His father laughed, though his eyes remained slightly squinted with worry. He kissed Silas on the top of the head this time then left the room. Silas listened to the front door open and close then his father's pickup roar to life and pull off, spitting gravel.

Silas closed the laptop, the videos still too much mental stimulation, and rolled over to face the wall. He wished he could completely disconnect, like taking a computer offline, but try as he might, he couldn't completely stop the loop of thoughts that ran through his head like the news ticker at the bottom of the screen on CNN. His strategy was to simply not look directly at the ticker, letting it fade into the background.

Picking a spot on the wall high up near the ceiling, a place where the faded wallpaper had ripped off when he'd pulled down a Jonas Brothers poster after he'd outgrown that musical phase and concentrated on it until the whole world seemed to be encompassed in that one small spot, nothing existed but that rip. Though he hadn't felt particularly tired before, he started to drift off and let himself surrender to it. However, on the very cusp of sleep, the buzzing of his phone snapped him back to consciousness like a splash of cold water to his face.

Silas burrowed deeper into the covers, determined to ignore the phone. It could only be one of a few people, and they could all wait twenty-four hours. Mostly likely it was Finn, and he would understand Silas's need to take a mental health day. The

day after the comedy show last week, he had received a couple
of texts from Franco, apologizing for how things turned out and
that he had never intended for such an outcome but thanking
Silas for coming. There had been nothing from Franco since
then.

On the other hand, Silas and Philip had been texting a
great deal over the past week, even joking together about their
position as outcasts and continuing the "nothing worse" game.
They had moved beyond mere cautious friendliness and seemed
to be becoming actual friends. Certainly, more than they had
been as part of the larger group. Now that they'd both been
ostracized and all secrets had been revealed, they really knew
each other and were discovering they had much in common.

The phone continued to buzz, not continuously but in
rapid-fire succession, suggesting a cascade of texts coming in.
Annoyed, Silas grabbed the phone to turn it off, but when he
saw who the messages were from, he snapped up to a sitting
position so fast he nearly knocked the laptop out of the bed.

Gus. A string of texts from Gus. Actually, one text so long
that it came through as several. As usual when that happened,
they came in out of order—1/6, 5/6, then 3/6, 4/6, 6/6, and finally
2/6—and Silas had to piece them together like a puzzle to read
them.

With shaking hands, Silas tried to hold the phone steady
as he reassembled the pieces into a coherent, if misspelled and
garbled, message.

*"Your probly surprised to hear frm me Im frankly surprised to be
messging u but I have something to say Katie told me wht happned
at the standup show. shes actually told me alot lately talking to me
abut how I can be how I can intimdate people even if I dont mean to
how I can com cross lie a snob or someting. Shes right I now that its
overcompnsation on my part. She sems to think part of the reson you
did what u did is cuz u were afrad u wouldnt be excepted and that I
may hve contributd to u feeling that way. I didnt wanna hear that at
frst but now I think she culd be rite. Kris tol me u mentioned me makng
a crak abut tech schools the first time we meet I honstly dont remember
that but it sonds like something I wuld say. If im being real then yeh
I can see how that mght make you fel u had to lie I dont know why u*

kept lyng thugh but Katie says I cant relly understand what its like for u and her feelng like outsiders in our lil group. So I want u to know that im not mad at u and I forgive u. that doesn't mean were friends agan cuz were not even though I fogive u doesnt men I want u as part of my life I cant do that. But im not mad at u anymor and I dont hate u or anything hope that can be enuf for u. u dont have to respond to this messge I wuld rather u didnt"

Silas had to blink several times to clear the tears from his eyes so he could finish reading the message. Despite the final request, his thumb hovered for a moment, itching to write some kind of response, but in the end he turned the phone off and lay back down, finding the spot on the wall again. It provided him no comfort now.

With a grunt, he sat up again and grabbed his laptop. He hadn't done much writing since December but creating stories had always been the easiest way for him to channel anxiety and frustration and fear. He'd been seeking escape and overlooking his most trusted escape route.

He opened a blank Word document and started typing, giving almost no thought to what story he wanted to tell. He started with an all-too-familiar premise, someone lying to their closest friends, and let the story flow through him. What he ended up writing bore only superficial similarities to his own plight, but a part of his brain recognized this was still his way of dealing with his own dilemma. He tried not to focus on that too much, however, lest it destroy the delicate magic.

Silas spent the next two hours writing an entire twenty-five-page story he entitled "The Smallness of Lies," and in doing so he succeeded in both facing his problems and escaping them at the same time.

Magic, indeed.

CHAPTER THIRTY-ONE

Silas found it a bit odd being back in the Village Grind after so long. This had been the first place he'd ever spent time alone with Kris, the site of their first sort-of-kind-of date. These associations made the coffee shop bittersweet for him, like coffee itself. Although in time he hoped the sweetness would become more prominent, right now it was the bitterness that overwhelmed him.

Of course, he didn't want to tell Philip that, so he hadn't objected when the young man suggested they meet there for drinks.

"Wonder if Katie's working today?" Silas said, sipping his frappe and looking around.

Philip, the steam from his coffee rising up like smoke in front of his face, shook his head. "She doesn't work here anymore."

"What happened?"

"She decided she wanted to focus solely on school this semester. She got into Furman for fall, you know."

Silas had just taken a sip and began to cough and sputter. "She did? Do you know what date she sent in her application?"

"No clue. Guess you still haven't heard anything, huh?"

"No," Silas said, staring at the rain trickling down the plate-glass window in rivulets. "But I keep reminding myself that there's nothing I can do to affect the outcome. Que sera sera."

"What is that, a drag queen on the RuPaul show?"

Silas sputtered again, this time with a laugh. "No, I think it means 'what will be will be.' That's what I tell myself over and over."

"Does it help?"

"Not one damn bit."

"Well, if it means anything I'm rooting for you. Would be nice to have a friend on campus again."

"Everybody still giving you the silent treatment?"

"Gus has sent me a few texts from Washington, actually," Philip said. "I think Katie's been a help on that front. I run into Franco and Shelia from time to time, and they're always nice and polite, but we don't hang or anything. They're in that early stage of their relationship when they pretty much only have time for each other."

I remember what that was like, Silas thought but said, "Paige and Kris?"

Philip took a drink then grimaced as if the cream in his coffee had soured. "Paige is still pretty furious. She's started hanging almost exclusively with the lit mag crowd these days. I can only imagine the kind of angry poetry she reads about us at those Hub City open mic nights."

"I shudder to think. And Kris...?"

Philip cupped his coffee mug as if drawing in its heat, despite the fact that vents pushing out hot air kept the interior of the Village Grind practically tropical despite the drizzly coldness outside. "At first he would literally turn and walk the other way if he saw me on campus. Like I was diseased, and he didn't want to catch it."

Silas waited out the following pause, because he knew the story wasn't done yet.

Philip picked up a couple of sugar packets, shook them then put them back without adding them to his coffee. Obvious stalling technique, though not particularly effective. Finally, he met Silas's eyes and said, "We've talked a few times lately. Nothing too heavy, and he's still obviously a little edgy around me. He did say that while he's still pissed about how I handled the situation, he believes my heart was in the right place."

"What does he say about me?" Silas asked, not sure he really wanted to know the answer.

"He doesn't really talk about you. He talks *around* you without specifically mentioning you. In fact,... "

"What? Tell me, I can take it."

"Well," Philip said, "one of the conditions of our tentatively talking again is that I'm not supposed to bring you up and I'm never allowed to say your name."

"Ouch!" Silas tried to keep his voice light, but that hurt. As if Kris wanted to erase Silas from existence.

Philip took his spoon and beat it lightly against the side of his mug, creating a musical sound that rapidly became annoying with repetition. "I doubt we'll ever be real friends again. I think I'm too much of a reminder to him of you."

"Ouch again. By all means, don't pull any punches."

Putting down the spoon, Philip fixed him with a serious gaze. "Don't worry, I won't."

Silas nodded, wondering if he and Philip could ever be real friends again because they each reminded the other of Kris. If there was a way, it had to start with honesty, the brutal kind. "Good, you shouldn't."

"What do you say we change the subject?" Philip said.

"Fine by me."

"So, where's that Finn guy? Think he'd want to meet up with us today?"

Something about the way Philip asked the question made it sound not-so-casual, and his sudden fidgetiness made Silas suspicious. "You know Finn is straight, right?"

"Yeah, I know," Philip said with a nervous giggle. "Doesn't mean I can't think he's cute. Nothing wrong with a doomed crush."

"I've had my share of those. To doomed crushes."

They both held up their mugs and clinked them together like wine glasses in a toast.

Behind Silas, the bell above the door jangled as someone entered the coffee shop. He saw Philip's eyes get wide, and Silas glanced over his shoulder and froze.

Just inside the doorway, Franco and Shelia stood, equally frozen, staring back as the umbrellas they carried dripped onto the floor. This lasted for several seconds that stretched out into whole universes of time, and then Shelia said to Franco, "Go get us some drinks. You know what I want. I'll be sitting over here with these two losers."

Franco looked at her for a moment, as if trying to gage if she was being serious, then he allowed himself a smile and hurried off to the counter.

Shelia grabbed two chairs from an empty table nearby and dragged them over to Silas and Philip, crowding them in on one side of the table. After settling into the chair closest to Philip, she looked from one to the other and her lips slid into that familiar smirk. Oh God, how Silas had missed that smirk.

"Do you guys mind if we join you?" she asked. "I mean, if you do, too late because I've already made myself at home."

Silas and Philip shared a bemused smile then Silas said, "By all means. Pull up a chair and stay a while."

"I pulled up two, actually."

When Franco returned with the drinks, he sat next to Shelia and said, "So what are we talking about?"

"I was merely butting in where I wasn't invited and making myself at home," Shelia said.

Franco laughed then leaned over to kiss her on the cheek. "That's what you do best."

"Still in the honeymoon phase, I see," Philip said.

"I'm the aloof sun around which Franco's attentive planet revolves," Shelia said, but the affection in her eyes when she looked at Franco was clear.

Franco downed half his chai latte in one chug. "Okay, so either of you two read *From the Dust Returned* by Bradbury?"

Silas raised a hand.

"Told you," Shelia said, bumping Franco with her shoulder. "Silas was sure to have read it."

Franco nodded. "I never disagreed. Anyway, we've started up the little book club thing again. Just me and Shelia. Gus said he'd try to read along but he's pretty busy up in the Capital and all. You two want to join in? We're only two chapters along, so would be easy to catch up with us."

"Sure thing," Philip said, a grin spreading across his face so wide Silas mused the corners of his lips might meet in the back of his head. "I'll see if they've got a copy at the lib."

"Yeah, I'm game," Silas said. "It's been a long while since I read the book, so it's probably due for a reread."

Shelia started talking about how she wanted to change

her major to Asian studies, but it would mean postponing her graduation and continuing on at Furman, and Silas marveled at how natural this felt. The camaraderie, they slipped back into it as if there had been no break in it at all.

Of course, Silas was aware that the one person he most wanted to feel this with was not here, but he tried not to dwell and simply enjoy the moment.

CHAPTER THIRTY-TWO

Silas stretched out in the tub. Or at least he did to the best of his ability considering the cramped nature of the trailer's bathtub. He had to bend his legs more than was altogether comfortable, and the width allowed for precious little elbow room. This was why he rarely took baths, but sometimes nothing relaxed him quite as much as a warm soak with a good book.

Despite the narrow dimensions of the tub, it felt good to submerge his body in the warm water, steam rising to cloud over the medicine cabinet mirror with a streaky film. He held the book high enough to avoid any splashing as he read.

Silas had first read *From the Dust Returned* maybe three years ago, and he had forgotten how delightfully charming the Elliot family, comprised of monsters and witches and ghosts, truly were. Like many of Bradbury's other novels, this one was really an interconnected series of short stories, and Silas devoured them hungrily, like delicious Halloween candies.

The combination of Bradbury's lyrical prose and the almost sensual undulations of the water had the desired effect of relaxing Silas and melting away the stress that had built up in his body. He imagined this would be the same result of a deep tissue massage, though he'd never had one. This was the poor man's equivalent, a luxury both simple and profound.

After fifteen minutes, he began to drowse, his eyelids pausing more and more on the downswing of each blink. When the book drooped toward the water for the third time, Silas snapping to attention just in time to avoid a literary dunking, he closed the book and reached over to place it on top of the closed toilet lid. Then he allowed himself to sink down further into the water. This necessitated a further bending of the knees and his neck bending at an awkward angle, but these minor discomforts did not prevent him from drifting into that NetherRealm between conscious and unconscious. His thoughts stretched like hot cheese on a pizza, taking on the rounded edges of dream, but he remained at least peripherally cognizant of his body and the tub around him. The sensation was akin to floating, and he allowed himself to be carried away on the current.

A knocking at the bathroom door roused him sometime later. He wasn't sure how long he had hovered on the border between sleep and wakefulness, but it had been long enough for the water in the tub to turn cold and he shivered as he called out, "Yeah?"

"Just checking that you're okay," his father said. "You've been in there over an hour."

Silas gripped the side of the tub and pulled himself up out of the water. "Getting out now. Thanks, Dad."

His father's footsteps clomped back down the hall toward the living room, and Silas grabbed the towel from the rod above the sink as he stepped out onto the threadbare bathmat. After toweling off, he took the bathrobe from the hook on the back of the door and shrugged into it. He brushed his teeth and gargled with the cheap mouthwash his father bought that tasted like he imagined battery acid would then retrieved Bradbury from the toilet lid.

Sticking his head in the living room, he said, "Dad, I'm going to do a little studying and then turn in."

His father answered without looking away from the TV. "It's not even nine o'clock on a Friday night."

"I'm going to Asheville with Finn tomorrow, and Philip is joining us for a movie on Sunday. So I'm getting my studying in tonight. See, I'm not the egghead you fear I am."

The flicker of the TV cast a ghostly glow over his father's face as he turned with a smile. "You're making sure you have your school work done before having any fun. I'd say there's still a bit of egghead in you."

Silas walked over and bent to give his father a quick hug. "Good night. See you in the morning."

"Sleep well, buddy."

Back in his room, Silas changed into the sweats he used as pajamas in the winter then settled in at his desk. One big upside to no longer leading a double life was that he had a lot more time for his studies. His phone sat on the edge of the desk, plugged up and charging. Glancing at the screen, he saw he had a missed call and a voicemail waiting.

Opening the call log, he actually pushed back the chair and rose to his feet in a dramatic gesture right out of a movie when he saw the missed call had come from Kris. Half an hour ago, while Silas had been dozing in the tub.

The voicemail was over five minutes long, and Silas felt torn. Part of him wanted to listen to it if for no other reason than to hear Kris's voice again, but another part of him wanted to delete it unheard because he could imagine the things Kris had to say and none of them were pleasant.

Silas paced around the room for a few minutes, sat back at the desk, got back up and paced some more. He played different scenarios through his mind then rated them on probability.

Scenario 1: Kris had decided to forgive him everything and wanted them to resume their relationship where they'd left off. Rating: highly unlikely.

Scenario 2: Kris had been so traumatized by the experience that he'd dropped out of school and joined the merchant marines (if such a thing still existed) and was shipping out tomorrow morning. Rating: less likely, but still more likely than scenario 1.

Scenario 3: Kris's sense of anger and righteous indignation had grown to the point that he could no longer contain it and he felt he had to unleash it on Silas. Rating: *ding ding ding* we have a winner!

Silas finally sat on the bed, legs folded beneath him, and with shaky hands hit Play on the voicemail, pressing the phone tightly against his ear. A few seconds of silence rolled out, and when Kris began to speak, the slurred nature of his words indicated he was drunk. Not tipsy, not buzzed, but sloppy drunk. Some of his words were garbled and hard to understand, and Silas had to listen to the message three times to get it all.

"I didn't mean to call you. I mean, obviously I *meant* to call. This isn't a butt dial or anything. I guess what I mean is I don't know why I'm calling. I shouldn't be calling. I promised myself I'd never talk to you again. I've been trying not to even think about you though obviously I'm having fuck-all success with that one. I thought getting plastered would take my mind off you, but instead it just knocked my guard down or something because you're the only thing on my mind tonight. I know that Franco and Shelia are still spending time with you, and even Philip, too. Part of me is mad at them for crossing enemy lines or whatever, but another part of me is glad to know you have people there for you. That's the thing that's got me so twisted in the head. I am so beyond pissed at you, and yet I still worry about you. And then I get pissed at myself for worrying about you. I should hate you, and I sorta do. And I sorta don't. When I heard your voice on your outgoing voicemail message, it felt like a homecoming or something, but then I reminded myself that you've done horrible things. Then this little voice inside reminds me about Andy. You know that I've done horrible things, things I can't ever take back but which I don't want to define me the rest of my life. Maybe you're feeling the same way."

Kris stopped talking and silence played out for almost a full minute. During his first listen, Silas began to think the rest of the message would be taken up with only the sound of Kris's breathing, but then he continued, his next words wrapping fingers around Silas's heart and squeezing.

"I guess I still love you. I *know* I do. I don't want to, and I keep telling myself to stop, but you can't really talk yourself out of these things. That doesn't mean I forgive you, because I don't. And I'm not sure I ever can. Maybe that makes me some kind of hypocrite, and if so then I'm just gonna have to own that. It's how I feel."

Another pause. This one much shorter, only half a minute.

"I understand that you didn't do any of this maliciously. Oh, at first I thought you did, that your intent all along was just to fuck with my emotions for some sadistic reason, but I don't believe that anymore. I think it was an unfortunate series of mistakes and misunderstandings that snowballed out of control, like you said the night you came clean to me. Of course, things didn't get to that point independent of nothing. You're the one who let it get out of control. You could've stopped it, but you didn't. I know you had reasons that probably seemed like good ones at the time but doesn't change anything. We can't go back."

A final pause, this one also around half a minute.

"I do appreciate that you haven't been blowing up my phone and email, trying to get me to talk to you. I needed time to really work things out on my own, and you seemed to know and respect that. It's so *you*. Anyway, guess that's all I have to say. Just wanted you to know that I do still love you and part of me always will, but I can't see any way to forgive and forget. Bye, Silas. I wish that—"

Another ten seconds of silence then the message ended without Kris finishing that final thought.

Silas's heart trip-hammered in his chest and his breath came in hitching gasps, as if he were running a marathon and not sitting motionless on his bed. He considered listening to the message a fourth time but resisted. If he allowed himself, he'd do nothing but replay the message over and over until he grew old and frail right here in this room. Reliving the moment and not wanting to move on beyond it to see what the future held. A modern-day Miss Havisham.

But no, there would be no moldering wedding dress for Silas. The question was how would he move on from this moment, what path into the future would he take? His fingers itched to call Kris back, actually talk with the young man.

However, he recognized that might not be the best course of action. Right now, Kris was on the far side of inebriation, therefore limiting the possibility of any kind of meaningful discussion. Besides, even if they did manage to hold a conversation, would Kris even remember any of it tomorrow morning?

Still, Silas felt the need to reach out in some way, to acknowledge Kris's gesture and respond to it. Of course, what kind of response could he give that wouldn't come out in a rambling, incoherent way. For someone who loved language, when it came to speaking, he often found himself tongue-tied while his thoughts fled from him.

With a burst of inspiration, Silas hurried to his desk and

got on his laptop. He only seemed to really have a command of language when it was written down. The process of sitting at the computer, his fingers cascading on the keys, helped him pull his thoughts together into a cohesive structure. So an email, that would do nicely.

He pulled up his Gmail account and entered Kris's Furman address. For a moment, Silas pondered how lucky he was that his lack of a Furman email hadn't given him away sooner, but it seemed college students used their email for school work only. Communication happened via text or social media these days. An advancing technological world that not only made it easier for people to stay in touch but also made it easier to lie about who you really are.

Shaking his head to dislodge this digressive train of thought, Silas began to type. He didn't think too much about what he was going to say, just as he never outlined his stories. He simply let it flow instinctually. The email came out in a glut, a block of text with no paragraphs, a stream-of-consciousness epistle that came from his gut and not his brain.

I got your message. I know it couldn't have been easy for you to call, no doubt why you needed so much liquid courage to do it. I want to start off by assuring you that I'm not expecting anything and I'm not asking for anything. But I do want to thank you and let you know that what you said meant something to me. And I love you, too. If you believe nothing else I've ever told you, I hope you know that how I feel about you is real, was never a put-on or an act. I'm not going to make excuses for myself or try to justify what I've done, because there is no excuse or justification. I was wrong, period. I don't know if Philip mentioned to you, but I have applied as a transfer student to Furman. I haven't heard back, but I'm keeping my fingers crossed. In fact, I think I'll attach the essay I wrote to go with the application because it might be something you'd be interested in. No pressure. Anyway, if I do get in and we're on the same campus next semester, I don't want you to be afraid that I'll be following you around, harassing you, trying to get you to change your mind about us. Essentially I'm going to let you lead. If you want to talk to me, that will be great. If you don't, I'll respect that. Much as it kills me, I have to accept that I've ruined any chance of us being together as a couple and that's something I'll have to learn to live with. I don't expect your forgiveness because frankly I don't deserve it. However, I'd be lying if I didn't say that I hope beyond reason that someday we can at least be friends again, but I won't push it. Regardless of what happens between us, whether or not we ever even talk again, just know you are a special man and I wish you all the happiness in the world.

Silas read back over the email, considered making some changes but ultimately decided to leave it as it was. Raw and unpolished, but also unfiltered and infused with a certain unvarnished truth. He almost hit SEND but remembered he'd promised to attach the essay from his Furman application. The only other people he'd let read it were his father and Finn, but he was proud of it. Like the email itself, it was raw and unpolished but also unfiltered and true. Out of all the possible topics, "Tell us how important the concept of honesty is to you" had instantly inspired him.

Clicking on the paperclip icon, Silas quickly located the file on his computer, attached the essay, and sent the email before he could second guess himself.

I'm a liar.

I know most people are to at least some degree. If a man's wife asks if she looks fat in these pants, most men are going to say no even if she does. You don't want to tell your grandmother to her face that you hate the homemade cookies she's always making for you. And let's not even get into the whole "size doesn't matter" thing.

So yes, in a way we're all liars, but I'm a liar on a much grander scale. I'm not talking little white lies, but big dirty slimy ones.

I pretended to be someone I'm not. Literally. Not like I pretended to enjoy classical movies when they really bore me to tears or that I think Thomas Pynchon is a great writer when I actually can't make heads or tails of what he's talking about in his novels. No, I told people close to me, people I love, that I was a Furman student when I really go to Greenville Tech.

If I had to guess, I'd say this confession is probably a first in one of these admission essays. At the very least, at this point I'd guess I have your full attention.

I don't think of myself as a bad person, not even now, but I am a liar. It started out feeling small and inconsequential, but the speed at which it escalated into a full-blown disaster has left me breathless. And the inevitable collapse of the lie, leaving my life in a bit of a ruin, has taught me something about honesty. A very valuable lesson.

And what I've learned is that honesty is the most important thing, and it's an all-or-nothing proposition. There is no such thing as a little white lie or a harmless lie. All lies hurt. Half-truths and lies of omission are not any better or less damaging. Small lies lead inexorably to bigger lies and those to even bigger lies, the way that streams lead to rivers and rivers to oceans. I've used the phrase, "it snowballed out of control," and yet what that ignores is that if you never make the snowball and start it rolling in the first place, it has no chance to grow.

So am I saying that you should tell your wife those pants make her look fat or your grandmother that her cookies taste like ass? Well, there are better and more tactful ways to get those points across, but essentially yes, the goal should always be honesty. Because once you start down the road of dishonesty, however slight it seems at the time, you quickly learn there are few off-ramps from that road. And it's a road that leads nowhere good.

So you ask how important the concept of honesty is to me. Extremely important, in a way it can only be to someone who has been a horrible liar in the past and seen the devastating consequences.

And that's the truth.

CHAPTER THIRTY-THREE

Silas rolled the dice, getting a five and a six. He moved his game piece, an open book, eleven spaces, landing on Timmons Arena, one of the yellow properties.

"I own that one," Finn said smugly, sifting through his impressive stack of cards to locate the correct one. "Let's see, with three dorms that means you owe me four hundred and fifty."

Silas handed him a five hundred and got a fifty back, placing it with his rapidly dwindling cash reserves. "Jesus, I'm almost broke."

Finn fanned himself with some of his game money, batting his eyes like a Southern belle. "You don't own any of the prime properties, not my fault."

Philip rolled next, moving his bell tower piece to one of the Campus Mail spaces. He drew a card and read it out loud. "'Your alarm didn't go off. Roll again and move back the number shown on the dice.'" He rolled again, landing double sixes. "Of course, now I roll doubles," he said though he was smiling. He moved his piece back, landing on the Parking Ticket space. He doled out seventy-five bucks to the Study Away fund.

The three of them sat on the floor in Silas's living room, spaced around the coffee table on which the board game had been set up. Philip had supplied the game, Furmanopoly, which was a version of Monopoly but with Furman landmarks replacing the properties from the original Parker Brothers game.

Taking the dice, Finn asked Philip, "When did you get this game?"

"First week I was on campus. Saw it in the bookstore and thought it was so cool."

"Then how come it was still in the plastic wrapping when you brought it over?"

"Only after I shelled out the thirty bucks did I discover that no one else at Furman thought it was cool. Apparently, the idea of playing this game is actually kind of geeky. This is the first chance I've ever had to play it."

"I think it's cool," Silas said. "Even if I am down to my last couple hundred dollars. Hell, it may be the closest I ever get to actually attending Furman. I'm convinced at this point that they found my application so laughable that they aren't even going to bother wasting paper with a rejection."

"You'll hear from them," Finn said, rolling and advancing his Paladin piece to the Study Away space, collecting the stack of bills that had collected there. "Even if they think you suck, they'll at least send you a letter to tell you so."

Silas punched him lightly on the shoulder. "You're so comforting, you know that?"

"I try."

Silas reached for the dice, but Finn snapped them up first. "I rolled doubles. I get to go again."

"You have the golden touch," Philip said with the kind of smile he used to reserve for Kris. Finn seemed aware of Philip's crush, and he handled it admirably, indulging it without encouraging it.

Finn rolled a one and a two, moving three spaces to the Rose Garden which he already owned. "Speaking of that golden touch, I'm almost finished with my adaption of 'The Smallness of Lies' and I think it's our best collaboration yet."

"I can't wait to see it," Silas said. "I still think it's a weird one for you to want to make into a comic."

"What's so weird about it? The story has a real Richard Matheson quality to it."

Silas could concede that point. "The Smallness of Lies" tells the story of a compulsive liar who begins to shrink a quarter of an inch for every lie he tells. Once he realizes what is happening, he tries to give up lying but finds he can't, that it has become such second nature that he does it without even thinking. He eventually lies himself into microscopic oblivion, the final lie that does him in for good being, "I don't deserve this."

"It's a great story," Philip said. Silas had let him read it only the day before. "You should let Franco and Shelia take a look at it, too. I think they'd dig it."

Silas shrugged. "I don't know. Maybe."

He hadn't actually seen Franco or Shelia since the Village Grind a week and a half ago, but a group text had been created in which they, Silas, and Philip discussed *From the Dust Returned*. Discussion on that particular book was starting to wane, and now Silas thought maybe he'd suggest they read *The Incredible Shrinking Man* by Matheson, which would be the perfect segue into asking them if they wanted to read his own story of impossible shrinkage.

Silas rolled and moved to another Campus Mail space. Drawing the top card, he sighed with relief before reading it to the others. "Social Probation. Go Home. Do not pass GO DINS. Do not collect 200 dollars."

Home was this game's version of Jail, which was a comparison not likely to please most parents, and Silas was more than happy to move his piece there where he wouldn't have to shell out money for at least the next three turns.

"You guys want to go to Barista Alley later?" Finn asked. "We can have ridiculously overpriced drinks and make fun of all the hipsters with their lumberjack beards."

"Yeah, especially the women," Silas added, and they all laughed.

"Sorry, I need to head out in an hour or so," Philip said as he grabbed the dice. "I have plans later with ... um, a friend."

The evasiveness told Silas that Philip's plans were with Kris, and he was trying to be sensitive. Silas wasn't sure if Philip knew about Kris's drunken message and Silas's follow-up email or not. Silas hadn't mentioned it to the young man, but had Kris?

A week had passed since that night, and until this morning Silas had received no reply to his email. And the one he got this morning had consisted of only six words. "Friends someday? Possibly, but no promises."

Silas hadn't responded to that, nor would he. Any further moves would have to be made by Kris. And if no moves were made then Silas would have to accept that with good grace. Hard as that might be.

From outside, the sound of crunching gravel and the familiar growl of his father's pickup caught Silas's attention and made him glance toward the kitchen and the clock above the refrigerator.

"Damn, we've been playing this game for almost three hours," he said. "It's like a black hole of time suckage."

His father's footsteps clomped up the front steps with urgency and then he burst through the door. The door actually careened into the wall with such force that Silas worried the knob might punch a hole in the thin plaster. His father stood there, actually panting, his eyes wide and unfocused until they landed on Silas. Worry about the wall dissipated and transformed into worry for his father. Had something terrible happened? Had he been fired from the hardware store?

"Dad, what's wrong?"

His father held up a hand, in which he clutched the day's mail. "It's here, buddy."

Even though his father played a version of the pronoun game, Silas didn't have to ask for further clarification; he instantly knew what the "it" was to which his father referred. He stood abruptly, banging the coffee table with his knee but not feeling the pain, and took the envelope his father gave him. From the Furman University Admissions Office. He'd always heard a fat envelope meant acceptance and a skinny one meant rejection, but he didn't know if that had any merit to it or was just an urban legend.

In the movies, kids who got their college letters never had the nerve to open them and always asked someone else to do it, but this was no movie and Silas ripped right into the envelope and pulled out the letter. He read it over once then a second time.

"Well?" Philip said.

"What's it say?" Finn asked.

Silas released a breath he hadn't even realized he'd been holding and read the letter aloud.

FALL 2019

CHAPTER THIRTY-FOUR

As Silas left his final class for the day, relief shuddered through him at having made it through his first full day of the new semester. He'd been ridiculously nervous headed in this morning, feeling almost as if he were starting his freshman year all over again. But as the day wore on, the nerves settled and he began to feel more comfortable. At home, even.

He made his way down the stairs to the ground floor, another student in the herd, blending in. It occurred to him that he could really put the debacle of last year behind him and start fresh. He belonged here.

As he walked out of the building, he smiled to see a familiar face waiting for him.

"What are you doing on this side of campus?" Silas asked. "I thought you had one more class today."

Finn shrugged. "Yeah, but it doesn't start for a few. Thought I'd check up on you, see how it feels to still be stuck here at Tech with me."

Silas rolled his eyes. "I've told you a million times, I'm fine."

"And I'm still not sure if I believe it."

"Look, I wanted to see if I could get into Furman so that I wouldn't spend the rest of my life not knowing. Now I know. I won't lie and say it wasn't disappointing, but the important thing is that it wasn't crushing. It is what it is."

"Que sera sera?"

"Exactly," Silas said with a laugh. "Besides, there's nothing wrong with Tech. It's a good education, and when I'm done maybe I can get into USC Upstate. They have a decent creative writing curriculum, and the author Brock Adams even teaches there."

"Never heard of him."

"I'll lend you his book *Ember.* Some pretty cool post-apocalyptic shit that takes place around Asheville."

"Oh, speaking of Asheville," Finn said, digging into his pants pocket and pulling out a bundle of cash. "This is your half of our latest haul from the comics."

Silas counted it out, impressed. "This is the most we've ever gotten in a month."

"Yeah, 'The Smallness of Lies' is proving pretty popular. They asked me for some more copies."

"Cool," Silas said then glanced at his phone as a text came through. "I gotta go. Philip is waiting for me in the student lot."

"Rubbing it in that you're done for the day, and I still have another lecture to sit through? I see how you wanna be. What do you guys have planned?"

"I don't know, he texted this morning and asked what time I would be done because he had a surprise for me. Said he'd meet me at my car."

"A surprise, huh? Intriguing. If he wasn't dating that Music major now then I'd say he was going to ask you out in some over-the-top promposal way."

"You're just jealous that he isn't fawning over you anymore," Silas said.

Finn nodded. "Guilty. I admit, it was nice to be the object of someone's affections for a while. Happens so rarely."

"Well, I love you, only not in *that way.*"

"That's only because you've never seen me naked."

"Thank God for small favors, otherwise I might have turned straight."

"Hey, trust me when I say that my favors aren't *small.*"

They laughed then started walking together, Finn's last class being on the way to the student lot.

"Heard anything from Kris?" Finn asked hesitantly, realizing it was still a delicate subject.

"Not for a few weeks."

"Probably been really busy, getting moved back here and everything."

"I'm sure you're right."

Over the summer, Kris had begun texting Silas from Texas. Simple, innocuous stuff like "How ya doing?" and "Did you see the Elton John biopic Rocketman?" The text conversations happened about once every other week or so, nothing consistent and nothing all that personal, but it was something. An olive branch. Silas had even started watching *Buffy the Vampire Slayer* on the off chance he'd get the opportunity to impress Kris with his new-found knowledge of the show if it ever came up. Which so far it hadn't.

But radio silence lately, no texts at all since Kris had come back to Greenville for his junior year at Furman. Silas remained firm on his decision not to initiate contact but instead to let Kris always be the one to reach out, but it was a hard resolve to keep.

"Here's where I get off," Finn said as they approached the McMahand Building. "You call me later and let me know what the surprise turned out to be. If it's roses and a serenade, I want to be able to say I told you so."

Silas waved him away. "Get to class, goofball. I'll call you."

After Finn went into the building, Silas shot a quick text back to Philip. "On my way. Why the cloak and dagger bit? What's the big surprise?"

The reply came quickly: "You'll see when you get here. I think you're going to like it."

Silas stuffed the cell back in his pocket and continued toward the lot. Honestly, it was enough of a surprise for him that Philip wanted to hang out at all. He'd not been as available since he started dating Blake last spring. Silas was happy that Philip had found someone, even if Blake did seem a bit pretentious the way only Music majors could, but it would be nice to spend some one-on-one time together. The last remnants of the old gang.

Franco and Shelia were still going strong, Shelia having stayed on at Furman to pursue her Asian Studies degree (at least until she switched majors again), but neither Silas nor Philip heard much from them anymore. The book club had even fizzled out over the summer. Gus and Paige had both graduated, of course. Katie heard from Gus on occasion, reporting he was getting settled at Georgetown, starting the law program there.

Paige had dropped out of the group altogether, and no one had any updates on her since graduation.

Sometimes Silas felt a little like that woman who married John Lennon, the one that everyone blamed for breaking up the Beatles. Of course, that was bullshit. A million different factors probably combined to cause that breakup, a new love interest being only a single one. Same with Silas. He was a contributing factor, but life was full of contributing factors. You learned from them and moved on. Which was what everyone in the group was doing. Some moving on together, and others apart. Such was life.

Silas had become so engrossed in his own thoughts that he made it halfway across the parking lot before realizing that the familiar figure leaning against his Nissan wasn't Philip. Silas's footsteps faltered then quickened. He felt a swelling in his chest, as if his heart had become a balloon expanding with helium. In a moment, it would lift him right off his feet and he'd glide across the pavement without actually touching it.

He didn't know what this meant exactly, this unexpected visit, a next chapter or the prologue to a whole new story, and he didn't waste time trying to speculate. He simply wanted to enjoy this moment, this weightless feeling of joy and possibility. He picked up his pace even more until he was practically jogging toward the car.

Spotting Silas coming, Kris straightened up and smiled.

ABOUT THE AUTHOR

Mark Allan Gunnells loves to tell stories. He has since he was a kid, penning one-page tales that were Twilight Zone knockoffs. He likes to think he has gotten a little better since then. He loves reader feedback, and above all he loves telling stories. He lives in Greer, SC, with his husband Craig A. Metcalf.

Bibliography

From Gallow's Press
Sequel
Tales from the Midnight Shift
Dark Treats
The Hunt
Locked Room Misery (co-authored with Benjamin Kane Ethridge)

From Evil Jester Press
The Quarry
The Summer of Winters
Welcome to the Graveyard
The Cult of Ocasta

From Crossroad Press
Ghosts in the Attic
October Roses
The Advantaged

From Crystal Lake Publishing
Flowers in a Dumpster
Where the Dead Go to Die (co-authored with Aaron Dries)

From Sinister Grin Press
Fort
Companions in Ruin
From Cemetery Dance Publishing
Curtain Call and Other Dark Entertainments

From Apex Publishing
Asylum
From JournalStone
Outcast

From Great Old Ones Publishing
Halloween House of Horrors

From Etopia
The Exchange Studen
t
From Red Door Productions (self-published)
A Laymon Kind of Night
Whisonant/Creatures of the Light
Lights Out

Curious about other Crossroad Press books?
Stop by our site:
http://store.crossroadpress.com
We offer quality writing
in digital, audio, and print formats.

www.ingramcontent.com/pod-product-compliance
Lightning Source LLC
Chambersburg PA
CBHW030252200626
46816CB00002BA/607

* 9 7 8 1 6 3 7 8 9 7 6 9 0 *